Best wishes
Donna Fries

The Unraveling of Shelby Forrest

A Novel

DONNA FRIESS

Library of Congress-in-Publication Data
All Rights Reserved
Copyright 2015 Donna L. Friess

Friess, Donna L.
The Unraveling of Shelby Forrest
Donna L. Friess
1. Housewives – fiction 2. Loss (psychology-fiction, 3. Regret – fiction 4. Psychological Fiction
Hurt into Happiness Publishing 2015
32332 Suite 102, Camino Capistrano, San Juan Capistrano, CA 92675
ISBN-13 978-0-9815767-3-2
ISBN-10 09815767-3-7

Printed in the United States of America. No part of this publication may be reproduced, stored in a retrieval system or transmitted in any form or by any means, electronic, mechanical, photocopying, recording or otherwise without the written permission of Donna L. Friess. The uploading, scanning, or electronic sharing of this book without the permission of the publisher is unlawful piracy and theft of the author's intellectual property. Note: This book is a work of fiction. The names, places, and incidents are either the product of the author's imagination or are used fictitiously, and any resemblance to actual persons living or dead, or business establishments is coincidental.

Front cover designed by Diana Starr

To order books visit Amazon.com. Also available through Kindle Publishing and www.drdonnafriess.com or www.yourtimenow.org

Thoughts about Donna

Oprah Winfrey introduced Donna Friess and previewed her story on *The Oprah Winfrey Show* stating, "This is a story of power and unbelievable perversion…It was the cover story in the *Los Angeles Times Magazine*. This is a show you cannot afford not to watch!" Oprah Winfrey, television celebrity and social activist.

"Dr. Donna helped to save me from feeling like an invisible piece of nothing. Now I know and feel that I deserve to live and move forward to a fulfilling life. I just love her!!!" Ginni C., Coaching client.

"Dr. Donna Friess is the most inspirational person I have ever met. She imparts a divine influence on the mind and soul." Jack H., Former student, certificated drug and alcohol counselor.

"Dr. Friess is very spiritual and life changing." Elizabeth W., Single-mom.

"Dr. Friess is as beautiful on the inside as the outside." Lea M., Abuse victim, single mom.

"Dr. Friess saved my life." Sandra K., Group Participant.

"Twenty-two years ago when I was a student in Donna's class she planted a seed in my heart and showed me how special I was. Because of her inspiration and wisdom, I have become a successful coach and am loving life. Her influence on my life has been profound!" Marylou H., Life Coach

"Donna is solid gold. She is good and brave and willing to share. She is the blessing of God, too bright to behold for those of us who love misery (too many of us, I am afraid). She has taught me so much!" Lisa W.

"Daddy's Girls" – Subject of cover story for the *Los Angeles Times Magazine*. Lynn Smith, August 4, 1991.

"Out of Darkness - It took Donna Friess of San Juan Capistrano Decades to Reveal Her Real-life Story of the Tragedy of Incest," *Los Angeles Times,* Dennis McLellen, May 6, 1993.

"Millions of women will thank Donna for years and years to come. You are a wonderful inspiration for all women in the world." Linda W.

"What a tremendous thing Donna Friess is doing to protect children." Marilyn D.

"She is incredible! Thank you to Donna for all the courage she has instilled in others." Lydia F.

"Donna! I am in the midst of reading your wonderful book now! So many reasons why you are my hero!!!!" Marissa. P., Director Shelter for Women

"Donna Friess turned her hurt into a halo, her scars into stars, what an inspiration she is to all!!!" Rev. Robert Schuller, Founder of Crystal Cathedral, national figure in television ministry.

Dr. Donna Friess has utilized a horrible childhood life experience and family tragedy as her driving force to help the nation's incest victims. Dr. Friess is a friend and advisor to hundreds of victims and students. She is an inspiration to thousands, a wonderful fun-loving motivational speaker who enjoys surfing and playing with her grandchildren. I am very proud and fortunate to call Donna Friess my friend." Collene Thompson Campbell, Former Mayor, San Juan Capistrano, National Institute of Corrections, Appointed by the U.S. Attorney General.

Books by Donna Friess

Cry the Darkness: One Woman's Triumph Over the Tragedy of Incest

Cherish the Light: One Woman's Journey from Darkness to Light

Circle of Love: A Guide to Successful Relationships, 3rd Edition

One Hundred Years of Weesha: Centennial 2010

Whispering Waters: Historic Weesha and the Settling of Southern California
With Janet Tonkovich

A Chronicle of Historic Weesha and the Upper Santa Ana River Valley
With Janet Tonkovich

Just Between Us: Guide to Healing (out of print)

True Animal Short Stories for Children:

Oh What a Big Surprise!

Three Little Kittens Lost in the Woodpile

Zoe's First Birthday

There's Something Scary in the Shed

Starving in the Woods

Winning the Horse Race

Jessica the Seal

The Unraveling of Shelby Forrest

"Donna Friess has written a thoughtful, tightly woven story about Shelby's heart wrenching life journey making the two hardest decisions a woman can make in life! The story follows the trials around these decisions and how they affect those loved ones in her circle of life and love! There are surprises and tears, smiles and laughter, when I finished the story I was asking for more. The characters are complex and the story delivers the harrowing and heart-wrenching story of so many women that have had to make these impossible decisions. It is a must read for any parent." -*Micki Harris*

"I really liked the characters in the book and how they played out emotionally. At times I could really feel the raw emotions of anxiety, stress, and inner pain, but I also felt the love and it made me smile. The book flowed very well and kept my interest as it always took an unexpected twist or turn. I had a hard time putting it down. This book will appeal to women everywhere. This is a book that I would keep on my book shelf!" - *Dawn Schenderl*

About *Cry the Darkness*

Winner Indie Excellence Book Awards – Women's Issues 2014
Honorable Mention – Paris International Book Festival 2014
Honorable Mention – New York Book Festival 2014
Honorable Mention- Southern California Book Festival 2014

"A real contribution to women everywhere." *Changes Magazine.*

"It is a wonderful book!" Marilyn Van Derbur, Former Miss America, incest survivor.

"I couldn't put it down. It is inspirational!" *Alpha Gamma Delta International Quarterly*

"It is a gripping story…it keeps the reader moving." U.S. International University *Envoy.*

"A must read for everyone. One of the most important books available. It gives hope. Donna's life story is a beacon of hope and happiness for adult survivors of sexual abuse." Claire Reeves, Founder, Mothers Against Sexual Abuse.

Cry the Darkness is my most valued possession." Gina, Incest survivor and AIDS patient.

"It changed my life and gave me hope." Sonja, Incest survivor.

"I learned that I was not alone." Lydia, Mother whose daughter was an incest victim.

"*Tarer I morket.*" Best selling non-fiction book in the history of Egmont (Virkelightedens Verden) publishing, Norway, 1990's. Egmont Bogklub.

"An inspiration for those working for victims of childhood trauma." *Changes Magazine*

"Outstanding Donna! A good reminder that we DO have a choice in how we respond." Judy P., Reader.

Reviews: Circle *of Love: Guide to Successful Relationships*

"It is possible to take control of your life. It is possible to change. It is possible to become more like the person you always wanted to be. Dr. Friess provides a path for you to achieve what you want." Jun K. Student.

"Great book! One of the best interactive self help books available. Halfway through it, I bought copies for my family and friends." Jennifer H., Student.

"Dr. Friess is an amazing woman and her book reflects her unique ability to teach others how to develop, maintain, and enhance relationships. Her suggestions guide people to be more satisfied with their lives. I know my life has been significantly influenced by Dr. Friess. I will forever be grateful." Christy S, Student.

Circle of Love is a well written book filled with insight and compassion for the human soul. Each chapter highlights a vital ingredient for success in communication. It encourages the reader to respond honestly without guilt. I value each lesson learned! I will continue to use the tools and reference for success in my life." Julie P. Mother, Re-entry Student.

Dr. Friess' teaching and *Circle of Love* have been more helpful to me in a short time than decades of therapy. Dr. Friess gets right to the point. She helps her students and clients to reframe their lives and to understand what is *right* with them. This has been life changing for me. Lois W.

Donna Friess' teaching has given me hope. *Circle of Love* might be the most useful tool I have encountered in my journey toward wholeness after my children died. Ellen G.

To those I love

ACKNOWLEDGMENTS

The characters in *The Unraveling of Shelby Forrest*—apart from Waldo Wilcox, and Haji, the safari guide, and Richard Leakey—were fictional. Mr. Leakey was a guest lecturer at Cypress College when I taught there, the idea that he was at USC is a creation of my imagination. This story is set against the backdrop of the War in Iraq and the indigenous people of North America and Great Britain. The history and impact of the first inhabitants is often overlooked.

On a personal note, the controversy over sealed birth records is close to my heart. My own brother was given up at birth when I was nine-years-old. This left an indelible imprint on my psyche. (It was I who placed the call when we finally located him 50 years later.) I relied heavily upon interviews and conversations with adoptees and adoptive parents including James Roberts, Leanne Anteau, Christine Cvijetic, Dominic Arpaia, and books by Betty Jean Lifton.

I particularly want to acknowledge the critical insights which my "early readers" provided: Leanne Anteau, Carmen "Micki" Harris, Lisa Williams, Dawn Schanderl, Joy Kersey, Diana Starr, and Diane Ferruzzo. My daughter Julina Bert and granddaughter Jillian Friess were the first to see the manuscript and were most helpful. Certainly the cheering squad of Janet Tonkovich, Christine Baumgartner, Rhoda Glickman, Jacqueline Stack, Dorothy McIntyre, Mary Berberich, and Hilary Powell who read or heard parts and pieces encouraged me to continue. Barbara Koffman, Leanne Anteau, Bertateme Pitt, Lou Pitt and Robin Priess Glasser believed in my project and shared important contacts. I have relied heavily upon my sister Diana Starr for technical support and cover design.

Across my life, family members, friends, students, clients, and acquaintances have shared deeply personal stories with me regarding their life experiences. I appreciate their struggles.

Debra and Rich Griffith were invaluable sources for the medical, military details. Keely and Bill Yankie, Guisy and Nick Colucci helped me with U.S. Air Force details.

As the reference page reveals at the back, I have relied heavily upon archeological discoveries, and historical accounts of early man, indigenous people, their culture, and legends. My studies of the neuroscience of the brain as well as my doctoral work in psychology provided considerable direction and inspiration.

There probably would never have been any of my words in any books without the encouragement of my husband Ken. Not only has he always believed in me, he allowed me to read the "day's writing" to him each evening while he tried to eat his dinner! Ken has also been a critical reader and editor for my work. It is he with whom I kick around plot lines. It is he who is my great love.

Always my sons, Rick and Dan Friess, my daughters-in-laws, Jenny and Natalie as well as my daughter, Julina and my son-in-law Justin Bert inspire me to be the best I can be, as do my eleven grandchildren: Jake, Jillian, Meg, Jaycelin, Emily, James, Elizabeth, Ella, Ashley, Katie and Caroline. I find a deep purpose for living through all of you.

Thank you all for your faith in me and for helping me. Donna

CHAPTER 1

Airplane
May 13, 2005

As Shelby fastened her seat belt in preparation for takeoff, she smoothed her perfectly pressed designer slacks, tucked a lock of luxuriant red hair behind her ear, leaned back and took a deep breath. *How I dread flying* she thought as she slipped her book into the seat pocket in front of her. The image of the poster she had just seen in the airport bookstore flashed across her mind: **Life begins at the end of your comfort zone.** *Who writes that stuff?* She frowned as she put her reading glasses into their case. *How could they possibly know about what it feels like at the end of that zone?* The familiar knot, the anxiety she had learned to mask for years, coiled tighter in her stomach.

Visiting her mother and stepfather in Washington State always seemed to squeeze that knot. *Shelby, you have gotten about as far away from them as you can...the expanse of the entire continent.* She tried to relax and rationalize with herself, sitting back, struggling to stretch the knot loose. She could feel the dark cloud hanging over her head, the remnants of the hours with Mother. She knew she was in a negative space; she could feel her mother's disapproval in everything she did. That last put-down rang in her ears, "Shelby why are you wasting your time with those insipid Pony Girl stories? If you want to write, you should produce *real* literature, not that pap!"

You would think that after reading all those self help books, I would be able to insulate myself from her constant barbs, she thought as she closed her eyes and leaned back into the headrest. She tried to turn her mind off, but it started up again. The memory kept flashing up behind her eyes. She took another gulp of stuffy cabin air and reached up to adjust the nozzle above her head. It did not help. The images would not shut off. Her brain dwelled on the life changing phone call that had come two weeks before.

She could still hear its insistent ring; see her movements across the kitchen to answer it. Her breathing became faster, she felt herself so close to the edge of the abyss. The deep timber of his warm voice as it resonated across the line vibrated in her memory...*STOP IT! STOP IT!* She straightened up and opened her eyes, forcing the images behind the dark curtain of her mind.

Nestling her head into the headrest, she rotated her shoulders trying to get comfortable. She sat like that, with her eyes closed, as the plane filled with passengers. After a while, she sensed the presence of someone getting into the seat next to her. *Damn. I was sure that seat would remain empty. Haven't they already closed the doors?*

There was some jostling as the person settled in; the rustling of a newspaper. She kept her eyes closed and feigned sleep.

As the plane rolled out from the gate she clenched her hands on the armrests. She had flown this route every year for so long. *You wouldn't think it would still get me this uptight...*

Shelby's brain scanned those years; at first the empty ones, then the others. More than thirty with this annual visit back home to Bellingham, Washington. She didn't look forward to these trips home. She always felt like the outsider, working so hard to be the "fun" aunt to her many nieces and nephews. She missed out on their daily rhythms; the jokes, the everyday dramas with the kids' volleyball and soccer lives; but to stop coming would be to miss out on her sisters' lives completely. That was too high a price. She'd already paid the highest price possible.

"Oops! Sorry!" apologized the feminine voice in the next seat. "Excuse me. I didn't mean to bang into your arm. I'm a little nervous about flying. My eyes were closed and I just grabbed at the arm rest. Instinct. I didn't look first. Sorry," repeated the edgy woman next to her.

Reluctantly, Shelby opened her right eye to see who this interloper was. She noticed vivid blue eyes in a friendly face, an attractive older woman with shiny blonde hair. That was a mistake. Seeing that Shelby was not really asleep, the stranger continued.

"It's my first cross-country trip on my own in years…"

Oh Lordy, I've got a chatterer. She opened the other eye. Shelby turned very slightly toward the intruder and grunted an acknowledgement.

"So you're headed to Atlanta? Business or pleasure?" she continued. "I have a meeting in Atlanta. I'm on a national council. Working with crime victims. It's my first meeting."

Is there no peace? "Hmm. I'm on the way home."

"Oh. Where is home?"

Oh goodness. Chatting. "Hmm, Beaufort. Along the coast of South Carolina. You know it? Lowcountry."

"That must be marvelous. I've read those Pat Conroy books. I like the idea of scooting around those bayous in a motor boat instead of all the freeway driving I do. I've been commuting to work for thirty years," she confided.

Shelby turned her head further and took another look at the woman's face. Earnest, thoughtful eyes. A welcoming and comforting expression. Warmth radiated out of her. Energy. Vitality.

Loosening the angry wad of feelings toward her mother that gripped her, she tried to soften her attitude. *Mother is not worth me being this furious; I could use some of what this friendly woman has.* Her mother's stinging words replayed once again across her mind. Then just as quickly her thoughts turned back to that ringing phone as she saw herself walking across the kitchen to answer it.

As the massive jet engines revved up for take-off, the noise precluded further conversation. Shelby practiced her rote: counting to twenty, long and slow. Deep breaths. She hoped that once she was in the air she would calm down. *Fifteen, breathe, sixteen, breathe………...*she could hear the phone ringing. "Hello."

"Is this Shelby Wells Forrest?" A male voice. Resonating. Nervous. She could hear it in his rushed breathing... *Stop it!! Seventeen, breathe, eighteen.*

Suddenly she could feel the smooth ascent as the monster plane lifted itself from the runway. Air borne. Free. If only. . . For the millionth time her memory felt the heft of that bundled package; of that perfect baby boy. She inhaled, only to recall his fresh powdery baby smell; the weight she could still almost feel. His solid form tucked safely into her left arm.

Her breathing became irregular again. *I don't know how much more of this I can take. They are coming all the time now. Those memories. The firm weight. His baby smell.*

Shelby forced herself to take another huge gulp of fusty air. It was less stale than it had been. She exhaled slowly. She knew what it took to fool herself into believing that she was okay. *Breathe girl. Breathe. There's no way it can get worse. The bad times are behind you.* She worked hard trying to reassure herself.

Oh if only that were true. I'm not so sure. She answered to herself.

Thankfully the woman next to her reached for her own book and seemed to occupy herself. Shelby once again leaned back and closed her eyes. More deep breaths. She suspected that she was suffering the symptoms of Post Traumatic Stress Disorder, PTSD. The intrusive thoughts, the nightmares, the panic attacks. The world held sympathy for the soldiers who returned with it. What about her?

That ugly dialogue continued in her head. Around and around, looping, scolding, critical, sorry. She could not find the TURN OFF switch. She heard the metallic clattering of the drinks cart. She opened her eyes. The flight attendant was two rows in front. *What to have? What would help? How about a nice big bottle of vodka for starters?* queried her impatient inner self. *That could never solve anything.*

"Ma'm, what may I get for you?" asked the tired middle-aged attendant.

"Orange juice, please."

"Great choice. I think orange juice is generally underrated, don't you?" offered the perky woman next to her.

"Oh. I haven't given it much thought."

"I squeeze it for my grandchildren when they come over. We have some trees in the yard."

"Oh. That's nice."

"We have nine grandchildren. Seven girls. It is pretty crazy at our house. How about you? Any children?

With that Shelby gave up. There was going to be no stopping this cheery stranger. *Maybe she will distract me for a while. Perhaps it's not to be that I simmer here in my emotional cauldron.*

With a weak smile that did not reach her eyes she replied. "Four …sort of…."

Her voice trailed off. She'd never said that before. The tight knot in her gut let loose a millimeter.

"With so many girls, I'm on a quest to buy more stuff. You know china, silver spoons, crystal, so there's enough to go around when I'm gone," The lady enthused.

My God, she is light years ahead of me. She is thinking of the future, inheritance even, while I just want to get through the day!

In an attempt to steer the conversation *away* from grandchildren, Shelby asked, "So what's this meeting you say you're attending for the first time?"

The woman's face became more serious as she turned toward Shelby and replied, "We want to help crime victims. We're creating a DVD for law enforcement and for families dealing with trauma. We want to train those who work with victims to become more sensitive, especially when they're working with children."

"Really?" Shelby felt a shift in her attention away from herself for the first time all day. "What kind of victims?" she asked, finally interested in what the woman had to say.

"Mostly kids who have been abused, or witnessed something catastrophic. Lots of sexual abuse. The law doesn't really get how to deal with them. Authorities, parents; they frequently try to force the child to talk about it. To get what has happened out in the open. That's not how children work. They need for it to be safe and then, and only then, they might open up."

The woman continued. "Often the parents or authorities, in their urgency to *do* something about it, to fix it, rush it. Rush the kids. Traumatized kids need time. Some youths show symptoms, bed wetting, night terrors, while others show nothing. Flat affect. They reveal nothing at all about anything. It depends on the child. That's what our DVD will show. How to best work with victims so they are not further traumatized."

The delicate hairs on Shelby's arms flew to attention. Goose flesh. *This woman knows things. I can feel it.*

Engaged mentally for maybe the first time in days, maybe weeks, Shelby thought, h*ow long have I been this distracted? Oh. Since the ringing, ringing.....* She forced herself back to the present and asked, "So how did you get into this work. I've always had an interest in psychology; even dreamed about someday serving as a court appointed advocate for kids."

"It's important work. Domestic violence is still so common. Entire families in trauma," the woman took a breath and continued, "I once read a statistic that there are something like 50 million adults walking around in our country who were victims of some kind of childhood sexual assault. Most go untreated. My associates and I have been working to put more teeth into the laws. Make it harder for criminals to hide in their dark corners." Her words were laced with passion.

"But how do *you* know about it?"

"Oh, I know. Believe me I *know.*"

Shelby believed her. She felt somehow that this remark was only the tip of a huge ice berg. Her intuition understood that this woman knew things. Scary things. Sad things. This woman seemed to have moved forward despite whatever it was. Shelby took another calming breath, leaning back, she took inventory of the knot in her stomach. *How remarkable, I feel safer. The knot is looser. How can that be?*

"So in your professional opinion, what is the most important step for people who are experiencing trauma to take?" asked Shelby.

"Take it slow. A person must not be forced to face the upset before he or she is ready. We are learning that with domestic violence and child sexual abuse, keeping the secret is a big part of the whole trauma. If we can get the victims to feeling safe enough, talk therapy can really help them to begin to heal. Holding a big secret is devastating. Part of the devastation is the fact that the secret keeper can never fully relax, be herself; be authentic."

Shelby sat back and digested that nugget. A while later the lunch service interrupted her thoughts. Acting on impulse, she turned to the woman next to her and began. "You know earlier, when you asked about my grandchildren?"

"Uh huh."

"I said 'four... sort of.'"

"Yes. I figured you were talking about step-grandchildren or that, oh, I don't know, maybe you were estranged from them. I knew to leave it alone."

During the next four hours Shelby could not believe her behavior. Perhaps it was the anonymity of the situation, or the feeling of safety she felt with this stranger. Acting completely out of character, for the first time in her life, she told her story to this unknown woman. She told about that beautiful sweet-smelling little boy; about the few minutes she held him.

She had talked on and on. She told about school and meeting Grant, her husband, and their life together, their two girls and now the two grand girls, and finally about the ringing. She even dared to share the life changing moment in the conversation; as she answered the phone and heard, "This is Cody James, your son."

The stranger said nothing. She just looked at Shelby with understanding in her clear blue eyes. Shelby felt safe with her, and very sad. In a weird little corner of her mind, she half expected that if she told anyone, they would wig out in shock. This woman simply listened, and then in a reassuring gesture, placed her hand gently on Shelby's arm, as if to say she understood.

CHAPTER 2

September 3, 1969
Western Washington University
Bellingham, Washington

A wave of nervous excitement shimmered down Shelby's spine as she took her seat in the front row of the large lecture hall. To stave off the nerves, she checked her face in her tiny compact mirror. *Not too bad; blue eyes with a scattering of freckles across my nose. Heart shaped face, and happily, for once, my mascara is not dripping down my cheeks. Ah, and not a zit in sight! A good day!* She laughed to herself as she fluffed up the ubiquitous red curls framing her pretty face. She had waited so long to get to this point in her life. Her growing up years felt interminable under her mother's watchful eye and heavy hand. She could not believe that until her 18th birthday last month, she had suffered an 11 p.m. curfew and the stinging remarks of her friends. "We're out with Shelby. Gotta get our little girl home." For a brief second she wondered why she did not get nicer friends. *Que sera sera*, she thought, *finally, I am now officially an adult.*

Her dream had been to go away to college but her mother had insisted that living at home and going to the local university was the pragmatic road to her future. Shelby had not shown her disappointment, she knew that with a degree in her pocket there would be a way out of Bellingham. Oh she loved the small town, the comfortable feeling of knowing everybody when she went downtown or to a football game, but something inside ached for more; bigger, farther away, new people….

So here she was literally in a front row seat on the first day of the rest of her life. She scooted back into the uncomfortable classroom seat, noted the graffiti carved into its desktop, and took out her notebook, American History 101. *Well, that can't be too bad.* As she glanced up at the wall clock she noted that it was one minute past 10 o'clock, when suddenly the very air in the lecture hall changed. It felt charged somehow, energized. Her eyes scanned across the floor to the entrance. She saw beat-up cowboy boots. Her eyes moved up, long legs. Blue jeans. Past the plaid western style long-sleeved shirt. The sleeves were rolled to the elbow revealing strong arms brushed with light masculine hair. Her glance continued upward until her eyes rested on a strikingly handsome middle-aged man. He seized the lectern as his piercing blue eyes seemed to address each student. Immediately, his resounding voice boomed, "Good morning students! Welcome to American History 101."

Shelby felt her heart skip a bit. *So tall. So handsome!* Within minutes this professor, Shelby realized she had no clue about his name, had enchanted the students with his wry wit and crazy jokes about President Nixon and his anti-ballistic missiles. He teased the students about being prepared when the Soviets tried to blow us up. The students laughed. More jokes about decorating their bomb shelters so they could make the cover of *Bomb Shelter Beautiful Magazine*.

She watched and marveled that within about fifteen minutes he had the students sitting on the edge of their seats, eager for more. Excited to be there. *Wow*, she thought, *now there is a lesson. Most of my teachers have been so boring that we could barely stay awake. This guy is amazing.*

Before she knew it class was over. She looked down at her lined notebook pages. They were filled with President Nixon's daring first year. The hotly contested anti-ballistic missile debates, the Apollo 11 splash down, and the first trip by an American president into Communist Romania, but the biggest point of all; history is simply the story of the current events of bygone eras. Not boring. Not stuffy, but as lively and interesting as a designer bomb shelter.

Shelby thought about what he had said. Somehow she had never thought of it this way. *This seems so much more interesting than high school history.* At the end of class he told us that now we would start our studies at the beginning, the indigenous people.

As she looked at her notes, realizing she had been fascinated by what she was hearing, she could not believe that this was herself. *You gotta be kidding. I have never cared about history or politics!* She gathered her belongings and left the hall.

At work that night as she waited tables at the Cracked Crab, her brain kept going back to that class, to the professor. She had checked the schedule of classes, Dr. Thomas Steele. American History 101.

DONNA FRIESS

CHAPTER 3

September 19, 1969
Bellingham, Washington

Shelby absentmindedly wiped the plastic veneer of the beat up captain- style tables at the Cracked Crab, where she had been waitressing for two years, she looked up to see Professor Steele framed in the doorway of the crowded restaurant. Happy hour was well under way on this late Friday afternoon. She was surprised to see him. As he pushed through the old-style double bar doors, she noticed a contingent filing in behind him. All were dressed in dark colored form fitting bicycle racing jerseys. Her gaze followed his confident masculine stride as he moved across the ancient wooden floor planks toward the tables in the corner. Firm body. Lean and muscular in all the right places. He was laughing at something the man behind him had just said. As he pulled out a chair, his head turned and she caught a glimpse of the crinkles at the corner of his eyes as he laughed again. *So handsome. So buff!*

She was surprised to find that her breathing had changed. She felt breathless and nervous all at once. *Silly girl!!! What is wrong with you? He's old. He's married.* She took a big gulp of air as she purposefully pushed two chairs that were haphazardly scattered nearby, back into place at the table, all the while her eyes stayed fixed on his back.

Since that first day of class, her thoughts kept coming back to him. She'd made a few casual inquiries. It seemed he was very popular, the other students considered him to be one of the best at the university, a sort of collegiate rock star. She was not surprised, from that first day, she felt a fire within him, a passion. In the following few weeks he kept the students riveted, they hung around after class, asked a lot of questions. As the semester progressed, she noticed that the attendance in her other classes had dropped off, lots of empty seats, but not in history. After the first day she had moved toward the back of the lecture hall, *all the better to hide!* She hadn't thought it out, she just felt more comfortable hidden in the back of the hall. She knew she was being irrational, but she couldn't help it, nor could she turn off the pictures of him which floated across her mind when she tried to get to sleep at night.

The tinny sound of the bell from the kitchen brought her thoughts back. Her order was up. She would have to walk past his table. *Oh God.* She took another big breath, forced a pleasant business-like expression across her face, squared her shoulders, and strode toward the cook and her order. She looked straight ahead as she moved past his table. She was aware of laughter coming from the group, heard snatches of conversation. Big race, Victoria. 100 Miler. She willed herself to calm, she had a job to do. She gathered up the order and served her tables. Shelby was relieved when an hour or so later the pack of bikers got up and left the restaurant.

She got through the weekend okay. Worked the Saturday lunch crowd, went out with Nick, the guy she had dated a few times, and kept up with her classes. She forced herself to focus on her studies as she fought down thoughts of Dr. Steele.

Sunday was a research day. She could not help herself, she wanted this first paper to stand out, to perhaps introduce her to him. The course work in history included two research papers which tied into the final project and the class trip to the ruins of an ancient Indian village. The indigenous population in this part of the Pacific Northwest had been more substantial than in some other areas of the country. The class trip was scheduled for Thanksgiving weekend. She wanted her work to stand out, to be so on point, so thorough, that a teacher could not help but notice. She knew she was being vain, but she could not help it. This paper had to be *good.*

When she awoke Sunday morning she discovered that the topic for her term project had come to her. Growing up hearing all of her nanny, Nano's, stories about tribal life, had given her a heart for the indigenous people. She smiled to herself as she thought about some of the spirit world legends she had heard; the underworld spirits sneaking out through passages in the volcanic peaks, rivers of blood running down from the mountains. She laughed to herself. Oh how she loved her Nano and her tales, certainly hot lava would look like blood?

She inhaled. Paused, as she let her thoughts come into focus; she would write on the Russian colonization of the great Northwest and how it affected the native tribes. This might take some doing she told herself. All she really knew about the Russians was that they left behind those blue onion domed Orthodox churches. Those churches had intrigued her on a family trip to Alaska. She sprang out of bed, hurriedly threw on her WWU sweats and grabbed a cup of coffee, grunted hellos to her family, and drove to the university library. She had a paper to write!

Many late nights later, nights filled with exhilarating research, resulted in a 3000 word paper with which she was satisfied. On Friday, the due date, she felt a nervous flutter in the pit of her stomach as she turned it in with the rest of the class. It was her silent emissary and she prayed that Dr. Steele was not the sort of professor who handed the papers off to a TA, or who just skimmed them, looking for typos as the grading criteria. She took a deep breath and focused her attention on the lecture.

The next Monday as the class came to order, Dr. Steele greeted the students and asked about their weekends. Before long he got to the subject of their papers.

"This was one of the finest batches of preliminary research papers I have had the pleasure to read in some time. Mr. Finch, where are you? Please stand." Dr. Steele led some applause.

"Your theory of early hominoids and their crossing of the land bridge at the Bering Strait was brilliant. Mr. Finch argued that the American Indians came from ancient nomadic northeast Asians arriving about 14,000 years ago. Congratulations." He hesitated as he looked around the lecture hall. "Miss Wells. Where are you? Please stand."

Shelby was stunned. For a second she could not believe that she was hearing her own named said aloud. Her heart slammed in its cage. Thunk, thunk. On shaky legs she slowly rose from her seat in the back of the hall. Everyone turned and was applauding as he continued, "Miss Wells has looked at the touch point between the Russian trappers and the Nisga'a people. They are a fishing society and believe themselves to be the original people of the Pacific Northwest, having lived here for thousands of years. Miss Wells discovered some of their most sacred legends as well. Original, compelling. Brava Miss Wells."

Shelby gratefully fell back into her seat as the class applauded her work. Her ears were ringing and her face felt hot. She comprehended just snatches of what the teacher was saying, "the class field trip will give you all a chance to understand how highly developed the cultures of the indigenous peoples were. Get your calendars cleared for our big trip. We will leave the Friday after Thanksgiving and return the next Monday, late. I have field trip slips up here for you to give to your professors to excuse you from your Monday classes."

At the close of class Dr. Steele stood near the lectern, calling out each student's name as he returned the papers. Her heart began its familiar thumping. Finally, "Miss Wells." She walked down the steps of the lecture auditorium toward the front of the hall. She kept her head up, plastered a fake smile on her frozen face, and aimed for dignity. "Well done!" He remarked as she grasped the corner of the paper from his hand and filed by.

There was an awful buzzing in her ears as she continued outside, shrugged a few hurried good byes to her classmates, and walked to the parking lot and the safety of her car. In the privacy of her little Bug, she opened her notebook to check her grade and read the comments.

Well developed ideas. Original thinking. Nicely documented research. Please stop by my office this week during office hours. I want to talk to you....

Oh no! Talk to me. I don't want him to see me. I don't want him to talk to me. *Well idiot!! Then why the hell did you knock yourself out on that paper if you didn't want to be noticed. That is why you went to so much trouble in the first place. I do NOT get you Shelby Wells!!! You're so damned pathetic!* The annoyed voice in her head would not let up.

The next Thursday she finally summoned enough courage to drop by his office. She sucked in a huge breath, stood to her full 5' 4" height, and knocked a tentative knock against the door frame of his open door.

"Um. Ah... You asked me to stop by. On my paper you asked. I am,... um... Shelby Wells." Her voice felt rusty and sounded a bit squeaky. Surely not the confident demeanor she had practiced all week in the mirror.

"Ah yes. Come in. Sit down. Let me see...your paper..."

"The Nisga'a people, sir."

"Oh, I recall now. Hey thanks for stopping by. Your paper has so much to offer. I was particularly taken by what appeared to be primary knowledge of their social structure. How in the world did you discover the matrilineal culture? Reliable sources show that they had a patriarchal society?"

Shelby felt herself relaxing. This was a whole new world to have someone actually want to share ideas with *her*. Maybe college was going to be more than a way out.

Smiling, Shelby responded. "Yes, that's the common belief. The more I researched, it was clear that mainstream thinkers have concluded that this tribe, at least, followed the patriarchal social structure, but it wasn't that simple. I knew it wasn't, so I kept at it." She could feel her confidence growing. She was on safe ground. Ideas. Always safer than feelings.

"Clarify? What did you discover that led you to these conclusions?" He urged. The expression on his face was warm with enthusiasm as his sandy hair spilled across his forehead.

"Well, sir, my family has lived in these parts for a long time. I grew up hearing all these stories. Stories about the locals, a lot of legends, even myths." Relaxing now, she realized how excited she was about her research.

"In fact I am the descendent of explorers who were here in the 1700's. My family lore has always maintained that we are descended from Bering's second voyage in 1741. I'm sure there's some Russian DNA in my genes as well as some Aleut Indian."

Laughing, "That long? Well I bet there is. There were so few women in the early days of settling the west; explorers and early settlers often married indigenous ladies. But that was a long time ago. Your work has recency…."

"On my mother's side there seems to have been some money. As the population grew and more and more Eastern folks settled here, my ancestors became more affluent. They always had household help, mostly from the tribal people. I was lucky enough to be raised by the most wonderful human on the planet. I call her Nano. She was my nanny growing up. She is Nisga'a. I think of her as my heart mother."

Shelby paused. Maybe she was revealing too much. *This must sound so lame. Heart mother.* She stopped. She could feel that her cheeks had turned crimson.

"Go on. Go on!" urged Dr. Steele.

"Across all the decades, my long ago relatives somehow kept up ties with the tribe. My family continued the tradition. Anyway, Nano is the one who actually raised me, my mom was always so busy. Nano's grandmother is still living. I interviewed her!"

"I knew it!" He bellowed in glee. "Primary source! I'm delighted!"

***

Shelby was amazed that she managed to get through the office visit. She'd held her own. She was happy. The weekend passed quickly. She saw Nick for a study date Wednesday evening and by Friday she was back at the diner. As she turned from the kitchen pass-through with her arms laden with a large platter of cracked crab legs she noticed a familiar troop of men coming through the swinging doors. Her antennae went on hyper-alert as her heart once again slammed against her chest wall. *Oh God! Not again!*

There was nowhere to hide as she moved across the crowded dining room. She managed about fifteen steps when she heard, "Hey. Hey! Miss Wells. Hi!"

She turned her head slightly toward the greeting and gave Dr. Steele a tight smile as she continued toward her table. She lingered longer than necessary taking care of her customers and slowing down her breathing.

The tinny bell called out to her. Walking toward the kitchen she could not ignore Dr. Steele who was waving her over. There was no avoiding him. She moved toward his table with her usual plastic smile stuck on her face.

"Hi there," she managed through clenched teeth.

"Hey guys, this is the student I was telling you about, the one with the primary material: the Nisga'a interview. Meet Miss Wells. Miss Wells these are my riding buddies." He announced with pride.

In unison they responded, "Hello." "Hi." One tall man looked at her and announced, "We heard all about your research. Great job!"

Blushing no doubt to a lovely shade of bright red. She thought, *great, all the better to match my hair!* She forced a smile.

"Seriously Miss Wells," the man continued, "we're all fascinated by the fact that you have first hand knowledge of the Nisga'a. There were more than 10,000 of them in their hay day. A powerful force. They moved north. There's not as much known as we'd like."

The bell chimed again. "Ah, gotta go. So nice to meet you all," she managed as she escaped to the kitchen.

As she left the lecture hall on Monday, Dr. Steele called over to her. He was standing behind the podium as the students were filing out. "Hey I can hardly get your Nano and her grandmother off my mind. I keep coming back to what she told you, about the power dynamic in the tribe, that the tribal leader was so much more than a medicine woman."

"Yes," replied Shelby, feeling a wave of confidence. "It's especially interesting in view of the common thinking that most tribes were patriarchal, like we talked about before." Shelby felt a bit calmer than she had in his presence in the past.

"So Miss Wells, you tape recorded the interview right? What is the lady's name anyway?"

"Yes, of course I did. She is known as Bella. There was some thought that she was somehow related to the Bella Bella tribe which lived more north of here. She's not sure if that's true, but we all call her Bella."

Relaxing a bit, Shelby smiled, "I'm really enjoying this project. When I think about 100,000 indigenous people, many different tribes, living here by 1800, with the wealthier clans sporting colorful totem poles, I cannot help but get excited about it. As a kid growing up, any time my Nano and I would be in the car and pass a totem pole she went wild with excitement." Shelby laughed at the image of her little Nano, knocking on the window of the car, pointing frantically to one pole after another as they drove by.

"You know those poles started out as corner posts for their homes? Then they became ceremonial and even funerary containers," explained Dr. Steele.

"They were mostly carved out of cedar, and didn't last too long." He hesitated, "Hey, I would love to hear the complete interview. Any chance of that?" he urged. "Would that be okay with you? May I hear it?" His voice was tentative and his eyes were filled with hope.

"Ah. Well. I guess so. I could drop the tape into your mail box," she answered.

"How is the grandma's English? I think I could understand what was being said better if you helped me with it. Tapes can be confusing," his voice was eager.

"Would you mind coming in while I play it back, so when I have some questions you can help me with information?"

"Well. I don't know."

There was a long pause, he continued. "I'm sorry. This is a big imposition. I have failed to mention that I am writing a book on the migration of the tribes out of Washington and into British Columbia, the potlatch celebration and, the small pox epidemic that drove them out in 1862. I have some good material on the Bella Bella and the Chinook, but the clan line and the matriarchy is still not well documented. I know very little of the Nisga'a. This could be huge for my research," he added compellingly.

Shelby felt a sort of electric jolt shoot down her spine. *Oh Lord. Help me. This is getting complicated...*

"How about Thursday at 12:00 at my office? I will bring sandwiches if you bring the tape," he concluded.

"Uh. I guess I could come by then, but I don't need lunch. They feed me at the diner."

Naturally by Thursday Shelby was a mass of nerves. She could not eat, nor sleep; had not slept, in fact, but a few hours since that Monday conversation. Thursday morning she somehow managed to get through her English and speech classes on auto pilot. She had to keep talking herself down, *what is wrong with you? This is nothing. Certainly It's not as horrible as speech class and you've managed to survive that!*

She arrived at Dr. Steele's door at precisely 12:00. He was on the telephone and motioned for her to take a seat. Within minutes he hung up and greeted her with an open smile. Her pulse quickened.

"Hi. Thank you so much for doing this. So, you've got the tape?" he asked excitedly.

"Ah yes. Right here." As she reached across the desk to hand him the tape their fingers touched. Shelby pulled back as if she had been electrocuted.

"Sorry. I'm just so eager to hear this woman," he apologized.

As the tape rolled along, Shelby began to calm down. Fascinated by the narrative, Dr. Steele leaned back in his desk chair, and closed his eyes. With his hands clasped behind his head, he looked more handsome than ever.

Shelby felt comfortable enough in the privacy of his closed eyes to examine him more fully. *Square jaw, long lashes, nicely styled longish sandy colored hair. Youthful manner, for someone so old. How old? Maybe forty. Maybe less. Young kids. At least two of them.* She had overheard the girls leaving class one day saying that he was separated from his wife.

They sat there like that for some time, finally after forty minutes of watching him listen, still with closed eyes, Shelby began to feel anxious about making it to her next class.

"Ah, Dr. Steele. There are still three more hours of tape. I need to get to class," she interrupted.

"Oh, uh. Sorry. I was lost in it. It is fascinating. Your questions are right on. Engaging, yet probing. You could be a TV interviewer. The next Barbara Walters," he said, laughing.

"I can leave the tape………" she offered.

A bit disoriented, he quickly agreed. "I'll have it back to you by Monday.'"

Smiling, Shelby, answered, "That's fine just don't let your kids cover it over with Sesame Street songs. She laughed.

"Oh that's not a problem. I only see them every other weekend."

The happy hour crowd was building at the diner on Friday afternoon when he walked in. This time he was alone. He took a table in her section. Shelby had been half expecting him. She felt sick. There was no choice but to serve his table.

"Hey there, Dr. Steele. What can I get you?" She asked, faking calm as she stood above him to take his order.

"Please call me Tom. Dr. Steele seems like for an old guy. Tom. Please and may I call you Shelby?"

"Certainly." She smiled. "Your order?"

"Just a cheeseburger. No fries. Gotta watch my girlish figure!"

he teased as he patted his flat stomach.

"Got it."

"I came in to see you. It would help me so much to meet your Nano's grandmother. I am hoping beyond hope that you will set that up for me."

A wave of ice seized Shelby's heart. This was getting way too complicated. She felt excited and scared at the same time. Also there was something else. This felt like some kind of imposition on her dear Nano.

As if he were reading her mind, he continued. "I know this is asking a lot. If I were not stuck on the matrilineal aspect of my research, I would back off. This is so important. This could bust open the entire thinking about the social structure of those indigenous tribes."

Shelby put in his order and took some breaths. She tried to evaluate her feelings. Some kind of ego trip mixed with a dash of fear, topped off with a helping of an attraction she could not deny. No one before had ever really wanted to know what she *thought!* She decided that she would leave it up to her Nano.

By the time the order came up, she knew what to say. As she carefully set the plate down before him, she responded, "Let me talk to Nano."

***

A week later, the next Saturday morning, she found herself meeting him in the parking lot of the bird sanctuary at the southern point of the Bellingham Harbor. She arrived early, so that she could catch a glimpse of the bald eagles. They were so majestic. *If I were to choose an animal to be, I would choose an eagle. Soaring above. Studying the layout. Taking my time, and then when I was certain...*

Right on cue, Dr. Steele, Tom, arrived in his sporty little red car. She'd caught a glimpse of it before, from the window of the Cracked Crab. As he climbed out of the tiny car, she observed him as he straightened out his long muscular legs. He graced her with a broad grin.

"Hi! This is great. I really appreciate it. Can we drive to the cottage. Want to go in one car?"

"Not possible. We have to go through the eucalyptus grove and walk about a half mile around the shore line. There's no road to her house. She's expecting us."

Shelby led the way on the familiar footpath. She was keenly aware of him, his scent, a few feet behind her. She felt things in her body she had never felt before. Dangerous things.

To keep the conversation on track as they walked along, she asked about his research.

"Well it's a funny story," he began, "of course as a history buff, you can imagine that I love anything related to the past. Anyway, about a year ago, I took myself on kind of a survival hiking expedition. I was alone, scouting the back country. Kind of a solo version of Lewis and Clark," he laughed. "So late one afternoon, I was resting in my camp when an interesting character lumbered in. I was surprised to meet anyone so far into the wild. I could tell that he was a loner. We shared the fire and some conversation. He had incredible stories. The one I liked the best happened to him a month before we met. I could tell from his excitement that it was fresh in his mind."

Dr. Steele paused. Shelby turned back to look at him as they tromped along the path. He continued, understanding that she was intent on his story. "It seems he had been hunting a cougar that had been killing his cows. He got the thing. Biggest mountain lion he'd ever seen, but not before it killed one of his dogs and torn the eye out of the other. Anyway, when heading home, he had to climb down a rocky ledge carrying the lion's head and skin."

Dr. Steele paused for effect. "Somehow during his descent, he looked to his left and saw something he had never seen before. He discovered a fifteen foot ladder made out of logs leading to the top of the butte. He could not help himself. He put down his load, told his hysterical, injured dog to wait, and climbed up the ladder. He described what he found as an 'oasis in the sky.' The top of the butte was littered with beads, shards of pottery, arrowheads, a storage bin, and even some remnants of an ancient shelter. He was sure that the finds were seven hundred or more years old. That man and his discovery rekindled my fascination with the native people."

"That old timer is Waldo Wilcox. We've sort of become friends. He's going to let our class come to his ranch. He and his family own 4000 acres. Private land. No tourists. There's so much to see. He told me that he has not disturbed anything he's ever found. He says it's sacred."

Shelby was spellbound by the narrative, finally she replied, "That is an incredible story. I can only imagine beads and artifacts lying around. Once when I was a kid, after a hard rain, I found an arrowhead in the mud. I thought that was a big deal! Now I'm even more excited about our class trip. What an opportunity! This is going to be fantastic."

They walked in silence a while longer.

"So enough about me. Tell me about you, Shelby Wells."

"Oh there's not so much to tell. You know where I work, and I'm something of a dog person. My two white labs are my good pals. We walk the shoreline and hike in the woods every chance we get. I've lived here in Bellingham my entire life. I love it, but I'm desperate to see more of the world. To experience other ways of life, to learn about other people."

"So what are your plans?"

They were walking side by side now as the path was wider.

"Your class has inspired me. For sure, I want to study the indigenous people more fully. With just this paper, I got stuck between the Nisga'a and the Nisqually, the names are so close, but I couldn't find any proof that they were the same people. Maybe they were long ago. Today the Nisga'a seem to be only up in British Columbia and the Nisqually more around Tacoma. Anyway, I have a fantasy of somehow living with a tribe for a summer or something, maybe teaching English. I don't even know if they would let me."

She paused and thought about it. "Maybe I could be a history teacher, maybe in a university, a future with some adventure where I could apply what I was learning." She slowed her pace and looked at him.

Earnest blue eyes met her glance. A ripple of pleasure flowed through her body. She understood that he saw her as a person. She wasn't used to this.

"I know I want to travel. More than travel, maybe the Peace Corps. I don't know. But I do know that I don't want to live in this town for the rest of my life. I am one who has a MOTHER, a very controlling mother. I cannot see living in the same place with her forever!"

With a reassuring smile, Dr. Steele, replied, "My bet is that once you're out of school, things with her will sort themselves out. A career in teaching is a great idea."

With that they came to Bella's little house.

That night as Shelby tried to force her body to sleep, her mind kept running pictures of Dr. Steele, Tom, as he interviewed Bella. She could almost hear his humorous laughter. Bella's sage comments had charmed him. The interview had lasted for three hours. Shelby worried that she had burdened her old friend with this handsome stranger, but every time she tried to close off their conversation, one or the other would bring in something new. It had gone well. She had enjoyed seeing him in this situation, so much more relaxed than at school. All charm and good manners, and honestly, Bella seemed to come alive in his presence.

She had lain there in bed, the clock ticking off the hours. Finally when her mind almost turned off, when she could feel sleep around the corner, the other picture would run in her head, the one where she began to trip over a root in the path and had stumbled, when suddenly his strong arm had interrupted her fall. He caught her just in time, for the briefest of seconds she could feel his taut body against hers as he pulled her up.

This was not good.

The week passed in agonizingly slow motion. Her stomach roiled. She felt numb in class, but excited too. She continued to sit in the back of the hall, and he continued to entertain and inspire the class. On Friday she was not surprised to see him come into the diner. Once again he came into her section and ordered the same hamburger with all the trimmings, no fries. As she placed the plate in front of him, he caught her wrist with his right hand, stopped her motion, held eye contact for too long, as he said, "Thank you, Shelby. That is perfect. Just so wonderfully perfect."

Oh no. It's getting worse.

She brought his check a while later. As he was digging for his credit card, he said, "I transcribed Bella's interview. So much new information. I've been comparing her information with other materials I have, old books. I came upon a drawing of a totem pole that I believe might have belonged to her clan. She was telling me about the winter festival of giving. I think this pole was part of it, part of the display of wealth. The missionaries managed to stop most of those festivals by the late 1800's, but some of the totem poles somehow survived. I'd really like for you to see it," he explained.

"There's more. I have some artifacts too. I have two grinding bowls; one's in pretty good shape, the other is a big shard. I know you'd be interested. Also it would be helpful to know if the totem drawing jibs with the descriptions you've heard over the years. It might be Nisga'a. Bella might know..." His eyes were pleading and his tone hopeful.

CHAPTER 4

October 18, 1969
Bellingham, Washington

Shelby agreed to set up yet another meeting between Dr. Steele and Bella. Once again, they met at the parking lot and hiked to Bella's cottage. During the long interview, Shelby found herself mostly day dreaming, watching the animated discussion. She could hardly believe the thrill he was obviously getting out of talking with Bella. He seemed young and charged up somehow. They'd been on the topic of the ancient gift giving ceremonies for a long time. Wisps of conversation penetrated her consciousness: lavish shows of wealth, redistribution, banning by missionaries. All the while, Shelby could not stop herself from rerunning the moment, the week before, when she had stumbled and he had caught her. Her mind played it again and again.

On the walk back to their cars he once again brought up the grinding bowls in his possession and the totem pole photo in an old book. "Seriously I think you'd enjoy seeing them. That guy, Waldo Wilcox, the one who owns the spread I was telling you about, loaned them to me so I could photograph them for my book." Shelby was only partially listening. She was worrying about where all this big talk was going. They were walking side-by-side now. She glanced over and met his eyes.

His words were suffused with vitality as he continued. "When the Wilcox family finally built their ranch house, the tractor dug these objects up. I've been out there a few times. The valley floor is *covered* with pit houses." Nodding his head in amazement, he sucked in a lungful of crisp air, "such incredible artifacts;

ceremonial beads, arrowheads, spears." He stopped in the footpath. Shelby halted as well, catching his eye to acknowledge that she was still listening.

"Imagine holding a bowl in your hands that is a thousand years old! I bet you'd be fascinated. I can't describe how it feels, there's nothing like it. I would love to show you what he loaned me."

She could hear an alarm bell going off in the back of her mind, but she ignored it, thinking, *what possible harm could there be? I am interested in the totem pole photo, the arrowheads... besides his family will be there. It's the middle of the day for heaven sakes! It's fine.*

Before she knew what had come over her, she had agreed to follow Dr. Steele, Tom, back to his home to see those artifacts. She drove behind him, up a long driveway, and parked her car behind his. They had arrived at an old two-storey Victorian style house. It sat high on the bluff overlooking the harbor. As he opened the large front door, she admired its beveled glass window. She followed him in through the heavily decorated, but unoccupied rooms, and out to a workroom in the back of the property; behind the flower garden and well mown lawn.

"So where *is* everyone?" She asked nervously, surprised at the silence that engulfed the house. "I thought I'd get to meet your kids. I saw their pictures in your office."

"Oh... didn't I mention? ... They're in Seattle." He moved toward a worktable littered with beads, a spear, and some rough stone objects.

"Here they are." Shelby could hear the awe in his voice as he handed her a beautiful dark grey stone mortar bowl. It was about eight inches wide and perhaps five inches deep.

"Feel its weight." She noticed that indeed it was solid, maybe weighing ten pounds. She held it reverently as he continued. "I can't help but think of the thousands upon thousands of acorns it took to carve out this bowl." He paused, studied her face. "It makes me feel sad somehow." His tone reflected his words.

"Why, what do you mean?" she asked, surprised by the sudden change in his mood.

"For thousands of years the tribes lived their lives here, fishing for salmon, gathering clams and oysters, celebrating life with lively festivals, and then along came the explorers, then the trappers, the settlers, the missionaries. Before long so much was taken from them." His brow furrowed, "Imagine outlawing their most fundamental cultural events, forcing Western values…subjugating them…" Shelby detected indignation behind his words.

He was quiet for a long moment as he turned away from her. She felt uncomfortable in the awkward silence.

"Sometimes it all seems so hopeless." His voice had become a whisper. "We're here one second, in terms of the planet, and then, whoosh… we're just gone. It's so futile."

She could not read his face as his back was now to her; she was uncertain what to do about this sudden alteration of his mood. He had been so thrilled about Bella and the mortar bowl, but now he was melancholic.

Shelby remained silent, noticing that his head had dropped forward and his shoulders sagged, as he rasped, "I *get* it about history, but sometimes it seems so unfair, so hopeless… We are born and then we die. Our little lives are simply over in a flash. The end. *Fini* as they say in French…" His voice trailed off.

Shelby continued to stand there in the work room. She was not too sure what to say or do. An intriguing quote from high school lit class streamed across her brain. It was by Thoreau. Something about the mass of humanity leading lives of quiet desperation. She sensed a desperation in him. This was such a peculiar contrast to the charming Dr. Steele who had just interviewed the delighted

Bella. The despair emanating from him seemed to fill the room.

How odd. So there is more to this man than the charismatic professor he shows to us students. In an attempt to offer comfort, Shelby moved toward him and rested her hand on his left arm. Her fingers lingered there a long moment, slowly his right arm came around and gently pulled her into an embrace. As he held her, she felt that familiar banging of her heart as her stomach did a summersault. She struggled to breath.

Ever so gently, he tilted her chin up toward his face. He held eye contact with her for what seemed an eternity, and then slowly lowered his mouth to hers. For a very long while they stood like that. She was on fire. Adrenaline raced through her body but she kept still; almost afraid to move. Slowly he kissed her eyes. First one and then the other. Her heart hammered.

They remained like that until, finally, he slowly led her by the hand to the sofa in the corner of the workroom where he very gently lowered her down. They lay together. He traced her ear with his warm tongue. Her pulse quickened.

After a long while, he delicately removed her tee shirt, then her bra, finally her jeans and underwear. Shelby was afraid that she might stop breathing. She forced herself to take a breath. She felt frozen. Terrified to move, to break the spell. With feather-like caresses, he outlined her flat mid drift.

"You are beyond beautiful Miss Shelby Wells. I've dreamed of this. Of you this way…….." he groaned as he continued his butterfly strokes slowly moving up to her breasts.

Not even in her most wild Technicolor dreams, could she imagine these sensations. Of course she had kissed boys, even let one touch her breasts, but nothing, nothing, had ever felt like this. His touch moved down her body. She forced herself to take some breaths. She felt shy. There was no way she would let on that this was all new to her.

As he crooned, over and over again, "You're beyond beautiful," she began to relax. His hands moved down from her stomach. Down. No one had ever touched her there! At one point he had moaned out, "Shelby is it okay?" She took that to mean, was he permitted to continue. She had thought, *oh, yes, don't ever stop!* The rest of the afternoon was a blur of emotions and sensations stronger than any she had ever before felt.

Hours later, still captive in an exhilarating fog of emotions, she found herself at home in her room. She didn't dare to turn on even a single light; she did not want to break the spell. She lay in the dark for the longest time replaying each glorious detail, until sleep finally came for her.

In class the next Monday he presented his usual captivating lecture. She lingered around a bit at the end of class, thinking he would call her over, or give her a special acknowledgement, but he was merely his usual smiling self to all of the students.

At the diner on Friday she was sure that he would come by her section for his special cheeseburger. Every time the double doors sprang open she could not help but look up. Finally, around 5:30 she caught sight of him coming inside with his biking buddies in tow. He seemed engaged with the group and unaware of her. This seemed odd after what had happened on Saturday, but perhaps this was a way to keep their secret.

Shelby watched the group of men as they enjoyed happy hour and each other's company. Once she walked by and caught his eye. He winked. She felt better. Special. After awhile they all got up and left.

No contact was made about the weekend. That seemed weird to Shelby after all the excitement about Bella and Nano and………

She distracted herself with her homework, Nick, and the diner. Monday in class was a repeat of the previous Monday. He was charming to all the students. Shelby's stomach churned in a new way. Anxiety had replaced excitement.

What's up with him? she thought. *It feels like he's working awfully hard at playing it cool.*

Shelby decided to find out what was going on. She bargained with herself that if he did not make a date with her by Thursday office hours she would go see him. She was not one to confront others, but this was too important and too peculiar. The week seemed to drag by in slow motion until finally it was Thursday. *Knock it off Shelby. Put on your goddamned big girl pants and go see him. He's probably just trying to protect you from campus gossip,* she reassured herself.

As Shelby drove through the university parking lot, looking for a student space, she passed the faculty parking area, when her glance suddenly caught Dr. Steele climbing out of his tiny red car a few rows away. She pulled into a handicap space so that she could watch him as he came around to the passenger side of the car and opened the door for a pretty Asian-American girl. Shelby had seen her around. She knew she was a student. A petite and cute student. She could not take her eyes away. It was like watching a train wreck. She noticed that Dr. Steele's arm came around the girl's waist for the briefest of seconds. She studied their body language. They were a couple. She knew it! She could read it! If she had learned anything in her speech class it was that body language tells the truth!

She felt like she had been kicked in the stomach! Her head pounded and her mouth went dry. Suddenly her whole world seemed to shatter before her.

CHAPTER 5

May 13, 2005
Beaufort, South Carolina

"Grant! Honey, I'm home!" Shelby called out as she let herself in the front door of their expansive 1850's home. She dropped her keys into the antique bowl on the cherry wood plant stand in the entry hall, as her mind lingered for a moment longer on what the woman on the airplane had said, "Secrets are toxic. They can make us sick."

"Hey, there you are!" greeted Grant, her tall, good-looking husband, as he took her into his arms. "How was the trip?"

"Oh it was fine," she answered, leaning into his embrace. "You know Mom bugs me, but I enjoyed my sisters; the kids are all getting so big!" She smiled up at him. "I got to have lunch with Nano. It was nice. You would've enjoyed it."

"Too much of a whirlwind for me. Four nights and all that flying. No thanks."

"I'm starving. Anything in the kitchen?" she asked.

"The rest of my pepperoni pizza. Shall I heat it up for you?"

"Let me change out of these clothes. In fact, I'll grab a quick bath and then I'll have the pizza. What're you doing?"

"I was just going over the notes for the deposition I've been in all week. That money laundering case."

"Is it going okay?"

"Long and slow," he sighed.

As Shelby eased herself into the claw foot bathtub, the warm water flowed up around her body, finally covering her stomach. It reminded her of when she'd been expecting; the huge stomach protruding out of the water. It had looked like a volcano sticking up. She smiled a weak smile and leaned her head back against the rim of the tub and closed her eyes.

These trips home left her feeling this way; scattered, anxious. They brought up old stuff, but she knew that wasn't really it. She was used to being around Mandy and her two half-sisters and their bustling families. No, the phone call is what had done it. That deep nervous voice, "Is this Shelby Wells Forrest?"

She soaked in the deep tub longer than she had intended, letting the warm water soothe away some of the kinks in her neck. Her shoulders had felt like concrete for a while now. The horrible showdown with Grant before she left had not helped either. They had smoothed it over but it was still lying there under the surface, smoldering and unresolved.

She had been mulling it over for days. How does one finally tell her husband a truth that should have been told thirty years earlier? "Oh honey, by the way, it slipped my mind about the baby I gave away. Sorry."

And that is just about how awkwardly the story had finally come out when she told him two weeks earlier. By nature he was a gentleman; poised, and calm. He had not exploded in anger, he was perhaps more stunned than anything else. He asked a few questions about why exactly she had given the baby up. Those answers he seemed to accept, but he pressed hard on why he was just *now* hearing this. He was not one of the top prosecutors in the state for nothing. Her answers had been weak. She explained that she was terrified of him leaving her if he knew. Through sobs she repeated how much he meant to her, that she was afraid of losing him, the girls, their beautiful life together. He pressed a few more times and then had slipped into his silent punishing self.

As she lay in the tub that conversation was still vivid in her mind. She recalled his reaction, how the muscles in his jaw flexed in anger. There was something else there, an indefinable expression in his eyes. She had known that she had said enough. Too much. All her instincts had screamed, *"STOP! Shut up. Don't disclose any more!"* Crying softly she had pleaded with him to understand; he had walked out of the room. She had not dared to confess about the phone call.

They'd gone to bed with all of that between them, in silence. For the next few days they went about their activities acting as if nothing had happened. Small talk, and then it had been time for her to leave on her short trip.

And now, here they were two weeks later and nothing had been resolved. He pretended, and she acted fake. She understood that she had hurt him by keeping the secret all these years. On another level, deep within her psyche, a knowing was struggling to work its way to the surface. Some intuitive part of her had a deep, festering notion that Grant's turmoil over her confession, had more to do with something long ago with his mother. She couldn't put her finger on it, but she *felt* it.

Whatever it was, it was too vague for her to fully comprehend, and for the life of her, she could not figure out how to reconnect with him. She did know that now was not the time for her to revert into a protective silence of her own. *Show grace.* Those two words leaped into her thoughts. *Show grace.*

She thought of their Golden Retriever, Tessie, who lay on her back in supplication when she got into trouble. The image of her dog brought a smile to her lips. *Well I certainly won't cower in a corner or squirm on the floor. What to do?* She climbed out of the tub, dried herself, put on a fresh robe and padded out to the kitchen. *Maybe it will come to me.*

"Oh there you are. I made you a little salad to go with the pizza. I'll warm it up."

As she studied his courtly figure standing at the microwave she remembered just how much she loved him. Her heart softened around the corners. She had hurt him. She had not meant to and she sensed something else was going on with him.

Theirs was an old story: beautiful young girl working as a temp, then as a Girl Friday in the State Prosecutor's office. She works hard, develops her skills and before long becomes a competent paralegal. She was assigned to the "first years." They kept her busy. It soon became apparent that she was good at it. She came to admire the law, and the details of it allowed her to heal. She was a few years into this work, when the most senior paralegal had to take an emergency leave of absence. She was asked to fill in. That is when she came to work for State Prosecutor Grant Forrest.

At first she was so awed by his power and reputation that she did not notice him as a man. It had been challenging just trying to live up to the demands of his cases, but after a few months she began to admire his quick mind. He was classically handsome at 6'2" with dark hair and a strong build, but that was not it. She had learned her lesson about handsome. No, it was his brains. She could see that he was a creative thinker. A problem solver. The connections he made were astounding, but it was more than smarts, he was honorable. No dirty tricks. She knew that some of the others cut corners around the truth. Also he was perceptive about people. He was the most winning prosecutor in the district. He dug in and did not let go until he figured out a win. It was his mind that eventually won her over and the fact that he seemed to really see her. He was older, a whole decade, and he had pursued her.

The microwave beeped its completion. "Here you are milady," smiled Grant. It was clear to Shelby that he did not want to revisit the unpleasantness of their last real conversation. *That's fine with me, I am exhausted anyway.*

***

A few days later Shelby began to throw herself into her work. Across her life she had learned that the busier she was the better she felt. Action kept her mind focused on the present. The 50th Beaufort Water Festival was only eight weeks away and the committee was determined to make a bigger splash than ever. Shelby smiled at her little pun. She felt honored to chair this important event. She ran a mental list: the raft races and air show were locked down, but they still had not confirmed the headliner, nor completed the entries for the arts and crafts show. The steering committee was good, but still there was a lot of work left for her to finalize. *Good. The busier I am, the less time to think.*

As Shelby formatted the content that would go into the festival program, her eyes slid over to the Post-It mostly hidden next to the computer. The number was there where she had written it. She had checked it often, wondering what to do about it. The International Code 44 stared up at her. The United Kingdom, the largest USAF base in England, near Landenheath, close to Suffolk. She had Googled it. Six thousand employees, including Major Cody James of the United States Air Force. A charming little town of under 5000 people.

She was not certain how long she could continue the small-talk charade with Grant. It was one thing to tell him about the secret from thirty-five years ago and another to tell him about the phone call. If Shelby had learned one life lesson living with her controlling mother, it was duck and cover. Avoid confrontation at all costs. But that was then and this was now. *Shelby you are a grown woman, a grandmother. When are you going to woman up and do what you have to do? Make the effing phone call!* screamed her inner voice. She had not heard from that bossy part of her inner self for a long time. Mostly she went along to get along. She knew this was too important to fall back into those old behaviors.

CHAPTER 6

Sunday, June 26, 2005
Beaufort, South Carolina

Shelby had been awake all night. Today was the day. She would punch in the 44 International Code. She had to. She studied the illuminated red numbers on the clock next to her bed. 6:00. Perfect. She heard the purr of the engine as Grant's Lexus slowly moved down the driveway. He was off to meet up with his golf buddies. He would be gone for most of the day. This was her chance. Great Britain was five hours ahead. She would do it. First coffee. *I have to fortify myself for this. This single call will forever change the course of my life. It will be good in some ways, but it may set off a chain of events that I cannot even imagine. I may well be detonating a nuclear explosion in my marriage. One fact is certain, the life that I have led up until this morning may slide away from me forever. A big risk.* She stood up and shook her head trying to clear it.

Shelby rifled through her lingerie drawer and retrieved the throw-away phone she had purchased at the Radio Shack in Charleston the week before. She had paid cash. She turned it on. It hummed to life. She dawdled as she mixed the cream and sweetener into her coffee. She walked to her favorite spot in front of the bay window overlooking the waterfront park. She could see the sail boats in the distance. She tried to enjoy the first sips of coffee, but it was no use. She was too keyed up. She would no longer put off the inevitable.

She lay the Post-It carefully on the side table next to her. She purposefully put on her glasses and studied the familiar digits. Her stomach was churning and her face felt flushed. She felt the effects of adrenaline pouring into her blood stream. She took in a big breath and punched in the numbers. As it rang, she felt light headed. She did not know whether she was calling a cell phone or a house phone. She had no idea. Would a wife answer? A child?

She knew from that uneasy first call on that warm May 1st morning at 10:00 a.m., that there were two children, girls. *Were they little girls?* She really didn't know. The connection had been weak and Cody James was obviously overwhelmed with emotions as he stuttered out his sentences. The information she was able to comprehend between her own erratic breaths was sparse. He was in the military and there were two girls. He had been looking for her for a while now. He was born on June 26, 1970 in Atlanta. Shelby pulled her thoughts back to the present. She purposely had chosen this day, a day of beginnings, to finally place the call. Today her boy turned thirty-five years old!

Ring. Shelby counted. *One.* Ring. *Two.* Ring. "Hello," answered the husky male voice. Shelby noted that he didn't sound nervous this time.

"Hi. Uh... Cody. This is Shelby. Shelby Wells, ah... Forrest. Hi! Ha...ppy B..ir..rrr.rirth...day!" She tried for a cheery tone but sobs grabbed hold of her like a vice, tears pricked her eyes, as she choked out *birth d d d..ay.* It was the first time in her life that she'd had the chance to wish him a happy birthday. She couldn't take it. Sobs wracked her body. She fought to mute herself. She felt embarrassed.

There was an uncomfortable silence. No doubt Cody was collecting himself as well. "So hi. I wondered if I'd hear from you again."

More quiet as Shelby tried to settle her emotions. "I wanted to... I've looked at your phone number every day since you called. I feel awful." She broke down again. After a long minute, "Cody this is the first time I've ever gotten to wish you a happy birthday." The sobs again overwhelmed her. There was another long interval while she tried to collect herself.

"I've thought of you so much across the years. I've worried if you were okay." Another long pause. "Cody, I'm so sorry. Just *so* sorry." She broke down again.

"Hey let's not get all wrought up here! This is now. That was then. Yes, Shelby I'm okay. Well, better than okay. It's just that somehow for a long time now I wanted to find you. Find out who I am. I know that sounds crazy. I needed to do this, maybe because of the girls. I'm not sure… Is it a problem for you?"

His earnest words were edged with concern for *her.*

"Cody. I can handle my end. I was so excited that day you called that I didn't catch all the details. Is this a good time? Could you fill me in a little?"

"Well, I am thirty-five years old! Joke! That part you know," he teased. "I married my high school sweetheart, Amber, and we have two girls. Kaitlyn and Willow. Kaitlyn is four and Willow is two. Willow is becoming quite the talker. I've been stationed over here in the UK for three years. They're going to transfer me soon. My orders haven't come through yet. Maybe Lackland, Texas."

"So tell me about *you*," he urged. "What do you look like? How are you? Do I have any siblings?" His enthusiasm spread across the miles.

Relaxing slightly, as his excitement was contagious, Shelby began. "Whoa. Let's see, *me*. First thing… mystery upon mystery," she teased, lifting her voice, "I still, somehow, through the miracle of science, have maintained my signature red hair!" She snickered at her own joke.

"I'm fifty-three, married. We have two grown daughters and they each have a child. Both girls. Seems like a lot of girls running in our blood line. Cody, I'm one of four girls myself."

Cody laughed. "Hold on! Go back. Did you say *red* hair? My girls are both gingers and curly too. Is that from *you*?" His voice was filled with wonder.

Allowing her shoulders to let go a fraction, Shelby responded, "Am I hearing you correctly? Are saying *reds*?" She sucked in a swallow of air. "Goodness!" Another long pause. "I think you're saying that your girls have *my* red hair?" She hesitated. Caught her breath. "I almost don't know what to say, I feel…oh, Cody…I feel awed by this news." Her voice cracked.

After a long moment, "What about you? Last time I saw you there was blonde fuzz on your head. What color did it turn?" she forced herself to find a center of calm, though her heart was racing at the news that there were two little redheads out there….her little redheads…

"That famous dishwater color. Dull blonde. But my beard is pretty much auburn." He laughed. There was a long pause.

"Changing the subject. Shelby, I guess I can call you Shelby, right?" His tone grew serious. "It's good to hear your voice. I was afraid that when I finally got the records and found out where you were that I might have been too late, that you might have died or something….and when I didn't hear back from you after the May call…."

"Cody, I'm right here. I promise I'm not going anywhere." With that her words choked off. She took a deep inhale. "That's a promise. I'd love to get to know you." Her words were heavy with meaning.

"Maybe we could meet sometime?" she asked tentatively, worried she had shown too much, looked too needy.

"As I mentioned, we'll be stateside in a few months. We can set something up…" he paused. "You say two daughters?...I have sisters?…" Silence filled the airways as Cody grappled with this new reality; he was no longer an *only* child. After an awkward moment, "Hey, this call is going to cost you the national debt. Should we get off?"

"Cody there's so much to say. This one conversation can't possibly fill the void." Intuitively, Shelby understood that the intensity of talking was taking its toll on both of them.

"I want to know so much… I can't even formulate the questions. I'm so lame. I've dreamed of this…of hearing your voice…for decades…" Her words trailed off. She sucked in a deep breath. "I'll try to be better next time, calmer." Another pause, neither spoke. Finally, "Any chance you might email me some pictures of the girls, of you and Amber?"

"Hey, quid pro quo. I'd love to see what half of my DNA looks like."

"You got it. So Cody is this your cell or your house line?"

"It's the cell."

"What's your email address?" asked Shelby.

"Jamesfam@hotmail.com. Is this a good number for you Shelby?

"Ah. No. Actually this is a burner phone." Her tone was heavy, "Uh, I've a few things to work out here. It's complicated… Here's my email address: Shelbywells@aol.com."

"That's funny, I thought you took your married name, isn't that right?"

"Yes, but in the back of my mind I always knew that if you ever came looking for me I wanted some markers out there in the world so you could *find* me," she paused. After a moment, her words were hopeful, "Cody, may I call another time? By the way, what's Amber's take on all this detective work you've been doing?"

"She's my best support, my ally. Actually she's the driver behind this, has pushed me forward. She's interested for the girls' sake too."

"I'm glad. I guess we should sign off. So is it okay if I call another time? Do Sundays work?"

"Shelby, I appreciate the call. Sure, Sundays are fine. We can talk again." There was a pause, "Bye."

"Happy birthday, Cody. Bye."

As she closed her phone she had trouble sorting herself out. Mixed feelings; some guilt, a sprinkling of worry, topped off with a helping of triumph. She raised a tentative finger to trace her lips. A grin was fixed to her face. She was jubilant, but it was shadowed by a vein of dread lurking in the back of her mind.

As her heart skipped about, she stood up and shook out her limbs. Her body had been tense during the entire call.

The day is still young, she realized, *and there's no quiet Sunday morning ritual ahead for me, I'm too wired.*

Her brain began to replay the conversation. *Yes, two girls. Little girls. REDS!*

She dared to contemplate, *maybe somehow they could be my little girls............four, two..........a new talker. How ironic that they are the same ages at Gracie and Ellie.*

I wonder if there is a prayer that I could ever be a grandma to them?

Her more cautious, practical self warned her. *Slow down. One step at a time, lady. There's still so much in your life that is unsettled. Your girls, remember? Grant? You might soon be looking for an apartment, for a divorce attorney... There's no telling how this is going to play out.*

Slow down.

She decided to take the dogs out. She'd do her favorite four mile course along the harbor walk. She needed to figure out her next step, besides walking always soothed her.

THE UNRAVELING OF SHELBY FORREST

CHAPTER 7

June 26, 2005
Beaufort, South Carolina

As Shelby tied walking shoes on her feet, the dogs began their usual excited dance. Tessie, the younger dog, grabbed hold of Zoe's ear and pulled her toward the door. "Girls, cool it. We're going. Slow down," she laughed as they tumbled on top of each other. "Let me grab the leashes." The dogs nearly knocked her over in their urgency to get out the front door. She shook her head at how silly they were with their unbridled enthusiasm for all such walks.

At the corner of Craven and Church Streets, they headed down the hill toward Bay Street and the harbor. The dogs pulled at their twin extension leashes. She held them back as they passed the colorful antebellum homes on their street, King Street. She loved it here. Loved Beaufort. As she speed walked, she could not help but reflect on how exactly she had wound up here; so different, but also so similar to her hometown of Bellingham, Washington.

Both small towns: historic and picturesque. People knew your business. *But in Beaufort they had not known my business, my secret...* she reminded herself as her thoughts drifted back to her marriage and Grant. Shelby was keenly aware of the fact that since she had returned home five weeks earlier, Grant had made no overtures toward her. No bottom pats as he walked by, no sweet caresses of her cheek. There had been no lovemaking since she told him her secret. He was hard to read. He acted lovingly toward her, they were going through the motions, but under the surface it had all changed. Somehow he had slipped away from her. She knew that she had hurt him deeply keeping the truth to herself all these years. She also knew that as a stand-up guy, this was a devastating betrayal. Shelby was not sure this could be fixed and the worst part, of course, was that there was so much more to the secret; a man, a wife, and two tiny girls. It tied her gut into knots.

Her brain had been kneading it over and over all these long days. The busier she kept, the easier it was, but in the night it would wake her up and the tentacles of the anxious knot would grab for her heart. There was so much to lose.

She glanced to her right as she passed her favorite three storey historic home. A tourist might not know its secret: how it had lain in disgrace for decades, devastated by the Great Hurricane of 1893, barely escaped the Great Fire of 1907, only to be picked over by scavengers looking for firewood. It was not until the 1970's that restorations to the great ladies had begun. Today, this graceful old beauty seemed so relaxed, proud to once again show off her majesty, as she presided over her manicured lawns and gloried in the massive magnolia tree standing sentry in the front yard. Today that tree boasted full white blooms. Both the ground level and the second floor shared exquisitely carved white railings wrapping around verandas, somehow inviting a mint julep and a rocking chair. This favorite house on her walk had even been used in the 80's film *The Big Chill*. Yes, she had landed in paradise. Every street ended in a breathtaking harbor view; graceful sail boats bobbed in the water, elegant birds dived for their morning catch, and clear skies illuminated beautiful vistas in every direction. This was Grant's world and he had chosen to share it with her, share his family's historic home with her.

***

After the worst day of her life, June 26, 1970, she had returned to her "Aunt" Lily's Atlanta home. She stayed for a few more weeks until she was strong enough to comb the newspapers looking for something. She had been at her mother's best friend, Lily's home far too long, coming on to six months. Lily had been kind to her during the heavy pregnancy months, but it was time to move on, beyond time. She found a nanny job in Charleston.

The position was a new beginning for her. She didn't know a single soul in Charleston, had only ever babysat her three sisters, but on an intuitive level she knew that if she were ever to get past the agony of holding that sweet nine pound bundle in her arms, and then handing him to the nurse, it would be with a family. And she had been right. The couple's baby was five months old, a little girl, Cara, and she had immediately fallen in love with her. The family also had an old Labrador Retriever, which helped her cope with how much she missed her two dogs in Bellingham.

She had taken a room in a home nearby and enrolled in night classes at the College of Charleston where she double majored in history and business. When her upper division work began she had the opportunity to take more courses in her majors. There, she discovered that the College of Charleston had one of the very first business divisions offering a program they called "Word Processing." It was new, actually cutting edge at the time, a fancy way to type in text and then save it. The classroom was a maze full of computers. Shelby sat at her computer with a screen that showed what was typed. It was an amazing new technology. There was not a typewriter to be found in the Business Department. Shelby had been fascinated by it and was soon the fastest student in the department at processing words. To further hone her skills, she even enrolled in a few court reporting classes. She had no intention of becoming a court reporter, but she could see that these skills could be a path to her future.

By the time she had completed her degree, Cara was three and a half years-old, and the family was transferred out of the area for the father's work. It had been wrenching to say goodbye to her, as Cara felt like her own. Sometimes the baby girl would mistakenly call her "Mommy." Shelby could still remember the wave of pleasure that pulsed through her when she heard "Mommy." Those two syllables held a world of meaning to her, and for the briefest of seconds she would feel at peace.

As she and the dogs kept up their pace, Shelby allowed herself the pleasure of recalling Cara. There had been times when she would hold Cara on her lap, maybe playing Cara's favorite game of "What's this?" She could remember the sweet perfume of the child's soft hair as the game began. Cara would ask, "What's this?" as she pulled at Shelby's nose.

Shelby might answer, "Something to smell little toes!" and Cara would giggle as Shelby grabbed a bare toe.

"What's this?" and Cara would pat at her eyes.

"All the better to *see* a tasty little girl." Cara would explode into more giggles.

Finally, "What's this?" as she twisted Shelby's lips into weird shapes.

"All the better to gobble you up!" With that Shelby would tickle her tummy as if to eat her all gone…all of this to the music of Cara's gurgling laughter.

Smiling, she reminisced. There had been lots of games. "The Cara Years," as she had come to think of them, had been healing for Shelby on many levels. The family home had felt safe, and Cara was an enchanting bundle of joy. Often, as she played with Cara, teaching her the alphabet, Shelby's throat would tighten and a wave of grief would flood her. That happened when she let her mind drift to what her son might be doing. He would have been only four months younger than Cara, already talking and smiling, asking lots of questions. The child care had been a way to stay connected to him. In those days he was always at the edge of her thoughts. Through the safety of Cara's unconditional love, she had been able to move forward in life, studying during each spare moment.

***

As Shelby and the dogs continued along the waterfront park, she pulled her thoughts back to the present. A wave of calm came over her as she took in the beauty of the "tabby" shell pathways. She could imagine the colonists designing them throughout the park. They used slave labor to crush the oyster shells and then combined them with sand and water and poured the mixture into wooden forms to make bricks. The crushed shells created lime which held it all together. The tabby building material became an iconic type of cement in the Lowcountry. She loved it, partly because it reminded her of her girlhood, scavenging for shells around Bellingham's shore. That thought linked to memories of visiting dear old Bella after an adventure of collecting shells. Bella always gave her a graham cracker and a cup of hot chocolate. She smiled at the memory of Bella and of course Nano. She stopped the dogs at the water fountain and offered them a drink. Both dogs stood on their hind legs and lapped the water from Shelby's cupped hands.

Shelby this is good, a moment of happiness taking you by surprise. I know you are scared, scared of all you may lose, but you talked to him.

YOU TALKED TO HIM!! HE WANTS TO SEE YOU!

By the time she and the dogs had hiked back up the bluff road to the house, she felt better. She reminded herself that she had time. Cody and his family would not be stateside for a few months. She had a few months.

At home, she went into her office to check her computer. The in-box was heavy with messages. She held her breath as she clicked the Read Mail icon. As her eyes scrolled down the emails she came to Jamesfam@hotmail.com. Her breathing increased and her heart thudded as she clicked "open." The screen seemed to come alive as the images of two angelic little girls, standing with their arms around each other, came into focus. They were posed in front of the famous Stonehenge monument. The girls were dressed in matching navy blue sweaters over pleated red skirts. She noticed a familiar spray of freckles across the girls' noses and then their luxuriant bright auburn curls. Her heart banged against her chest. Holding her breath, she scrolled further, and there he was, her smiling handsome boy; square jaw, military hair-cut, blue eyes, with a joyous expression on his face. She could tell that he was tall, maybe 6'2" or so.

Shelby could scarcely believe what she was seeing. After all the years of imagining what he might look like, there he was! Tears sprang to her eyes. She knew this face. This was a reminder of a face she had admired years ago, Dr. Tom Steele, only this face had an open honesty to it. This was the face of a good man. She scrolled further to find his perfect family of four posing against the same backdrop: big, good looking daddy, beautiful petite, light-haired mother and two glorious little girls.

After a while she came out of the semi-trance she'd been in as she studied them. She scrolled through her own photos until she found a nice close-up of herself with Zoe and Tessie. Intuitively she sensed that small doses of information was a good way to proceed. There was no need, at the moment, to go into detail about Michelle, Laney and Grant. *I don't want to overwhelm him with what he's missed.* She selected the photo and pushed "send."

For the next hour Shelby sat, almost hypnotized, examining every detail of the precious faces in the photos. She imagined getting to know them. Her heart felt light and expanded with love.

CHAPTER 8

July 11, 2005
Beaufort, South Carolina

Shelby was dicing purple onions on the cutting board next to the deep old farm sink which she and Grant had salvaged when they had restored this ancient home. She smiled a little to herself as she continued to prepare her girls' favorite family recipe, her classic potato salad. The girls' and their families would arrive later in the day, and a certain level of chaos would take over. *A good thing*, Shelby thought, *maybe it will stave off the demons that keep running through my mind.* The Water Festival anchored the annual visit which brought her grand girls and her daughters, and their husbands, back home for two weeks each year. Her grandchildren could hardly talk of anything else. They had spent weeks working on their art projects for the arts and crafts competition, and the sons-in-law had been training for the raft races. It would be a marvelous vacation, so different from her sojourns back home to Bellingham.

This most recent visit home to Bellingham had been typical. Determined to not lose her place in that part of the family, Shelby continued her annual visits, but the time at home was never really satisfying. She loved her three sisters and their families, but no matter how many soccer matches and basketball games she attended, she still felt like an outsider. She knew that her mother was at the center of her discomfort. She could only imagine what was said behind her back. The disapproval wafted off her mother like a bad smell. She knew that her mother's controlling ways would never change. Sometimes she even questioned why she insisted on returning home each year, why she tried so hard. She chalked it up to her own dysfunction, but in her heart of hearts she knew a big part of it was getting to see Nano.

She could pinpoint the day that her mother's domination turned to disapproval. In her memory it seemed like yesterday. It was January 16th, 1970. The spring semester was just beginning when her mother discovered her bent over the toilet heaving up her Cream of Wheat breakfast. It had taken her mother about two minutes to put two and two together and confront Shelby. She could still hear that fatal life-changing exchange.

"Oh for God's sake! Look at you Shelby Wells. I've noticed you at dinner the last few nights. You've been moving your food around your plate. Your color has changed. You look positively green! Young lady you have gone and gotten yourself pregnant, haven't you?"

Shelby could still feel the sting of those words. She had been stunned! She thought she had the flu. She had been feeling horrible. The flu was going around. She recalled thinking, *pregnant? Could I be pregnant?*

Her mother had slammed the bathroom door shut, leaving Shelby to digest those words as the last of her breakfast came up. After a while, she washed her face and hands and almost in a trance, threw herself face down on her bed. She did not cry but her brain immediately understood that her mother was right. After a long while the tears finally came. The worst part was that she had never really had a serious boyfriend, had never really been in love. Now here she was, one stupid afternoon that removed her virginity. Pregnant. She had barely been able to grasp the fact. But the knowing slowly came to her consciousness; the missed periods, the tight jeans, the agonizing nausea, and then just as quickly, the awareness that her plans for her career as a history teacher in a far away university, had gone up in smoke, all for those throbbing hours with Dr. Steele.

Even now a lifetime later, working at her familiar kitchen sink, it was still so vivid. She recalled how the drama had unfolded. She decided to visit him during office hours. She chose the next Thursday to visit his office and to confront him. She had decided to drive her car across campus to his office, when she had seen him in the faculty parking lot with that girl. She had learned her name, Serena, and she had suddenly understood what Dr. Steele was.

In the next week, she had conducted a surreptitious investigation into his character. He had implied that he and his wife were separated, heading for divorce. She learned that his wife was merely staying in Seattle with their kids while she helped her mother through chemo. He was very married and apparently enjoyed a pastime of seducing his students. It had been difficult to learn that he had a reputation with the young women on campus.

Shelby's mind glided back across the years. She recalled the class fieldtrip to Ranch Creek the Thanksgiving weekend of 1969. She had made Steele her special study project. Under cover of about forty-five students from his two sections of History 101, she had watched. She watched as the students, including the pretty Asian girl, climbed into the bus. No surprise, the Asian girl jumped into a seat behind his. Ten hours later when they had arrived at the inn where they were staying Shelby positioned herself in a corner of the lobby area where she could observe him handing out the room keys. She had Barb, the classmate she was rooming with, get their key.

Dr. Steele had informed the students, during the briefing upon their arrival that he would be in room 102, just off the lobby, if they needed him. Shelby continued to watch as the students collected their keys and took their duffle bags to their rooms. The beautiful Asian girl smiled as she took her key and walked across the lobby to room 103, directly across the narrow hall from Dr. Steele's room. Shelby knew that if she sat in the darkened lobby spying, that in the still of the night, that girl would slip into his room.

It was then that she finally understood that she had meant nothing to him; she had been a mere distraction for a few hours, a conquest. What a stupid naïve fool she had been, thinking that she was special to him, imagining that what they had was the beginning of love. *Stupid! Stupid!*

She recalled that somehow she had managed to get through that class trip. She had felt numb, but she was a good actress, and concealed her hurt. The semester had ended. She earned her A and had not seen him again. In her mind it had been one ridiculous afternoon, but with her mother's declaration, it had become a life-dividing event.

Shelby shook herself back to the present and her potato salad. That was a long time ago. There was still a lot to do before everyone arrived. She could hardly wait to see Ellie and Gracie.

CHAPTER 9

July 12, 2005
Beaufort, South Carolina

Sun burnt and happy, Shelby delighted in tucking in her two little grand girls after their big day at the festival. Both girls were sticky from the cotton candy, but had been too sleepy to take baths. Shelby dampened a wash cloth with warm water and gently wiped the evidence from tiny hands and faces. Nothing pleased her more than when she had all of her gang under her roof. Her thoughts moved to her wonderful daughters. It pleased her so that they were each other's best friends and now even the little girls were becoming inseparable on these family vacations. Shelby prolonged the face wiping as the sleepy girls nodded off.

Oh she knew she was lucky. More than lucky. Her friends constantly said that they wanted her life: a handsome successful husband, two beautiful grown daughters, happily married, each intent on growing bigger families. There would be more babies. Shelby lingered as she tucked the covers in around little Gracie, aged two. *What a delightful bundle of energy and opinions she is with her sparkling hazel eyes and dark hair! Lots of opinions. A leader for sure.* Shelby laughed as she thought of the many orders that Gracie had handed out during the day.

She moved around to the other side of the double bed and tucked in Ellie, the polar opposite of Gracie, calm and agreeable. Ellie at four was a brunette with round, serious brown eyes and a thoughtful disposition; the easy one. For just a moment, Shelby pondered the future and thought about the little ones to come. This big house would fill up again, at least during vacations. Then without her permission two other little girls screened across her consciousness. Two red heads. Shelby's heart rate speeded up. The peaceful warmth she had been enjoying evaporated as reality set in. *If I'm still in this house…*

Shelby turned on the Mickey Mouse night light and quietly shut the door.

Down stairs she could hear the animated voices of her sons-in-law who were enjoying the warm evening on the veranda. They were recounting their victories in the raft races. She fought down the wave of anxiety that had taken over. *Stay in the present!* She forced a smile on her face and focused on the low hum of the guys' conversation. It was nice that they enjoyed each other. She walked into the kitchen where the girls were sitting at the granite island. "Oh Mom. There you are. Did the girls go down okay?" asked Michelle.

"They were so pooped out. I couldn't even get them into the tub and you know how they love that claw foot tub. I wiped the worst of the stickiness off. They were asleep before I turned out the light. I cannot get over how much they had both changed in just the month since I've last seen them."

"Mom, almost three months. You were in Washington. Remember?" corrected Laney.

Changing the conversation, Michelle said, "Mom, that was probably the most amazing Water Festival yet! You did a great job chairing the event. I hope you're proud."

"Mom, for sure it was the greatest! I had the best time. I loved seeing my high school friends. It's funny how we're all doing the kid thing. I really appreciate that I get to come back to my old life every year," added Laney wistfully.

"I know I'm only an hour away, but still, it's not the same as living here. It surprises me how many of my friends have stayed here in Beaufort."

"Honey, Beaufort is a piece of heaven is what I'm thinking," replied Shelby as she put her arm around Laney's shoulders.

With that Michelle got up and put her arms around both of them. "Momma it's so good to be home. Here you both are, my besties."

Shelby's eyes filled with tears. They stayed like that for a long moment.

Finally, breaking away, Shelby asked, "Does anyone need a snack? I know we've all been eating all day, but it has been awhile." With that she took the potato salad out of the refrigerator and sandwich fixings.

"Michelle would you see if the boys are wanting something to eat. Where is your dad anyway?"

That night in bed next to Grant's rhythmic breathing, she thought about her girls, about her beautiful family and the gripping need to see her son. *If I insist on seeing Cody and his girls, I may well lose what I have. Grant still has not touched me...*

Once again sleep eluded her. As she lay in the dark her mind rolled her problem over and over. She realized that she should have spilled the whole truth when she had the chance, that awful day in May when she told him about the baby in the first place. Now it seemed too late. She had already hurt him to his core. Grant saw the secret as a betrayal, that she had not trusted him with the whole truth during their entire marriage. Dark thoughts over came her. The children were raised, he was slowing down his career. What was there to hold him to her if he knew about the grown up Major in the United States Air Force; the two little girls? She witnessed what happens when handsome men are suddenly available. The women swarm around them.

She tried to calm her thoughts by reassuring herself that things always work out. *Do they Shelby?* asked her critical inner voice.

When Dad finally had had it with Mom's verbal abuse and bullying, did it work out? You'd been Daddy's special girl. He took you everywhere with him, told you that you could be anything, do anything. Life was your golden chariot just waiting to launch you as you soared across the heavens. So how was that soaring after Dad left? Your grades plummeted. In fact you were not really yourself again until those Charleston years when you were going to school at night and working in the Prosecutor's office. So maybe things do work out but sometimes it can take years.

Shelby hated it when her internal dialogue got around to her dad issues. She knew she had mom issues. Any of her friends could tell her that. Controlling, bossy, thinks she knows what's right for everyone, status climber. *Shit! Yes, mom issues.*

I can't stand knowing that I have dad issues as well. I won't go down that "if only" road; but... if only Daddy could have stayed.

The critical internal voice retorted, *you mean, if only he had been too weak to leave?*

Well, ...if only he hadn't remarried, had a new family, and moved so far away. If only... The internal conversation whirled around in her head.

Your self help studies have shown you that you have trust issues. You've also suffered abandonment. You need to move on. You are mired in all this.

I do have trust issues. Yes, damn it. Abandonment! I'm afraid that Grant will leave.........

After another ugly hour of arguing with herself she decided to get up. She was reluctant to pop an Ambien. The drug made the nightmares worse. A few days before the girls arrived, the really awful one replayed. The one where she was telling Grant about the phone calls, about Cody and his girls, when suddenly her teeth had all fallen out into her hands. They were black marbles. In the next scene she had somehow become the stained glass window in the sanctuary at church. She was frozen there in the colorful glass, forever watching her family walking across the church lawn, arm in arm, from her high vantage point on the wall. In the dream, she could see Grant giving Gracie and Ellie piggyback rides. They all seemed so happy.... getting along without her. Then she'd wake up shaking, gasping for air.

It didn't take a Freudian psychologist to analyze those images. Clearly her subconscious knew that a big price would be paid if she told more of her secret. Her mind was warning her that the *telling* would cost her all that she had worked for, Grant and the girls, and now the grand girls. Shelby slipped out of bed and made her way to the kitchen. No lights. There was enough ambient lighting to pour a half cup of milk, blast it for 30 seconds in the microwave and add a dash of vanilla flavoring.

Taking her place in her favorite chair in front of the bay window she drew a deep breath as she stared into the inky night.

When had her courage abandoned her? She knew. She just didn't want to admit what her parents' break up had done to her. She recalled that last morning when her dad had lived with them. His suitcase was packed and was placed by the door. She had raced up the stairs to where he was finishing getting dressed. She had wrapped herself around his leg, begging him to take her with him.

"Honey, you know you are my special girl, but I have to leave. You and Mandy will be better off with Mom. You'll see, I will see you for vacations. It will be okay. You'll always be my special girl." With that he had patted her on her ten-year old head, slipped his arms into his sports jacket and was out the door. Forever.

Yes, there had been a few weeks during some summers when she and sister Mandy had visited him. But she had always felt like an outsider, and then he married and had two more children. It was more painful to visit him and his new family, and endure not being a part of his life than to stay away. So she had stayed away. There had been phone calls, "How's school? How are your classes?" But there had been no real connection. Across the years as she thought about it, it felt like the light had somehow gone out inside of her. She remembered that she had once been so curious about everything, the indigenous people, Bella and Nano, traveling, kayaking, hunting for shells and labeling them, writings stories and entertaining everyone with them. She led the class in all her grades until the fourth grade. Then all that had simply stopped.

In her mind she divided time: "before Dad left" and then the "dark years" when he was gone. If not for having her best friend, Laura, to spend time with, she wasn't sure how she would have turned out, but she did turn out. Well sort of. *Maybe I have turned out,* she thought. *But I know that something important inside of me has always been guarded. I've not ever really let anyone all the way into my internal world. I've been protecting myself. I guess that's the trust thing again.* Shelby sighed and took a sip of the warm milk.

She remained sitting in the dark for a long time. Finally she asked herself, *Shelby, I think you've also held yourself back from yourself! I'm not sure you've been truthful with yourself about what you want.*

The internal conversation continued. *You've kept yourself so busy chairing festivals and training docents, writing your stories, and raising the girls, that I don't think you've seriously considered what **you** want. This is your life. Probably the only one you'll get and you are more than half way through it. What do YOU want?*

That line of questioning was not helping the anxiety and sleep issues. She sat very still. Finally, after a long while, *I want it all! I want Cody and his wife and little Willow and Kaitlyn to know Michelle and Laney. I want us to be a family! I want all of this to be okay with Grant!*

With that admission soft tears rolled down her cheeks.

CHAPTER 10

July 15, 2005
Beaufort, South Carolina

"Mom do you have energy to put the girls down?" called daughter Michelle from the kitchen.

Smiling, Shelby replied, "You betcha!" With that she went into the great room to gather up Ellie who was deeply involved with her new markers and a coloring book, and to search for Gracie. Sure enough Gracie was behind the corner desk surrounded with her stuffed animals, leaning against a very patient Zoe dog.

"Girls, bedtime. I'll help you get ready."

"Grandma may we have another 'tory? A native girl one? We love those!" asked Ellie.

"Sounds great! Why not? More Native Americans, huh?" laughed Shelby. "Gracie, are you ready for your bath?"

Fifteen minutes later the girls were ready for bed. As Ellie brushed her hair, she admired her image in the mirror. "Pretty," she declared to the mirror. Turning toward Shelby, "Pretty, oh Mamma Mia. Oh yeah!" Ellie's eyes twinkled in pleasure.

Shelby did her best to stifled the laughter that bubbled up inside when she thought of the things Ellie and Gracie came up with. *Mamma Mia, Indeed! Where'd that come from? She's only four. Oh what a heartbreaker she's going to be!*

The girls climbed into the double bed in the guest room. Shelby situated herself against the pillows, one adorable child tucked under each arm.

"Grandma, I like the one about the shell money and that funny man with the long hair. Will you tell that?" Ellie looked up at Shelby with clear brown eyes.

"Well once upon a time," began Shelby, sharing one of Nano's favorite legends.

A contented expression settled across Ellie's adorable face as she relaxed against her grandmother. Gracie looked up with a big grin, and then promptly inserted her two favorite fingers into her mouth, her index and middle fingers. A warm ripple of pleasure flowed through Shelby as she thought, *it doesn't get better than this*, and began her story.

"A long long time ago when the Earth was very young, before white people came, there was a man and a wife who lived in an Indian village near the ocean, far away in a place now called Washington. The man was a very greedy person. He loved shell money more than anything. One night he dreamed about where a vast treasure of *hiagua* was hidden high in the mountains, guarded by the mountain spirits. You girls remember that *hiagua* was their shell money?" Both girls eagerly nodded their heads yes.

"The man was very excited about finding the treasure, setting out the next morning to climb to the top of the huge mountain, a mountain covered in snow, where his dream told him the treasure was buried. When he got to the top, a voice told him where to dig, near three famous peaks. The man searched around and finally began digging with his antler pick. After a lot of digging, he discovered a *humongous* number of beautiful shiny shells. He pulled out hands full and discovered that they were strung on shiny golden strings. There was enough treasure to last a lifetime! He gathered up all he could carry, stringing them across his body, hiding the hole so that no one else would find the treasure and he headed back down the mountain."

The girls snuggled against Shelby, "As he trudged along, a loud voice, the voice of the Transformer, the king of the world, warned, 'you must leave gifts to the spirits of the mountain! You *must* leave gifts.'" Shelby used her deepest, rumbling bass voice. As she spoke, the sweetest memory of her Nano telling this story, using the same booming voice, filled her heart. She knew that sharing Nano's stories was a way of keeping her close. Another wave of contentment flowed through her. The girls leaned more heavily into her, as this voice of the Transformer was very scary.

"'Leave gifts!' But the man was too eager to get back to his village and brag, so he ignored the voice. He left *nothing* and kept hiking down the mountain weighed down by his heavy load."

"Finally the treasure became so heavy that he had to stop and rest. Soon he fell into an exhausted sleep. When he awoke his legs felt stiff. His back was sore. He touched his face and realized that moss was growing on it! He reached up to smooth back his short black hair but it was very long, hanging down to his bottom."

Suddenly Ellie and Gracie began to giggle. "His bottom," said Ellie laughing, no doubt imagining the funny man with the very long hair.

"Isn't that just silly?" asked Shelby as she continued. "Anyway, he got up, trudged down the mountain to his home, leaving all the shells behind. At his teepee a very old woman was weaving a basket. When she saw him, she greeted him with a smile."

"*Could this old woman be my wife?* He thought. *I must have been asleep for many long years.* Suddenly he realized that the spirit voice he ignored must have cursed him for not leaving gifts!"

"As he studied the old woman, he saw that she was at peace, and seemed rich with many dried salmon and hides on the line by her lodge. She explained that yes this was his lodge and she was his wife. With that he noticed that his desire for more and more shell money had cost him precious years with his wife. He no longer felt greedy, nor did he desire the beautiful shells. He smiled as he understood that he was the richest man in the world for the love that he shared with her. No shiny *hiaqua* could match that love. They lived happily ever after. The end."

Shelby glanced down at the girls who had now fallen asleep. Gracie was still contentedly sucking on her two fingers, and Ellie lips were curled into a smile. Shelby slipped out of the bed and leaned down to kiss each of the girls' soft cheeks. As she turned on the nightlight and closed the door, she thought, *Am I like that man? Am I so greedy as to want to know the love of all three of my children and all four of my grandchildren? Clearly I already have so many riches in the world. Maybe I am asking too much? Perhaps I need to thank the gods of the peaks for all that I already have and leave well enough alone?*

***

"Momma, thank you so much for a glorious vacation. Dale and Ellie and I had so much fun. The festival was better than ever and it was great having some quality family time," said Michelle as she hugged Shelby goodbye.

Ellie was wrapped around Shelby's leg and had started crying. "Oh honey, I know you don't want to go; Grandma will come up real soon and see you. What would you think if I told a story to your preschool class?" With that Ellie looked up through teary eyes, "Grandma could you tell about the funny man with hair to his bottom?" she asked.

Shelby sank to her knees and drew the child in for a last goodbye hug. She took a deep inhale of Ellie's sweet scent as she marveled at what marvelous mothers her two daughters were. "I'll come up and visit you real soon. I'll tell a story to your class and maybe we can go to the alligator farm again, would you like that?"

Nodding her head yes, Ellie's face broke into a smile. "I love you Grandma."

"I love you too."

Laney came out to the driveway with the last of the bags. "Mom, great time as always. The baby's not sure why we're leaving. She was getting mighty used to sleeping with her cousin. I hope she'll go down in the crib at home after all this big girl bedtime and being with Ellie."

Taking a big breath, Laney said, "Mom I hate to leave. You know what a help you were these two weeks with Gracie? I really appreciate it. I feel like I've actually had a vacation. I've probably been working too hard trying to get my food business going. I've been having a lot of sore throats…Anyway, I hope we didn't do you in with your hands full of the festival and all." She hugged Shelby a last goodbye.

"Daddy," Laney called to her father who was galloping around the drive-way impersonating a horse with Gracie giggling from her perch on his shoulders, "time to buckle the horseback rider into her car seat!"

Grant galloped over and swung Gracie to the ground. "Yes ma'm. Also it might be time to take this old steed back to the barn," he remarked, his eyes sparkling in mischief as he looked at his daughter.

As Shelby observed the scene playing out in front of her, she felt the familiar sense of falling in love all over again with her husband. This came from watching his tenderness with his girls and now his grand girls, his involvement in their lives… She took a deep breath and loosened her shoulders as the truth of what he meant to her filled her heart.

Grant was shaking hands with his sons-in-law who next hugged Shelby.

"Shelby, Grant. Another wonderful vacation. Thanks again for all the hosting and all those home cooked meals," offered Laney's husband, Conner, as he climbed into his big SUV.

As the vehicles pulled out of the driveway, Grant put his arm around Shelby "I hate to see them go," he confessed. "I always love the craziness of a full house."

"All that chaos didn't get to you? The dogs and the kids?" asked Shelby.

Grinning, Grant offered, "Ah, well if we are being completely honest, let's just say a bit of quiet won't bother this old guy. I always hated it when I heard grandparents say, 'love seeing them come, and love seeing them go!' That seemed so harsh, but perhaps there's a tiny element of truth to it," he added, smiling, as he drew her into an embrace. "Besides, now I have you to myself." Their eyes met in a knowing way.

Shelby melted into his arms thinking, maybe *the punishment has passed. Maybe I am back in his good graces.* She leaned her head against his shoulder as they walked back into the house.

"Grant, we haven't had a minute alone to chat since the kick-off gala for the festival," began Shelby still curling into him. "Why don't I pour us a glass of wine and we enjoy the veranda for a while."

A short time later, sitting on the porch swing, Grant began, "Well it was sure your big night. Your welcome remarks were funny and set the tone for the rest of the evening. It was rather a big deal, my dear girl, and you did an incredible job. Be careful or they will have you chairing the event every year!" he warned smiling into her clear blue eyes.

"Oh yes, for sure, they love free labor. I think once in a lifetime is plenty! I know that you get that it took a big effort, but it demanded way more of my time than I'd thought. I feel guilty about the girls. I wasn't able to visit them as often as I like. Gracie's clinginess sort of proved it."

"Shelby, the kids are *fine*," reassured Grant. "You worry too much."

"I hope they are..." She paused, "What did you think of Frank Preston as commodore? Were his remarks as lame as I think they were?" asked Shelby.

"He was okay. Everyone knows he's a bit of a blowhard, but he's done so much for the city. It was probably his turn," answered Grant. "I thought the theme, the Southern Side of the South" was clever. Who came up with that one?"

"Cindy Burke. She's a hard worker. That theme seemed to attract more attendees than usual. They estimated 50,000 across all of the days. Anyway, I'm glad I did it, glad it's over, but all that aside," Shelby held his eyes, "Grant, I want you to know how proud I was of you up at the head table. I'm already the envy of the other gals on the committee, and then you really topped it off when the dancing began. No one was brave enough to start it. Probably Frank should have, but you saved the day when you took my hand and simply led me out on the floor. I felt like royalty the way you were waltzing me around the room."

"Well you were the star, you *are* the star of this ol' boy's heart," concluded Grant as he squeezed her hand, the one he had been holding.

"I'm not sure I tell you often enough how much I appreciate you putting up with my committees and the fundraisers that go with them," added Shelby as she returned his hand squeeze.

"Well tit for tat, what about the thirty years of you charming my colleagues at hundreds of boring functions? I know the other guys can't figure out how an old goat like me, landed such a hottie." Grant paused and then laughing said, "I don't think I shared this with you. A few weeks ago in the locker room at the club, I overheard a conversation on the other side of the lockers. I only got a snatch of it, but someone referred to you as 'Grant's trophy wife.' It blew my mind! Clearly they weren't privy to the years of your capable work as the best legal secretary the office had ever seen, nor had they any idea about your grasp of the law, and I assure you, Madame, they've no idea of your writing life, or your docent work. Anyway, I couldn't help my reaction when I heard that!"

"You gotta be kidding!" Laughing out loud Shelby continued, "Sir, I take it as a compliment! Perhaps this old grandma has a bit more tread left on her tires!"

Grant began to laugh, enjoying Shelby's reaction.

Shelby added, her eyes dancing with delight, "It's sort of preposterous, but seriously, I take it as a compliment! Those guys must think I hang out in the gym all day and when I'm not doing that, I'm supervising my household staff while munching down bon bons!" More laughter.

"Honey, you are pretty *damned* gorgeous! I think they're jealous," added Grant.

"Hey, what if next time I'm at the club, I nonchalantly mention how my wife restored our 175 year old home? No wait. How about I casually mention about the time when I was on a case out of town, and came home to find you up to your elbow in the downstairs bathroom drain? Remember the terrible sewer back-up?"

Merriment played across his face. "When I got home I couldn't believe what I was seeing." Grant chuckled at the memory. "You had pipe wrenches, plungers and a drain snake littering the bathroom floor and your arm was literally up to the elbow in the toilet!" Grant's amusement continued as he recalled the image of his very ladylike redhead as chief plumber. "You got it out too. I forget, what was stopping it up?"

"Laney'd dropped her phone down the toilet!" Both Shelby and Grant smiled at the memory. Grant continued, "Or I could tell the guys about your archeological digs or the history museum." He smiled. "I'm teasing. Let them think what they want. But in a way it objectifies you. It sort of bugged me which is why I didn't mention it before."

Also you have been mad at me for weeks. She thought silently.

He turned toward her and gently lifted the curl on the left side of her face and tucked it behind her ear. "I love your new hair cut. In fact, I love you Shelby Forrest," he murmured as he bent down and kissed her fully on the lips. "How about we go upstairs?"

A ripple of pleasure flowed through her as she returned his kiss. His mouth was warm, his tongue inviting. She was a perfect fit against his strong muscular body. Across her life with him, his embrace had sheltered her from the world. And *always* this part of their marriage had been the crown jewel.

Maybe I have my husband back? Perhaps the hurt and rage from learning my awful secret has finally lifted.

Maybe things will be okay, for now...

DONNA FRIESS

CHAPTER 11

August 1, 2005
Beaufort, South Carolina

Shelby arrived early at the museum. The 'Indian Artifacts from 1500' exhibit was set to open the next weekend, and it wasn't ready. It was her job to make sure that it was historically accurate and creatively put together. She had overseen the summer exhibit for the past five years. She looked forward to it every year.

There was a lot going on at the museum and in another month or so, it would be time to train the next class of docents. Five women had passed the rigorous interview process. Shelby used her key to get into the back area where the collections were housed. She set her latte down on a plastic topped table as she examined the progress on the display. The tools and pots looked good. The Catawba tribal women were famous for their beautiful pottery. She loved the providence of the pots: they had been in heavy demand by the early colonist who insisted that a good gumbo could *only* be cooked in a Catawaba pot.

Looking around the room, she admired an ancient hoop leaning against the wall. The indigenous tribes loved sports and gambling. This hoop, made of twigs wrapped in soft hide, was a replica of the hoop used in an early game. The people rolled the hoop in a straight line past the tribesmen. The warrior who could get his spear cleanly through the hoop, won the competition. The problem was how to demonstrate the tribal peoples' love of gambling. As Shelby pondered this, her memory transported her back to another gaming tribe. She sat down and took a sip of her coffee as she recalled their 1998 family trip to visit the Maasai of the Serengetti, the purpose of which was to study the Maasai culture and observe the first ever inter-tribal "Olympic" competition. She could only imagine how much betting had been involved in those games. A mental image of the Maasai warriors and their jumping competition came to mind. She smiled thinking of all that jumping and the singing that accompanied it. The champion managed to get three feet off the ground. The shocker was at the end of the three days of competition, when the women of the tribe invited, she laughed to herself, *Invited is a bit mild, rather they dragged us into their jumping circle, and insisted that we jump!!*

She smiled to herself. *What delightful memories!*

She continued to reminisce; the more she and her daughters got into the jumping, the higher they went. Shelby could still visualize her glorious Michelle, at 5'8", as she out-jumped them all, to the hilarity of the Maasai women. It had thrilled her that her exquisite brunette daughter was able to gain such height! She smiled just thinking about it.

As the vision of the colorful Maasai athletes flashed through her mind, more details of that trip came into focus. Her pulse quickened as her thoughts transported her back to that time. It was the first day of the safari, a big, bold family adventure. She recalled that they were in Arusha, Tanzania. It was the first day of the tour and the members were assembled quietly on white metal lawn chairs outside of the dining room at a resort where they'd spent the night. The guides, Haji and Neko introduced themselves to the group of ten strangers who would comprise the tour guests. Haji opened with a welcome in Swahili. He greeted the group with a huge smile, white teeth gleaming against ebony skin, saying, "Jumbo" and surprisingly at least five of them, including her two cheeky and dazzling daughters, chimed in with "Hakuna matada." That was all it took to break the ice; the whole crowd fell into spontaneous laughter, as all were familiar with the Lion King movie. Shelby found it amusing that a few simple words garnered such respect.

A memory floated by. She'd purchased a beaded bracelet from a local. As he handed her the change, she replied, "Jumbo." He stared at her and, finally, with great awe, asked, "Ma'm where you *learn* Swahili?"

Crazy. Enjoying the luxury of the mental trip into the past, she allowed the memories of that trip to spool forward.

The guide, Neko, was explaining how much he enjoyed leading tours, that this tour was a pilot program focusing more on tribal culture than wild animals. Before long, he asked each member of the party to introduce themselves. Grant's deep Southern drawl filled the air as he replied, "Grant Forrest, Beaufort, South Carolina," and along the row went the introductions, until finally Shelby heard a voice from the row behind her, "Tom Steele, Los Angeles, California."

Her head had swiveled around so fast her neck made a cracking sound. *What?* It felt like her blood had stopped flowing. She had not been able to believe it. It was all she could do to maintain her cool and not fall off her chair.

What were the chances? One in six billion? Well maybe not. The entire population of the planet cannot afford to travel. Well, one in two billion? Ten of us out here together for two weeks! Ohmygod! With that she recalled that she had sunk further into her little lawn chair.

As Neko and Haji continued their orientation, she managed to calm down her racing heart. After about twenty minutes the meeting broke up. All were to check out of their rooms, and meet at the Range Rovers at 10:00 a.m.

As the group gathered around the vehicles, Shelby had finally settled down enough to notice the woman with this Tom Steele of Los Angeles: older, well groomed, and nice looking, in a plain, grey grandmotherly way. *How old would they be? A quick addition problem; let's see in 1969, almost thirty years ago, he was probably 43 years old. So, early 70's? Not bad. What did the lady say her name was? Hum... ah. Adrianne. Adrianne Steele. Not a girlfriend. A wife. Probably the first wife. Interesting.*

The tour members seemed to naturally divide between the Rovers. The four of them and a couple from Australia stood next to one of the trucks. From the cover of her bush hat, she studied Tom Steele as he handed his duffle bag to Neko, then turned, facing in her direction. She knew he couldn't see her where she was, standing in the shadow of a graceful acacia tree. She studied him. He had maintained his regal bearing, not stooped shouldered as were so many older people. The hair was grey now, but still dropped boyishly across his forehead. She could make out the blue of his eyes, Robert Redford eyes, but the crinkles she remembered at the corners were now canyons that cut down his cheeks. The jaw line had become fleshy, deep lines surrounded his mouth. He was still handsome, but a faded version of his younger self.

Shelby realized very quickly that she needed a strategy in place to cope with this unexpected and nightmarish occurrence. She decided to employ the tactic of amnesia. She knew from their trek through Nepal two years earlier, that spending twenty four/seven with tour mates tended to create a certain type of chumminess. For a moment she thought of all those group meals. Grant was naturally outgoing and made friends easily. She would pray that he did not turn Tom Steele into his new best friend.

Shelby took another sip of her latte and settled more fully into her chair as she continued to explore the old safari memory. She was enjoying herself, in that way that people do who are picking at a scab.

The first stop on the way to the Ngorongoro Crater, had been at Lake Manarya. They were to trek through the banana plantation and then enjoy tasting banana beer. As they tromped through the plantation, she noticed that the tour members were spontaneously getting acquainted. Far ahead Grant had fallen into step with Tom Steele and the local guide. Shelby now recalled just how upset she'd been imagining their conversation, how knotted her stomach had been with anxiety. She recalled arguing with herself: *for God's sake Shelby, it was thirty years ago, he probably has no memory of you, much less of that fateful afternoon in his workroom. Chill lady!*

That night at the lodge there was a welcome dinner. All the tour members were seated at one big table overlooking the magnificence of the world's biggest crater. Haji and Neko did not take their meals with them, needing a break, no doubt from the barrage of questions. Michelle, graceful and smart at twenty-two, had leaned over to her mother and whispered, "Mom, I read that the astronauts can see this crater from space. It's that gigantic!"

Shelby had responded with a smile, but her real attention had been focused on what might happen, having Tom Steele as a dinner mate. As the wait staff took their orders, the burly sixty-something Australian man, Edmund, in his heavy accent lifted his wine glass, "G'day mates, um, 'cheers.' How about a wee toast to a once-in-a-lifetime walkabout? Hear hear!" Everyone along the long table raised their glasses.

"Chums, how about we go 'round the table and share what we hope to gain from this expedition. Give us a bit of a chin wag, heh?" He chortled at his suggestion and paused a moment. "My area is sorting out the lifestyle differences between the Aboriginals who live in my country from these here, Maasai."

Shelby had struggled to understand what he was saying through his heavily accented English. "My" country sounded like "me." His wife was up next and talked about her interest in the African culinary arts. Before long it was Tom Steele's turn, "The body of my life's work has centered upon the indigenous people of the western United States. I foresee an examination of the parallels with the African tribes. Perhaps I shall write about it, certainly study the common denominators, formulate hypotheses, and perhaps develop a new paradigm."

His words sounded so pompous. *Asshole*, she'd thought.

Around the table the responses continued, Michelle had spoken up. "Uh. Hmm. Somehow I've become fascinated with the birds.

Ah,… but I goofed up today! Um, sorry! I let that bird out of the cage and told Haji of my interest!"

The group snickered at her little pun." Oh boy did he jump on *that*," her remarkably attractive face broke into a smile. "Just this afternoon on the drive here, I got a real ear full; my own private bird seminar!" she teased. "He kept stopping the Rover to show me different kinds of birds, and I was hearing the *moans* from those in the back of the truck!" She was laughing and the others joined in.

Laney, Shelby's very sweet, petite, light brunette daughter, was next. Gracing the group with her most blazing smile, she said, "I begin my senior year at the university in September. I'm up for adventure before I settle into career mode." Her voice was alive with excitement as her wide brown eyes sparkled in anticipation.

When Grant's turn came around, elegant as always in his Carolina drawl, "I'm so happy to meet y'all. I've always had an interest in photography but more recently I'm focused on the human condition. These days I'm striving to show our lived experience through images, faces in particular. This is a great opportunity for me." He smiled comfortably around the table.

Shelby was proud of his response; it revealed his gravitas and a bit of his soul. *He's so poised and handsome,* she'd thought.

When it was her turn, "I'm a volunteer curator for our local museum. My specialty is Native American artifacts. I, too, am interested in the Maasai way of life. It's such a privilege to be allowed to be among them, to participate in a sort of living museum. I feel humbled to be a part of all this."

She'd said more than she'd wanted. She didn't want to be conspicuous. The waiters reappeared. *Saved by the food!* Lively dinner conversation moved along in soft rhythms.

A few days later, after an afternoon trek across the grazing lands of the Maasai, the tour members were relaxing with cold drinks on the veranda of the resort. The Steeles were seated at a small table near Shelby and Grant. Tom began, "It sure was something to see those boys decked out in their bright red blankets driving the goats back to the compound. I wonder how long they can maintain their way of life?" he had pondered.

As Shelby's memory continued to zero in on that trip, she recalled they were several days into the safari at that point and her concern about being recognized by Dr. Steele had faded. She was feeling more like herself, less edgy, less uptight. She recalled how she'd answered his speculation.

"I don't think there's a *prayer* that they'll be able to remain as they are!" She had been surprised at how snarky she had felt. "I read that there are already four million cell phones in Africa. With solar technology coming, my guess is that in the next ten years, forty million Africans will have cell phones. The Maasai already discourage their children from learning more than rudimentary math. They don't want them going past the second grade for fear that they will leave the tribe." Her eyes had challenged Steele's.

Fueled by annoyance, she had continued, "Once technology, computers and cell phones are more affordable, *how* will they be able to keep the modern world out?" She had paused and inhaled sharply. Her volume had increased, "Furthermore, by letting us in, they are in a way setting themselves up for assimilation; their youth can *see* what we have and I promise; they will *want it*!"

"That's pretty doom and gloom." Tom had answered, his own challenge clipping his words. "You think they'll experience what happened to the natives in America?"

"Well I doubt the government will *infect* their blankets with small pox," her words had been taut with sarcasm, "or put a price on their heads, but yes, I think it will be the end of them. That's why it's so important, that we, who write, get as much of their way of life preserved as possible!" She had concluded with more vehemence than she had expected.

Now, as she sat in the workroom with her latte, she wondered just when her passion for native peoples flamed so bright? She answered herself. *What do you think? It's because of Nano, the one who really raised you. You're more Native American at heart than anything else.* She smiled to herself in the privacy of the backroom. *Yes, and that is a very good thing!*

Once again her memory pulled her into another day on that safari. The group had visited the Leakey Museum, studying the history preserved in ash, foot prints of early hominids imprinted 3.5 million years earlier. The earliest evidence of humans had been fascinating and most of the group wanted to see more. They decided to climb down to the site of one of the more famous excavations. Ever watchful of Tom Steele, Shelby noted that Adrianne Steele had stayed behind to rest on a bench in the shade. Shelby's vigilant eyes had stayed on him as he speeded ahead of the others, catching up with Michelle.

Shelby, too, increased her pace, drawing closer as they hiked down into the canyon. She was near enough to overhear him talking to Michelle. Shelby's stomach recoiled as she sensed the oily charm oozing out of him. *Oh for God's sake. Does this creep ever stop?* She heard his professor voice, working hard to impress her daughter. He was saying, "The Leakey family put Africa on the map. Before Mary Leakey's find of the first hominid's skull in 1959, there was no real evidence of the genesis of mankind in Africa. They found stone tools in earlier digs, and were convinced that humankind began here, but they needed more proof, so you can imagine what it meant to discover a skull." Shelby was aware that he was droning on and on. She wondered if Michelle was now brain dead from it all. She dropped back and chatted with the Australian man's wife, Enid.

About half an hour later, she found that she had caught up once again to Michelle and Tom Steele. He was still at his lecture. "Then two years after Mary's discovery, another, larger hominid skull was discovered. This one was probably the tool maker. He became known as *Homo Habilis, man with skill.*" Steele paused in his tutorial to ensure that Michelle was listening. Shelby heard a faint, "Uh huh" from her daughter.

He continued, "The entire Leakey family was fascinating. Imagine three generations of paleontologists. What a legacy! I had a chance to teach with the son, Richard, one semester when he was a visiting professor at USC. Quite a guy. Discovered *Homo Erectus,*" he concluded, clearly pleased with his little speech.

Shelby could practically see his chest puffing up. *Asshole,* she had thought once again. *Try paleoanthropologists, you twit. At least get it right.* As she walked along the dusty path, she had began to realize that the angst of the past week had been in vain; all that freak-out over some big Tom and Shelby reunion, of Grant learning that he'd been more than a professor to her... Shelby recalled that she had shaken her head in disgust, thinking, *the bastard doesn't even know I'm alive!* That truth had enflamed her emotions even more fully. She was furious!

That night after dinner, in the big dining room, the resort staff entertained the hotel patrons with an elaborate tribal dancing demonstration. The audience thrilled to the raw passion exhibited by the spontaneous chanting and stomping taking place in the center of the room. The dancers were garbed in feathered headdresses and brightly colored skirts or pants. It was a rowdy and exciting show. Toward the end, the dancers pulled in audience members to join in the fun. The hotel patrons bravely gyrated, trying to keep up with the dancers, until finally they were allowed to sneak back to the safety of their seats. The waiters were pouring tea and coffee. The audience part of the exhibition was over.

Suddenly the room throbbed with even more energy. The air crackled as the drum beats grew faster and faster. The grand finale was beginning. All eyes were once again riveted on the dancers. From the corner of her eye, Shelby detected some movement down at the end of the long table. *Oh for God's sake!!* She was aghast as she observed Tom Steele rising to his considerable height and reaching across the table for Michelle's hand. Shelby could not believe it. *The audience participation part is over, you idiot!* her thoughts screamed, as he led Michelle out to join in the wild exhibition. Hips swaying, feet stomping, arms flying in time with the rhythmic beat, they held their own. The dance was intense as it grew faster and faster ending in a great crescendo of noise and movement. Instantly a mighty burst of bravos was shouted out by the audience. Many stood up; whooping and whistling. When everyone around her stood, Shelby was forced to as well. She plastered a smile on her face and clapped, after all it was her vivacious daughter who was the star. In her head, once and for all, she got that Dr. Steele was a player, a user of others. A cad. A sleaze ball. Bottom slime.

Even as old as he is, he's still chasing after the young women! He's disgusting.

Shelby was aware that she was allowing her dark side free reign in her head, and she didn't care!

As Steele walked Michelle back to the table, elegant as ever, she took her seat, but as he made his way around the table to take his chair next to wife, he miscalculated its placement, and suddenly, and most ungracefully, he plopped on his rear!

Commotion. There was a scuffling of chairs as his table mates scooted back and tried to help him up. Shelby did her best to conceal her delight, as the group around him raced to make sure he was okay. "Hey, Tom, you okay man?" they chimed.

For the remainder of the trip she kept a close and annoyed eye on him.

As she took a last sip of her now cool latte, another memory streamed by. It was farther into the trip. Grant had stayed up visiting long after she and the girls had turned in. Later, back in the room, getting ready to take a shower, he reported, "I was talking with Tom and Edmund. Tom's an interesting guy. He held an endowed chair at the University of Southern California for ten years before he retired a while back." Grant glanced across the room at Shelby. "Apparently his research was seminal regarding the matriarchal culture of some of the tribes of the Pacific

Northwest. He says it changed the course of thinking; got him a cushy position at USC. I'm surprised you haven't heard of him with all of your studies." With that Grant walked into the bathroom and stepped into the shower.

Let's see, oh handsome husband, mused Shelby, her sarcastic self had taken over. *Perhaps I have heard of him. Oh yes, I wrote about the maternal social leadership, about the importance of the medicine woman to the Nisga'a tribe in my first paper. In fact, I took him to meet my Bella. MY BELLA WAS THE PRIMARY SOURCE!*

Continuing her dark rant, *Dearly beloved husband, I have **purposely** kept his goddamned name out of my head and out of any conversations for the past thirty years! It was enough to find him on the Internet and see the title of his book. It's become a classic in academic circles. Yes, darling. I have heard of him, not only did he not give me any credit in his book, he ignored Bella's contribution all together... that irks me the most! Ah yes, and there was the matter of the nine pound reminder of our little afternoon tryst.* Shelby had enjoyed her macabre thoughts.

She could hear the museum coming to life on the other side of the workroom door. It was time to get to work. Almost ready to close this chapter on those old memories, she lingered a moment longer, recalling the most heated argument she and Tom Steele had engaged in during that African trip. It was the old debate over the arrival of humans to North America.

Back then in the 90's the newly discovered Kennewick Man found near the Columbia River in Oregon, was one of the oldest and most complete skeletons ever discovered in the Americas. It proved that there could have been multiple migrations of early man; that they could have come by tar-lined boats well before the Ice Age.

Standing now and organizing herself for work, she recalled what a rampage she'd been on. *I ranted on about the ancient finds in Chili, the stone tools from California's Channel Islands, the navigable kelp forests along the coast of the western seaboard. I mercilessly insisted that the new DNA evidence proved that early man lived on the Bering Land Bridge, but of course, that's not what the argument was really about. I had always felt used and discarded by Steele. It was a way to get even. All the while, Steele had stuck to his old-school argument of one big migration over the land bridge 14,000 years ago. Once again he had dismissed me.*

I have to get back to work. But I do take great pleasure in being vindicated in my old position. The recent carbon and DNA studies are finally in on my old buddy Kennewick Man. They support the position I took all those years ago against Steele. Scientists now lean toward the concept that humans were in the Americas some 20,000 years ago.

I'm proud that I argued my position, that I stuck up for myself. It finally gave me some closure regarding Steele's character. It allowed me a window into his personality; not only was he a scoundrel, he was closed off. Everything was his way or no way. I was correct in never having divulged to him about the baby; I meant nothing to him.

Poor Grant, I doubt he ever did figure out what had come over his usually agreeable wife. Why I was so contentious!

Lesson learned, my dear, she reminded herself as she threw away the last of the cold coffee and walked over to apply the finishing touches to the display.

CHAPTER 12

August 12, 2005
Beaufort, South Carolina

The day was going to be another scorcher. She sometimes wondered if she would ever get used to the humidity, so completely unlike Bellingham, *ah but so wonderfully far away from Mother*! A mischievous grin crossed her lovely face as she tied her left shoelace. "Girls, come on, time for our walk!" With that, her two big Golden Retrievers came bounding into the foyer. "You're so funny. Where do you want to go today? The harbor?" Both dogs wagged and panted their approval.

As Shelby set out on her familiar power walking route, she thought about the weekend coming up. Grant was coming home early today, Friday, as Michelle and Dale had invited them to dinner. It was not a typical weekend thing for Michelle to cook for them. She wondered what was up. *Oh I so hope it's baby news!*

The week before when she had driven the 134 miles to read one of her stories to Ellie's class, she knew that Michelle had some appointments. She did not push, however she noted that her daughter was usually more forthcoming about whatever appointments or meetings she had. This time she had been a bit mysterious. Until this dinner invitation, Shelby had not given it any more thought. Frankly, she had to admit to herself, *I've been more concerned about my own problems...*

The "Ellie Day" at the pre-school had been wonderful. Her adorable granddaughter had been thrilled at having her own grandma there to read for the class. Shelby couldn't help the delight that played across her face. Ellie's little feet had practically danced with excitement. Of course the story *had* to be one of her Pony Girl stories.

As she and the dogs strode along, Shelby's thoughts scanned the crazy busy years when she was the mother and Laney and Michelle were the children. She could almost smell their fresh little-girl fragrance, and feel the softness of their little bodies pressed against hers during those bedtime story years. "Mommy, oh Mommy," the harmony of Michelle's seven year-old voice rang in her memory, as the vision of Michelle's brown eyes filled with longing for just "one more 'tory." Laney-girl, at four, would have looked up with exuberant eyes, "Momma, how about Pony Girl winning the horsey race?"

The harmony of their little-girl voices faded back into memory, but the feelings of joy she experienced raising them, being their mommy, remained. The mental film of their growing up years continued to screen across her mind; the soccer games, sabot races, science fairs, and Girl Scout camps. When they had been really little, a favorite game was the "roar" game played on hands and knees. Shelby would hide and when she heard one of the girls crawling by she would bellow out a huge ROAR! The girls would collapse in giggles. They loved it. These days it had become a tradition with the grand girls. Those growing up years of her own girls were certainly the busiest, happiest time of her life. She had, for once in her lifetime, allowed herself to mostly let go and surrender to the music of their childhoods. The pain of giving up that glorious nine pound bundle had been somewhat muted in those years, she thought of him, but the ache had softened. Mostly.

As she and the dogs moved along she realized that today she felt strong. *I'm having a good day. No nightmares last night.*

Her thoughts pulled back to when her daughters were little. Suddenly an image closed in on the first day of kindergarten for Michelle.

In her mind's eye she saw herself at the elementary school that day. She was unbuckling Laney from the car seat, preparing to go inside to the office, when a knot of four energetic junior high school boys sauntered along on the sidewalk next to her minivan. In her slow-motion memory, she lifted Laney out of the car, and as she did, her eyes fell upon a light-haired boy in the back of the pack. Her breath caught. Her heart somersaulted. Sweat broke out on her upper lip. She'd reached for the roof of the van to steady herself. She felt faint. For a millisecond her brain imagined that the light-haired boy was her son. The boys continued by, this boy was taller than the others, pink cheeked with fair hair falling across a high forehead. He was sturdy, good looking. She'd thought, *Maybe a basketball or football player.*

As they continued toward her, she caught the sounds of his laughter, something one of the others had said. The corners of his blue eyes crinkled. *Steady Shelby* she had admonished herself. *Get a grip*, but the panicky sickness had overtaken her. She stood, too long, with Laney riding her left hip

"Momma, what's wrong, you look funny?" asked Michelle from the sidewalk.

She fought down the panic. *Steady Shelby. It cannot be him.*

But he would be in junior high. He's thirteen now. It could be him...

After a few minutes, the alarm mostly subsided. She pulled herself together, rolled the van door shut, and reached for Michelle's hand as she reminded herself: *Today is the first day of big girl school.*

She forced that tough part of her psyche to close the Evan door. She had known not to name her baby boy, but somehow across the years, in her fantasies, he'd become Evan. *Get a grip!* She had squared her shoulders, taken a restorative breath, forced a smile, and marched with her girls into the school's office.

Pushing old thoughts from her mind, Shelby focused once again on the dogs and the walk. *Stay in the present!* They had just come upon a flock of seagulls perched on the rocks next to the water. Both Zoe and Tessie stopped to take stock of the birds. "You girls," said Shelby, "oh how you would love to be off leash." She smiled at the image of how fast those birds would scatter if she were to unbuckle the two leashes. They remained there, all three, looking out at the harbor, calm now in the humid summer morning. The sky was blue and the only sounds were of the water lapping against the rocks and the joyful screeching of the birds. After awhile, "Let's go!" she coaxed the dogs, knowing she had a lot to do before Grant got home around 2:00 and they headed to Charleston.

Her thoughts returned to the "Ellie Day" of storytelling and how serendipitously the whole Pony Girl enterprise had begun. She had Grant to thank for all of it, for believing in her. Years before when Michelle and Laney were just little girls, Grant would sometimes come home late from work and stand at the door listening to the involved goings on of the American Indians in her stories. He would remain there for a long time, absorbed in the plot until the girls fell asleep.

Eventually he began a campaign to get her to write down all those tales. Grant was nothing if not a formidable advocate. He kept up the pressure. "Honey I don't think you know what you've got there," he'd say. "The stories are original and well developed. They are exciting, hell, I even enjoy them! You simply *must* write them down, if only for our girls when they are mothers."

Finally when both girls were in school and she had some time to herself, and partly to get Grant to stop nagging her, she did. She created a character of a little Native American girl she named "Pony Girl." This little girl went everywhere on her beautiful spotted pony with her younger brother, Tangled Hair Boy, following behind. In the stories, Pony Girl and the brother, nicknamed Tangle, got into lots of mischievous escapades. Eventually she illustrated the stories with photos, and printed up copies at the local copy store. It was fun and she enjoyed giving them away as gifts.

One day Shelby attended her neighbor's baby shower. Her gift to the expectant mother was a set of three of her little books. The colorful books were passed around the circle of party goers as the expectant friend opened the other gifts. After the party, her acquaintance, Susan Parker, stopped her, "Hey Shelby can we chat a moment?"

"Sure Susan. What's up?"

"I hadn't known about your books. I took a long look at them when they were passed around. I'm impressed. They're pretty neat!" she enthused.

"Oh, thanks. You're sweet. They are kind of fun. Just stories I have made up for my girls," smiled Shelby as she gathered her purse and sweater.

"I don't think you understand Shelby. They could be commercial. In my other life, before the kids, I was a graphic artist. I think you've got something here. I'm not kidding. Also, you might not know that I am a rep for a line of children's clothes," Susan added.

"Oh, nice. No, I had no idea." Shelby reached for the door knob.
"How about I illustrate them for you and we become partners?" offered Susan.

Before long the little series of books celebrating tribal life became popular. Little Dowgy Press contracted to publish them and Shelby put them up for sale in the museum's gift shop. Surprisingly, one day the local tribal chief's daughter and her children visited the gift shop and fell in love with the little books. Coincidentally, that week, the History Channel was filming a special on her father, the chief, in its "A Day in the Life" series. The cameras picked up on his grandchildren reading Pony Girl books. Within no time at all, the books were in demand.

Now six years later, as a result of that exposure and in great part due to Susan's efforts, there were Pony Girl books in libraries and book stores across the country. Susan even negotiated with a paper products representative and some high-end children's boutiques now carried a line of Pony Girl party supplies. A children's television producer was talking about TV rights.

It all seemed dreamlike to Shelby; for her it was the stories and Nano's legacy that mattered. The tales held a personal intimacy, the best part of her childhood. She could almost hear her Nano's low voice as she made up her own stories, a mix of her fantasy and some of Nano's legends and myths. The commercial aspect of Pony Girl Enterprises simply did not compute in her head. She had trouble wrapping her mind around it. So far, she resisted the opportunities for promotional road trips, though she had consented to a few book signing appearances at local bookstores.

Whenever she considered herself as a professional author she would almost roll her eyes to herself. It seemed that surreal; fun, unexpected, satisfying, but surreal. The additional income had been nice, allowing for some big trips and a nice nest egg for the grandchildren's college. She used her maiden name as her pen name. She didn't know why, but she preferred to keep her writing life on the down low. There'd always been something inside of her that did not want to be noticed, a timid, scared something.

On writing days, she would sit at her computer with the dogs asleep at her feet, and clear her mind. Sometimes the memories would be so vivid that she could almost hear Nano's low chant singing, *The Earth is our Mother, care for her. Speak the truth but only of the good in others. Life is sacred, treat all things with respect.*

She could visualize Nano taking her and Mandy for adventures in the woods where they might come upon a clearing where Nano would teach them the blessings to the Earth. She could even remember that Nano called them the Earth Prayers to the Great Spirit. Those comforting memories always left Shelby feeling renewed and oddly at peace in her own skin. She admired how Nano and Bella had lived in the world, how they viewed it as sacred.

As she and the dogs strode along, now heading back up the hill to the house, she examined her own childhood. She could not exactly put her finger on it, but she knew there were some damaged, dark corners in her psyche. She had studied everything she could get her hands on for years trying to understand herself. She knew that toxic mothers bred kids with issues.

Issues. Oh she knew she had those! Let's see: lacking a real voice in my own destiny, blind obedience to her rules, low self esteem, insecurity, feelings of worthlessness, and the grand poohbah of them all, trust. If I added them up the list would be long.

She visualized her mother. A beautiful and powerful force was she: Avery Alexander, Queen of Bellingham. Avery exhibited the ideal on the outside, self possessed in her designer clothes, perfect hair and make-up, and slim shape. She chaired the city's most important committees and was a force to be reckoned with at the PTA. The outside world saw perfection, but for those on the inside, the view was the polar opposite. Where mother appeared concerned and loving to her friends, she was controlling and cold to her children. If one were to disobey, or upset mother, there would be a price to pay.

Shelby mined her memory and stopped at the day in high school when she and girlfriend Laura had driven to Seattle without telling their mothers. It had been one of her very few rebellions, and even so, they were home when they said they'd be. But when her mother checked the odometer on the car and discovered the high miles, a major blow up occurred. At the end of the yelling, she was fined and put on restriction. Shelby knew that her school friends broke more rules than she had, that it was seriously not *that big a deal*, but at her house it was. She lost the use of the car for the rest of the semester. What was interesting to Shelby was the realization that even then, Avery made it about *herself*, about being humiliated if her friends ever found out that her daughter was disobedient.

Shelby recalled a typical chaotic event from her childhood. It happened one Christmas when she was little and her dad still lived with them. She was probably about seven years old. A few weeks before the holiday, she overheard her parents agreeing, no buying gifts for each other; they were saving money for an Alaska trip, *only buying some things for the girls.* Shelby remembered the conversation because she had been so relieved when she knew there'd be presents for her and Mandy. On Christmas morning things started out just fine. Shelby and Mandy, excited as always, jumped on their parents' bed and were greeted with hugs and smiles, then everyone had gone out into the living room, where they opened their presents as usual. Then the trouble began.

The moment Mother realized that Daddy did *not* have a gift for her, she locked herself in the bathroom and would not come out. Shelby and Mandy had drawn little pictures and shoved them under the door as they pleaded with her to open the door. A knot tightened in her stomach as she relived that day, knocking and crying at the bathroom door. It had been a horrible scene; a huge drama. As a child, Shelby did not understand her mother's terrible reaction to the lack of a gift; she had *heard* them agree to *not buying gifts*. It was not until adulthood when she revisited the scene, that she realized that Mother must have been hurt because Daddy didn't *make* her a gift: a poem or a painting. Mother must have expected him to read her mind, perhaps he had, and his own passive-aggressive resistance kicked in. Who knew? All Shelby knew was that it had been awful. Thankfully, for the most part, Mother was off doing her own thing, whatever that was, and Shelby's care was left to Nano who loved her unconditionally.

She and the dogs returned home, it was time to get into action mode. She had a lot to do before they headed north to Charleston. She unhooked the leashes, checked the dogs' water dishes and slipped upstairs to take a shower and pack for the overnight trip.

Six hours later, nestled comfortably in Grant's Lexus, the conversation turned to Michelle and the dinner invitation. "I wonder what the occasion is?" remarked Grant.

"She was sort of mysterious about her appointments last week when I was up there. I'm hoping for a baby announcement," offered Shelby. "When Ellie turned four, I thought to myself that it's already a big spread in age between siblings, but I kept my mouth shut."

Grant looked across the front seat as if to urge her on. "I know she's been trying. I think they've been having trouble conceiving and the last thing she needs is pressure from me," confided Shelby.

Grant reached for Shelby's hand.

Their talk turned back to the case that Grant was working on, the money laundering. "Those crooks just keep on doing the same thing, and then they're so surprised when they get caught. The principals in this case have a chain of car washes, lots of opportunities to wash cash. I guess," he said smiling. "Anyway, we've got 'em. I will be glad when it's over. I think they are going to plead out next week."

After a while, Grant reached over and turned on the satellite radio and resumed holding Shelby's hand. Elton John's somber words for "Candle in the Wind" filled the car. Shelby grew quiet as she concentrated on the words. She closed her eyes and leaned her head against the window. "Lived your life like a candle in the wind, burned out long before your time…"

Shelby had been devastated by Princess Diana's death eight years before. "the truth brings us to tears…never fading with the sunset when the rain sets in…" As the lyrics washed over her, she thought about how brave Diana had been; standing up to Buckingham Palace; making a difference in the world. Shelby remembered news coverage of the princess walking through the land mine fields of Southeast Asia calling for something to be done about the millions of mines that were still hot, waiting to explode on innocent villagers. Diana had been brave. It was time for Shelby to be brave. "The truth brings us to tears." Sir Elton John was finishing "…our golden child…whispered to those in pain." Shelby knew that whatever "footsteps" she took in the future would change her life forever. She wondered if she could find the courage Diana had shown. She'd have to reach down deep, her own candle had not quite been snuffed out by a childhood filled with chaos and drama, but it certainly had not flamed as brightly as it might have.

As the beautiful, sad song ended, and the car purred along the miles, Shelby's memory once again went back to her growing up years. She had hated the yelling scenes, her mother screaming at her dad. She recalled a typical incident in front of the hotel in Anchorage, something about they *had* to drive to Denali Park even if it meant twelve hours in the car. Screaming, yelling, withholding affection. Making scenes. It had been awful.

She understood from her self-help books that for many small children, it's more important to obey and be in mommy's good graces, than to try for independence. Shelby always knew that to disobey mother was to be a traitor. As a young girl it was just much safer to avoid the scenes and do what she was told: blind obedience. She mostly stayed under the radar. She was doing okay until her dad could not take it anymore.

That last night with Daddy in the house was seared into her brain. She and Mandy were cleaning up from dinner. Dad got home late, when he mentioned to Mother that he wasn't going to interview for the principal's position, that the timing was off. That had been the beginning of the end. Her mother's scalding rant played across her mind, "You goddamn weak bastard, you promised you'd apply last year. *Now* is the time, why the hell aren't you going to interview?" Mother's abuse didn't stop. She'd kept it up, finally screaming, "Get the fuck out!" She'd yelled such commands in the past, but this time, with the third "get out," her father quietly turned around, walked upstairs, packed his bag, left and never did return.

In the weeks that followed, Mother begged him to come back. But Dad was done. Eventually, Shelby became deaf to it her mother's tirades and tears. As long as she kept her head down, it was relatively quiet at home. That was until the day that mother caught her throwing up in the toilet.

Shelby felt shell-shocked that ugly morning as she hung her head over the toilet vomiting the last of her breakfast, thinking she had the flu, then realizing that there was truth in her mother's accusations, that she could be pregnant.

Before Shelby knew what hit her, she was packed up and moved. There had been one huge argument in which Shelby prevailed. After that win, there were no more discussions. Her mother invented a story which was told to her sisters and stepfather. Everyone seemed to accept that story. And the secrets began. She had been too distraught to put up more resistance, and unable to imagine a different scenario, she went along with it.

It was not until decades later, that Shelby came to understand that toxic people often employ an insidious crazymaking tactic against their victims. It is called "mind raping." Her mother had done that to her, telling Shelby what her own *feelings* and *thoughts* were regarding the pregnancy; when she had *insisted* on termination. It had been all Shelby could do to assert herself against *that* solution. In lieu of that, she had gone along with her mother's second alternative, putting the infant up for adoption.

Giving up that baby had been the most crushing devastation to Shelby's life, but great insult was added to the psychic wreckage a few years later when her mother tried to convince her that the pregnancy had all been a dream; one of those lucid dreams that seem real, that it had never happened! That was when Shelby knew that no matter what, she was *never* going to live within two thousand miles of her mother!

Eyes closed, and her head resting against the window, she gave a little prayer and thanked God for her ability to have stopped the destructive cycle; for not treating her girls as she had been treated.

She took a deep breath and acknowledged God's firm guidance in helping her to raise her girls exactly the opposite of how she and Mandy had been raised. She understood that by providing the kind of childhood for them that she had craved, she was also helping herself to feel more whole. She opened her eyes and sat up straight in her seat. *Enough of all this excavation into ancient history. It's the past*

Shelby leave it there, she ordered to herself. *Get back to the present.*

Turning toward her husband, she said, "Grant, isn't it lovely that Michelle has invited us for dinner? We both know something is up. This is not like her, and especially on a Friday night. I hope it is good news; good *baby* news!"

Shelby looked across the front seat and made eye contact with him. He raised his eyebrows in a question and squeezed her hand.

CHAPTER 13

August 12, 2005
Charleston, South Carolina

"Momma, Daddy, would you like to sit right here," invited Michelle as she motioned to their seats and pulled Ellie's tall chair up to the table. "It's so great to see you two. We appreciate you driving all the way up here on a Friday afternoon. I hope the traffic wasn't too bad?"

Once the five of them were seated, Dale offered the blessing, "Bless us, oh Lord, and these thy gifts we are about to receive. Make us truly thankful, thank you Father. Amen."

The "amens" were whispered, and then Michelle passed the platter of fried chicken. "Hey Cricket, y'all made my favorite," commented Grant, smiling at his lovely first-born.

"Daddy, I had to make something special to lure you up here on a Friday night," beamed Michelle to her dad.

Ellie chimed in, her enthusiastic little-girl voice a delight to the ears, "Grandma the other kids at my school liked hearing about Pony Girl when you came to my class. I was telling the teacher about Tangle Boy and how he went fishing and caught a robin!" Eyes dancing, Ellie's face broke into a huge grin. "That is so silly. What a bad boy to fish for birds!" She was laughing now. "Grandma, Miss Jennifer wonders if you could tell that 'tory next time. Would ya Grandma?"

"Ellie, honey, that's a lot of driving for Grandma," reminded Michelle to Ellie.

"It would be my honor. It's fine. Michelle. I love it. Yes, I'm happy to come, Ellie. I enjoy being involved. Michelle, it's fun for me, feels a little like when you and Laney were kids." Smiling at her daughter, she replied, "Have car, will travel!" as she laughed.

The dinner conversation moved along companionably, everyone enjoying the time together and the celebratory vibe that stirred the air. Shelby cleared the table and Michelle brought out a lemon meringue pie. "Daughter you are spoiling us!" declared Grant as he held eye contact with his daughter and softly sang the few words to their song, "*My* ...brown-eyed girl," as she handed him a slice of pie.

"Oh Daddy!" she giggled.

Once everyone was served, Shelby noticed that Michelle sent a poignant look to her husband. Taking that as a cue, Dale began, "Grant, Shelby, ah, er... We've something to share with you."

"Mom and Daddy," interjected Michelle, "it's been a long road," she hesitated. "We haven't said anything much, tried not to over-think it or make it even bigger, but now we've some news. Good news!" she paused.

Dale jumped back in, "You'll be grandparents again after the first of the year!"

Dale and Michelle grinned as Shelby leaped out of her chair and hugged them both.

Grant lifted his glass. "Hey! This calls for a toast. Congratulations! That's great news! Cheers!"

"Mom, Dad, I need to share this with Laney and Conner. I'm going to make the call. I wanted you to be the first to know, but I want to dial my sis in on this. They'll be so happy!" exclaimed Michelle.

Later, as Shelby was rinsing off the ceramic plates and stacking them in the dishwasher, Michelle slipped into the kitchen and put her arm around her mom's shoulders. "Momma I didn't want to upset you before with how much trouble I've had trying to conceive this baby. I had a few early miscarriages."

Shelby turned from the sink and wiped her hands on a towel and studied Michelle's face. "My friend at school adopted a little boy from the Ukraine." She paused, "We considered looking into that, and we began checking out the IVF route."

Shelby reached for Michelle's hand. They held eye contact. "Mom, it was pretty awful for awhile. I was scared and freaked out until I found this new obstetrician,… a wonderful, smart woman."

Shelby kept still as she squeezed Michelle's hand in understanding.

After a moment, Michelle continued, "The new doctor understood that I needed a few months of supplemental estrogen. Anyway, it worked." She inhaled. "I was really beginning to stress over the age gap between my kids…over all of it…"

Their eyes met. "Mom we're so *relieved* and thrilled!"

"Oh baby, I'm sorry you've had so much trouble. I didn't realize, but I've purposely kept quiet about the next child sensing that the last thing you needed was pressure from me."

"I know. I appreciate that. I would've told you months ago about this new doctor, but after your trip to Bellingham you seemed distracted." Michelle paused. "I worried that maybe things weren't right between you and Daddy. Then I thought you were just overwhelmed with the Water Festival, and I didn't want to add to *your* stress. Anyway, now you know the good news!" concluded Michelle as she leaned into her mother's embrace.

After a few minutes Shelby asked. "Are you thinking about

names?"

"It's early yet, but we're past the critical twelve week mark. I've been thinking more about giving up my teaching contract than about names. I'm not sure how many more babies there will be; I want to be home more with this one than I managed with Ellie."

"That's a big decision. Teaching jobs aren't all that easy to come by these days, but I've never regretted the choice to stay home with you girls. Grandmother Avery, even though she didn't have a career, never seemed to be at home. Nano raised me. I wanted to be there for you girls, and I was."

"Remember our neighbor, Lucy? I've never forgotten something she once confided to me. When her son was born she had to return to her teaching position when he was just four weeks old. I remember her words in her strong Alabama accent. 'Jeffrey wasn't even as big as a li'l ol' roast, and I had to leave 'im. It tore me up somethin' awful. I cried all the way to school.'" Shelby paused and looked at her daughter. "That sad little admission has stuck with me all these years."

Yes, because Lucy was so broken up about not seeing much of him, but at least she got to come home to him at night, while you had no idea where your baby was...

Shelby forced her thoughts back. "If you do decide to give up your contract, I don't think you'll be sorry."

Once again looking into her daughter's serious brown eyes, Shelby added, "You could always take a year's leave of absence, and test the 'stay-at-home waters.' See if it works for you."

Both women finished up with the dishes. When the kitchen was mostly under control, Ellie sailed into the room, "Grandma, how about a 'tory?" she begged.

"All right, little one, let's get you ready for bed. Come on, I'll help."

Snuggled against the headboard on Ellie's soft bed, Shelby began the story. As she related the tale of Tangle Boy, another part of her mind tumbled across the evening's conversations. *Apparently I've not been that successful in masking my agonies over Cody and telling Grant.*

She mulled over Michelle's words. As the story ended, she looked down at Ellie and realized that she was sound asleep. Her stuffed animal, Lambie, was wrapped in her arms. Shelby turned off the lamp next to the bed, tucked the soft blanket up around the sleeping child, and leaned back against the headboard as she examined her thoughts. *One never really knows what is around the corner in life.*

What an irony. While my world is torn asunder struggling to know what to do about four beautiful people practically knocking at the door, hoping to be a part of our lives, my wonderful Michelle has been desperate to figure out how she could get her hands on another person to love...

My dear God, you like to challenge me don't you? I'm ready for an answer anytime you want to show me the way.

Later the next day, Shelby and Grant bid their goodbyes with hugs and kisses. As they drove out of their daughter's neighborhood, Shelby noticed that they weren't heading for the Interstate, the way home.

"Honey, Grant, where're you going?" she asked.

"Ah. That eez for me to know and for you discover, my dear," replied Grant in his seriously bad French accent.

Within a fifteen minutes, Grant pulled the car into the valet service in front of the historic and luxurious Charleston Place Hotel.

"Grant, what? What're you doing?" she asked in an incredulous voice as she nodded her head and felt a grin of disbelief spreading across her face.

"What's up, sir?" she asked again.

"This is a little pre-anniversary get-away for us. In my book, thirty years is a very *big* deal!" His eyes sparkled with mischief.

"Well, mister, it's a bit elaborate for my current wardrobe; slacks and a tee," worried Shelby.

"Is that right? What if I showed you a second suitcase in the trunk with some of your favorite evening outfits, a bathing suit, and workout clothes?" asked Grant, sporting a very big 'I've thought of everything' smile. "Ellen, was only too happy to stay an extra night with Zoe and Tessie."

"I booked the bridal suite and we have dinner reservations at the Charleston Grill at 7:30. It made the Forbes most distinguished list this year. So what do y'all think?" he asked, exaggerating his drawl and continuing to grin.

"Why handsome sir," she replied in her thickest fake Southern accent, as the valet opened her door, "I might just be the luckiest little ol' gal in the world." Now dropping the accent, "You really are such a romantic! I love you Grant Forrest!" she replied, lifting herself gracefully out of the car.

Sunday afternoon, as they headed south to Beaufort, Shelby leaned against her headrest and relived the last twenty-four hours. Grant had been his warm, loving self. Dinner had been a magnificent culinary adventure, after which he had even taken her dancing. The dancing had been a surprise. A nearby rooftop club featured an oldies rock band. They'd listened for a while, but when they played The Village People's "Y.M.C.A.," Grant had stood and ushered her out onto the tiny dance floor. They'd laughed out loud as they reached up to demonstrate the big "Y" in YMCA. It had been fast moving and exhilarating. Their enthusiasm attracted some other dancers and they all stayed on the floor for the entire set, including a rambunctious rendition of "Shout!"

When the soul single, "You Are the One for Me," began, Grant folded her into his arms. He'd whispered, "It's true you know. Shelby Forrest, you are the *only* one for me." His voice was jagged as he'd said that, then he nuzzled her ear, making promises of what was next on the evening's itinerary. Shivers had shot down her spine.

She was pleased that back in their suite, she'd managed to have a truce with the angst that haunted her, and was able to surrender to his skillful lovemaking. It had been carefree and even a bit wild, and after, she had slept curled up in his arms, like in the old days.

As the Lexus rolled along the highway, Shelby realized that she was proud that she had managed to stave off the avalanche of anxiety that lay threatening, waiting to suffocate her. She had been *mentally present* all evening. When her brain tried to wander over to the topic of Cody, she had pushed back.

Now, as the miles clicked by, she could allow herself think of him. He and Amber and their girls were returning to the States in about another month or so. The get-away night reinforced how much she had to lose if she insisted on having a real relationship with him and his family. She sensed from the little she knew of Cody, that if she bailed on him, he would understand, would sense how complicated it was for her, and that it would be okay with him.

The minute her thoughts went down that road, another thought roiled up; *but you already bailed on him.*

Really, you would do that again?

CHAPTER 14

August 16, 2005
Beaufort, South Carolina

Thrashing against the sheet that covered her, bathed in perspiration, Shelby felt as if she were in a deep pool, swimming up to the surface, to consciousness. *Oh just that awful nightmare again,* she thought as she shook the horror of those black marbles, her teeth, falling into her hand, the consequence of telling Grant the rest of the truth. Every time she had this dream she was relieved to wake up and realize that it had only been a dream.

She sat up. Grant's rhythmic breathing was steady next to her in their big king size bed. The digital display read 3:30. *Oh God, too late to take a pill.* The worst part of the dream was that she was frozen, a part of the stained glass window in the church, with a clear view out to the world. This time, however, what she saw from her perch was not Grant giving piggyback rides to his girls, but two little red-headed girls holding hands with a tall fair-haired man as they walked away. She'd dreamed that image the week before, walking away. She knew why these episodes were coming more frequently. She felt like a pressure cooker about to explode. Amber and Cody would be moving to her continent in a matter of a few weeks and she had made little headway in figuring out her next move.

The guilt she felt was almost paralyzing. During that emotional birthday telephone call in June, she'd implied that she would be calling frequently, maybe even the next Sunday, but when that Sunday had rolled around she couldn't face it. Her stomach had fisted tight, and she'd gagged trying to drink her morning coffee. It had been easier to decide *not* to call on that day. Somehow with the Water Festival and the girls returning home, it continued to be easier not to call.

Maybe I will call today. Her thoughts stopped. What would she say, *Your sister Michelle is having a baby; she's had a hard time conceiving. We're a cozy family here. I love my husband with all my heart but I don't trust him to stay with me if I tell?*

Shelby slipped silently out of bed and padded down stairs to the kitchen. She pushed the on button to the coffee maker, as she was far too early for the machine's auto response, and went out to the garage to take care of the dogs. As she stood in her thin pale blue nightgown waiting as they took care of their morning business, she noticed the yard was bathed in light. She looked up to realize the moon was nearly full. Three more days and it would be a full moon. *I love the full moon. This Sunday will be a full moon. I will call him then. I promise.*

Having made a decision, Shelby and the dogs went into the house to wait for daylight. With her comforting brew in hand, the dogs settled back to sleep at her feet, and she began to think about the last week. She felt a bit like a person on a merry-go-round, only this one was whirling faster and faster, threatening to throw her off into outer space. She was thrilled by Michelle's announcement, reassured to be back on an even keel with Grant, and relieved that the Native American exhibit had opened without a hitch. But the biggest issue to face her in thirty-five years still lay writhing and raw at the edge of her soul.

Calmed by the dark, she leaned back in her favorite chair admiring the view shadowed in moonlight. She knew it was time to pick at the slim thread that was holding her together. Her struggle had intensified last Monday. She'd been in the coffee room at the museum, taking a break, sitting at one of the little round Formica ice cream tables when she noticed a hard bound book lying face down on the next table. She could almost make it out. There was a photo of the author on the dust jacket on its back. She'd leaned across the space between the tables and lifted up the book. As she studied the author photo, a wave of recognition swept through her. She'd seen that face somewhere; a nice looking older blonde woman. And suddenly it hit her. That was the woman she had sat next to last spring on the flight home from Bellingham! A hot jolt of adrenaline had burst through her. Her head had spun.

Sitting in the break room, almost in the slow motion of a sleep walker, she had slowly turned the book over, *No Longer Alone: The Power of Telling the Secret,* by Charlotte Lewis, Ph.D.

So that was her name. Charlotte. It suited her. I told her..........

Shelby had remained there in the empty break room for a long time. In the entire world only her mother, Lily, and this Charlotte Lewis, had ever known her secret, and now the anonymous stranger on that flight had a name. Of course the woman didn't know *her* name. That thought reassured her for the moment, until she realized how completely irrational she was being. A stranger on an airplane was not going to search out Grant and tell her secret. The book was about telling your own secret, not a random stranger's.

Seriously Shelby, she'd thought, *You've got to get a grip. Ah, you're forgetting something; Cody and Amber also know...*

She'd scanned the Table of Contents: The Fallout from Secret Keeping; The Secret as a Time Bomb Waiting to Detonate; The Secret Keeper's Inability to be Authentic. She read more; shame, lack of trust, living as an imposter. The Table of Contents was full.

As she studied the book, her thoughts came to a story she often read to Ellie, *The Velveteen Rabbit* by Margery Williams, where the most dearly cherished little stuffed bunny dreamed of becoming real. The wise old skin horse had warned that for a toy to become real, it had to be truly loved. One day while the little boy and the bunny were playing in the nursery, the little boy held the velveteen rabbit close to his face and whispered to him that he was real. The bunny was thrilled by this news. One terrible day, however, the boy forgot him and left him outside. As the rabbit lay in the flower bed, the real rabbits came upon him, and made fun of him, for he had no back legs. He was made of one piece of cloth. Discovering that he was not real was hurtful; his defense was to pretend to the others that he *was* real. Later, when the boy found him, he felt real again, tucked into the bed covers feeling loved.

One awful year, the little boy contracted scarlet fever and all his toys had to be burned due to contamination. The bunny was so sad to be headed for the burn pile, that he shed a real tear. From that tear the nursery fairy appeared and did her magic. Because bunny was well loved, the fairy made him real and he got to live in Rabbit Land with his new jumping legs and long whiskers. One late autumn day he was resting near the flowers in the boy's yard when the boy caught sight of him. The boy stopped and thought, *Why he looks like my bunny that was lost when I was sick!* The boy never knew that it really was his bunny, come back to check on him, made real because the boy had loved him.

Shelby wondered that morning in the break room, as she wondered now, if Cody were the boy come back to make her real.

Sitting silently undercover of early morning darkness, Shelby continued to pick at her truth. She worried whether she would measure up to his expectations? She'd always loved him with all her heart, but would that be enough to make up for.... Her thoughts trailed off.

If the story represented them, surely she was the worn one with the "hairs rubbed off her tail." She grimaced, *yes that sounds about right*, and recalled the wisdom from the skin horse as he taught about becoming real, "it does not happen all at once, it takes a long time to become real...uncomfortable things happen to you." That seemed an understatement. *So how long will it take? I may be running out of time.*

As she continued to needle at the wreckage of her psyche, she sensed, once again, that across her life she'd kept something important back. Once close to her sister, Mandy, she'd never shared her secret, nor really let Mandy in since she left

Bellingham. After her dad moved away and remarried, that closeness with him had simply vanished. She knew she held back from her writing. She'd gone along when Susan wanted to have the books published. It was fine; she acknowledged that it was her imagination behind the stories, but surely the power source that drove their success was Susan Parker. Shelby dreamed of creating a serious book on Native American myths and legends, had even completed most of the research, but never started the writing.

I feel like I'm waiting for something; that underneath all this waffling is a powerful woman screaming to emerge. Shit! she thought to herself.

As she continued her psychic probing, she considered her courtship with Grant. She respected and admired him, adored him, really. She loved him, but still she held back. She recalled one particularly rough spot years ago, when the agony of all she had withheld from him had tormented her. It was during the long hours in the birthing room waiting for their first child, Michelle. Grant had sat by her bed, holding her hand, waiting for the contractions to become more frequent, all the while she feigned ignorance of the whole process. That had been bad; looking into his big sincere brown eyes, feeling his nervousness through their entwined fingers, while she pretended. But then Michelle had arrived in her squalling glory, and it was a busy time. She was able to push it all back into its dark corner in her mind.

She got that she was resilient; had figured out early-on to get away from her mother; had completed her education, became competent in the law offices, and raised a beautiful family. She understood that she nurtured herself as she cared for her daughters, and that at her core there was a tough-mindedness that had served her well.

She took a sip of the now tepid coffee as her mind skimmed to Cody. Suddenly the drama of Cody's existence swirled to the front of her memory. After her mother discovered her morning sickness, she'd packed her into the car one Monday morning and driven her all the way to a Seattle clinic for a pregnancy test, the long distance assuring Avery that no one in her world would know of this shameful situation.

A few days later, when the test results had come back positive, there was a terrible fight. "Shelby, tell them you won't be in next weekend at the Cracked Crab. I'm taking you to Tijuana. Abortions are easy there. We'll fly into San Diego and rent a car. This will be over by next week." Avery's authoritative tone brooked no argument. Somehow, even though Shelby thought of herself as a weak, compliant figure of a woman, she'd fought back.

"No, Mother, we are *not* flying to San Diego," her voice had been edged in steel. This was so out of character for Shelby, that Avery was stunned.

"Don't talk back to me young lady. You've brought dishonor to the door step of this family. How do you think your father will hold his head up at school? As principal he has to live to a higher standard. This will reflect badly on him, on all of us. I will not tolerate this insubordination. You will give notice about the weekend at work." Avery's words were taut with rage.

The icy syllables cut through Shelby's heart, but she did not back down.

"No Mother, I'm not going to kill this baby. I'll go away somewhere. Raise it on my own. I'm not getting rid of it. Abortion is not something I would *ever* consider. And Derrick is *not* my father!"

"Derrick has been a hell of a lot more of a father to you than yours! He's not run off to Idaho and started a new family. Let's stay on the subject. You're the slut here. The promiscuous little bitch! How dare you take the moral high ground!" Avery spat out her contempt.

"Promiscuous? Hardly, that was my first and only time," retorted Shelby.

"Whose is it? Maybe it's time to get married. We can be in Reno or Vegas in a few hours. Who is the asshole anyway, that guy Nick?"

"No. There's not going to be a shotgun wedding!" A cold calm had fallen over her. "No. Not Nick. I'm leaving. I'll go to Dad's." She had stormed out of the room.

She and her mother did not speak for the next few days. Finally, calmer, her mother had come into her room one night. "You can stay with Lily in Atlanta. She needs help. She was diagnosed with rheumatoid arthritis. Has trouble with her hands and getting around. Being roommates all those years, we have each other's secrets, she won't tell anyone." Avery paused to let her plans sink in.

"By all means, do *not* tell your father. He'd have a fit. I won't have him hanging *this* over my head! I think I can still get him to help pay for some of your college expenses, even though you will be changing schools. I repeat, do *not* tell your father. This is the best plan. I called Lily. She welcomes the help and we'll find an adoption attorney. Lily has a room for you."

Avery had lowered her voice, "Shelby, you can still have a future, and you will help a family who cannot have a baby. This does not have to ruin your life," she had paused and inhaled. "If you absolutely refuse to go to Mexico, this is the best way out."

The decision had been made and Shelby had won. There would be no Mexico and she withstood her mother's pressure and did not reveal the father's identity.

Settling back into her chair, she thought, *I'm proud of that. I didn't let anyone talk me into getting rid of my baby. I stood my ground.* For a moment Shelby basked in that victory, but her thoughts pressed on. She'd known that without skills, education, support, or a husband, that the best course of action *had* to be what was best for the baby. The infant had to be given up, the only caveat was the promise for its' education. And so on that agonizing June day in 1970, she passed the worst test of her life; she dug deep into her soul and found the resolve to hand over the sturdy little bundle.

Shelby was clear about her weaknesses, but she also recognized a seam of toughness that lay beneath her docile exterior. She figured out a path that would allow her to cope with the loss of the baby; she had to be with a family. She would become a nanny and go to school at night.

It had been easy to find a nanny position. Lily gave her a reference and she enrolled in college. Those "Cara Years" had been her saving grace, as tending to Cara was a way to remain connected to her son. One day, while Cara was still an infant, an epiphany came to Shelby. She remembered it well. Cara had been fussy with an ear infection; Shelby was rocking her to sleep. As she gently rocked back and forth, her mind had rerun that fateful day in 1969 which had derailed her life forever. As they rocked, her mind poured over just how she had ended up holding another's baby instead of living in the sorority house, and studying history at the university as she prepared for a career teaching.

To and fro she had gently swayed, and as she did, she relived that life changing afternoon. Her mind came upon those sweaty minutes with Tom Steele, to the urgent moment. She could still almost hear his raspy voice. "Is it okay?" as he groaned into her ear. She'd answered that it was. Suddenly, Shelby realized that he had *not* been asking about her virtue and continuing; he was asking if it was safe! Was she using *birth control?*

As that awareness filled her mind, her pulse had quickened. The pregnancy resulted because of a *misunderstanding*! She remembered what she'd thought as she soothed Cara: *Ohmygod! I have to **own** what happened!*

Shelby checked the clock. Daylight was still some hours away. She padded into the kitchen and poured a half cup of warm coffee and then returned to her chair and her thoughts. She remembered all of it so vividly.

As the years passed she would catch herself looking for her son in a crowd. He was never far from her thoughts, and yet she had cobbled out a way to live her life. She married and raised a family. She enjoyed her life; her husband and daughters, the granddaughters, and her work at the museum. She felt a part of the community. Her writing centered her, as did her dogs.

Across her married life, there had even been times when the girls were little and she was rough housing with them, or when she was remodeling their house, that she would lose herself in the moment, and would almost be free. Yes, she had gotten by across the years. She had kept *very* busy, but this new situation, with the frequency of her panic attacks and nightmares, was forcing her to acknowledge that the secret keeping was not working very well. Perhaps the call to Cody, which she promised herself this next Sunday, would help.

With that she noticed that dawn was breaking. She would work some on her current Pony Girl story and then take the dogs out for a walk.

CHAPTER 15

Sunday, August 19, 2005
Beaufort, South Carolina

Shelby waited until noon to place the call to the U.K. Grant had plans for a full afternoon of golf. Now was the time. As she expected, adrenaline was surging through her; stomach in knots, shoulders tight as slabs of cement. *This is about normal these days. No wonder I've put this off for so long.* She punched in the International Code 44 and the string of numbers that led into the labyrinth of her heart, digits that would allow her to talk to Cody. Considering the decades she imagined doing just this, a part of her watched from the sidelines, fascinated by her ambivalent behavior.

As the phone began to ring, Shelby worried that she would not be able to hear over her thumping heart. It sounded horribly loud in her ears.

"Hello."

"Cody, it's Shelby. How are you?" Her voice was breathy. She fought through it. "Are you getting ready to come back to the States?" she asked in a rush.

"It won't be long now 'til we transfer." The deep masculine timbre of his voice put Shelby a bit more at ease. She could feel his competence across the miles.

"The specific orders will be coming in; our best guess is Lackland near San Antonio. That could be interesting. Amber likes history and has been studying up on the Alamo."

"That's so great. Is this a good time to talk?"

"It's fine, quiet around here. Amber is getting dinner and the girls are in Scooby Doo land," he reported with a smile in his voice.

"I've been wanting to call for a while now, but honestly I feel so emotional about all of this. I don't want you to see me as a big cry baby. I've gone over our last call a million times. There was so much I wanted to know. I didn't ask the right questions. First of all, could you tell me what the girls are doing now, I mean, like their development. How much is Willow talking? Is Kaitlyn starting to read?" Her eager questions spilled out.

Shelby sensed that the girls and the here and now were safer subjects than the past.

"Willow is using whole sentences now. A few months ago, if you asked her 'how does a doggie go' she would say 'woof woof.' Now she'll offer a long string of words. She's a riot, a hoot really. Miss Kaitlyn is more restrained and, yes, she is fascinated by books, trying to read. In fact Amber's sister gave her a book, something called Pony Girl, a storybook about a big adventure. I thought of you. The author's name's the same. Anyway, Kaitlyn is beginning to recognize words on the page, and she can sort of write her name. She gets a lot of the letters, but not in the correct order. She writes me cards. I get a kick out of them. She puts her signature along the side of the page. She has her own unique style."

Shelby recognized affection and pride in Cody's voice.

"I love hearing about them. They look adorable in their photograph." After an awkward pause, Shelby asked, "Is Amber okay with the move back?" She was still steering the conversation toward the present.

"She is. She misses her mom. This will be good," he answered, ending the Amber discussion.

The tumult within Shelby continued its uprising. She passed over the Pony Girl topic. *This call can't be all about me.*

Daring to learn more about Cody's life, her tone became more serious as she changed the direction of the conversation. "Can you tell me a little something about your childhood?"

"I had a fine childhood. My parents were older when they adopted me. Mid 40's. They loved me. They always said that getting me was when they finally felt like a real family. They provided me with every opportunity, actually sacrificed for me. Lots of special summer camps. I always liked science. They made sure I had enrichment programs."

"I'm glad to hear that. Did you fit in with them? I always worried whether you were comfortable with your family, if the fit was right."

"Well, they were a lot older than my friends' parents. Once at open house in middle school, a kid teased me that my dad looked like my grandpa. That was hard. I never forgot it. Anyway, my parents were good people. Kind. I did fine."

Cody was not about to share with her that he'd always felt like a mismatched puzzle piece or that his dad's favorite parlor game for dinner guests was showing off Cody's unusually keen memory. Realizing that Shelby was already something of a basket case, he knew to keep those realities to himself. He had no need to further contribute to her obvious angst.

"What do you mean *were?*" she asked.

"I lost them a few years back. Car accident," he answered.

Shelby thought *Heavens! I've been so tied up with my own issues about telling Grant and the girls, I haven't even considered what could be going on with him.*

"Cody, that's terrible, I'm so sorry, I had no idea."

"I'm better now. It was rough for a while. That's when Amber started pushing me to find you. I think she thought it might help."

"And here I have been non-communicado succumbing to my own stuff. I want to do better with you, but I've felt overwhelmed, paralyzed. A part of me wants to jump on a plane and be there in five hours, while another part of me knows that the timing's not yet right on my end."

There was silence at the other end of the line.

"Cody, I'm glad they took good care of you. I'm sorry, not only for your loss, but for the girls. They don't have your mom and dad. Is this too painful to talk about?"

"I'm okay. The girls are young, I don't think they really understand yet. We'll see Amber's mom when we come stateside. We're getting along. Amber takes good care of us. Please don't worry. We're fine. Excited to move home."

"I bet you are," Shelby waited for a long moment. "About that, your moving back," she waited to collected her thoughts and then plunged in. "I don't know any other way to say this, but to say it. I've painted myself into a corner. After you called the first time, I told my husband that I once gave a baby up for adoption. He's a straight shooter and the fact that I kept your existence from him all these years has cut him to the core. He feels betrayed. In hind sight I needed to tell him right then that you had located me, that you'd called, but I was so intimidated by his hurt and anger that I clammed up. He's a prosecutor. He pressed me, but I didn't have the guts to say more," she concluded in a shaky voice.

There was another long silence at both ends of the phone. "Will you give me a little more time?" Her tone was pleading.

"Shelby, whatever you *need*," a hint of frustration laced his words. "We're fine. Always were. Amber sustains me, always has. She's my high school sweetheart. Don't worry. This was never to pressure you. We will have new phone numbers when we transfer. What do you want to do about that?" he asked.

"I will do my best to call before then. You have my email, could you send the phone number to me, your address too?" She could feel a hot neediness in her words. It was embarrassing. It was time to end the conversation.

"Is Amber holding your dinner? Should we get off?" she asked as she sensed the impatience building in him.

"I hear dishes on the table. Yeah, I should probably go. I appreciate the call. Was a little afraid that I'd scared you off." His tone had shifted, though the words were light, Shelby understood the gallows humor that lay beneath the surface, simmering with emotion, and something else.

"Bye Cody."

"Bye."

Closing her burner cell phone, she realized that she still didn't know what he did in the Air Force, nor how long he has served.

Oh Shelby you are such a goose, she scolded herself. *He might be a fighter pilot for all you know. He could be killed in Iraq by the time you get around to facing up to all this. Also what was all that about fitting in? I know you were thinking of the girl down the street who was a bad match in her family, but Shelby you never fit in at home, either. And you were your mother's natural child.* Her inner voice was critical. *Yeah and look what a mess I am..........*

She put the phone down and looked out the window. She admired the colorful rose bushes in the back yard, while her brain whirled to the growing up years with her mother. The two of them had been like oil and water from the beginning. *Maybe the troubles you've had with Mother are not so much about the fit of the two of you. Maybe it has a lot to do with the way Avery is. Look at her relationship with Michelle and Laney. From the start she insisted on being called "Grandmother Avery," never the cozy "granny," or "grandma" that other grandmothers seem to enjoy.*

As Shelby continued mining her thoughts she realized that her mother had no real relationship with Michelle and Laney. Nothing. There was an obligatory gift at Christmas and a check on their birthdays, by their teens, just the check.

Interesting.

Enough of this, she thought, *we're nearly out of food. What does any of this have to do with Cody and his adoptive family anyway? I'm going to the market.*

CHAPTER 16

August 19, 2005
Lakenheath, Suffolk, England

Cody closed his phone and thought, *this is just such total bullshit,* as he stood his full height and walked into the kitchen. Amber was putting the casserole on the table.

"Cody, what is it? You don't look so good."

"Screw it. That was Shelby on the phone. This call was better. She didn't spend the entire conversation crying, but my God, that woman is a mess! Says she's painted herself into a corner, that she's overwhelmed, feels paralyzed. She's obviously terrified of telling her husband and daughters. I'm so fucking tired of the secrecy surrounding all of this. I have half a notion not to tell her when we move, nothing, not our address or phone number. Let her come looking for us when she's ready. All this bullshit about 'she thought of me every day of her life.' Please. Here we are. I don't see her coming through that door." Cody took a deep breath as Amber came into his arms.

"Honey, she has lived with this secret for thirty-five years, I doubt she ever imagined that she would actually see you again. Think what this must be like for her. Even though the "Unseal Birth Records" movement is growing, it's still almost impossible to get those records opened. She wouldn't expect you to find her." She paused. "Maybe we need to give her some space." Amber pulled back from his embrace and looked into his brilliant blue eyes.

As she reached up and cupped his face between her hands, she said, "It's hard for us to imagine the times back then. I once had a lady professor who told the class that back in 1970, when she was expecting, it was not okay to be teaching, to be seen in public. She said no one ever acknowledged her pregnancy. It was a taboo, and Cody, she was *married!* We just can't imagine; the secrets, the shame. Cody, let's give her a *chance*."

Cody and Amber stood like that in the kitchen for a long time. "Cody, you've always said 'it's us against the world.' We'll be fine whether she comes into our lives or not. I know this is easy for me to say, but it's true." She smiled up at him. "Do you want to call the girls or maybe sit for awhile, maybe have a beer? I can put the dinner back to warm."

"No. I'm okay. I'll go get our Scooby Dooers," said Cody.

A few days later Cody had some time between patients at the medical center. *I've always done better when I can wrap my brain around a problem*, he thought. *Let's see what the medical literature has to say about Shelby. There are some advantages to working in the largest military medical facility in all of Europe.*

He smiled to himself as his mind transported him back to another library. He thought of his undergraduate years. He lingered in the old school memory. *Go Dooley!* He thought of his alma mater's crazy mascot, "Lord Dooley, the king of unruly," and it made him smile. In his mind's eye he could see himself in the quad at Emory, the skeleton streaking across campus, trying to scare students. Lord Dooley, dressed up in flowing black robes, as he roamed the campus each spring during "Dooley Week." Cody chuckled.

Okay, enough of that. Let's see what this library has to tell me. He took a seat at the bank of computer terminals. He would start with the psych literature, then on to the medical journals.

In his brief psych rotation during medical training, he'd been impressed with Eric Erickson's work on the stages of human development. He'd start there. He scrolled through the search engine: Erikson, "On adoptees as a new species."

I'm certainly not going there! I had an entire childhood of feeling like a freak.

Cody continued his search: Trauma literature. He scrolled further: The unwed teen mother. Cody randomly opened a document. *The trauma of giving up one's baby is equivalent to a death, however in American culture, there is no emotional support for the mother who is often an unwed teen. Unlike a death, there is no social support to help her cope with her trauma and her grief. She is forced to go it alone, maintaining her secret and disavowing her psychic holocaust. For her, this is very likely the most devastating experience of her life. She has nowhere to go, but to bury it. This often leads to Post Traumatic Stress symptoms. She may never feel whole again.*

Cody sat quietly at the computer terminal. *Grief. I haven't really thought of it that way. Could it be that perhaps Shelby has been in grief for thirty-five years? What would that feel like?*

Her words echoed in his mind, "I've painted myself into a corner." He knew the heartache that consumed him after his parents' death had almost undone him. They'd loved him completely; done everything within their power to allow him to soar. He loved them back, but at the same time a burden of guilt hovered over him. He knew why; across his growing up years, he was embarrassed that they were so different from the other kids' parents. It wasn't just that they were older; there were few books in the house, they never traveled. They weren't like him. He'd been hoarding books and dreaming of exotic locales since he was a young child. By his fifteenth birthday, he stood over six feet tall, towering over them. When they died, the guilt for all of *that* overlaid the sorrow, consuming him in a nightmare of anguish and pain.

Could Shelby have experienced something like that? Has my finding her pushed her over the psychic cliff into acute trauma?

Cody lifted his head from the computer, staring at the wall across the room. For the longest time he was lost in thought.

Maybe I need to back off. Amber has encouraged me in this search to help me to feel better. She can't know the guilt I feel over Mom and Dad. I've let her push me...

He continued to focus on the blank wall.

Looking for Shelby was never to ease the pain over Mom and Dad. The driver for me was losing that teen patient. She was a great kid.

Cody felt his stomach constrict as a mental picture of her came into view. She'd been so damned cute with her pixie hair-cut and her enthusiasm for World Cup soccer. He recalled that she'd drawn sketches of the dress she planned to wear to her winter formal.

She suffered Marfan Syndrome, the genetic disease that affects the skeleton and cardiovascular system. She was actually his buddy Ron's patient, but he'd been involved with the case. The girl had presented with chronic fatigue and shortness of breath. The medical team had been clear on the diagnosis, but her heart had given out before they could find a viable treatment. She'd been so young; a real sweetheart.

The fact that it was hereditary scared me into seriously searching for the genetics of my girls. Cody, this may be true, but you've failed to ask about her health, or that of her offspring. Why haven't you?

Cody thought about that for a while. It seemed so inappropriate.

Hello. I'm your long lost son come to know if you all have some horrific terminal disease that I should know about before it's too late. I don't care much about you or what is going on in your life. I'm just concerned about myself and my girls.

His sarcastic thoughts pulled him up short.

What's wrong with you? asked his higher self.

That's not what you're about. You care, and you've devoted your life to serving others. You're holding back to protect yourself. Also, it seems unlikely that her offspring are afflicted by a genetic disorder. If so they would not have reproduced.

Cody, you've answered your own question just by finding her.

The internal conversation continued.

You've dedicated yourself to helping people to live the healthiest, happiest life possible. Don't you think you could find some charity toward Shelby? She could have scraped you out, you know. A trip to Mexico in 1970 would have done the trick.

His higher self persisted. *Maybe Shelby was brave to go through with the birth and give you up. Maybe she is a hero.*

It's time for honesty. His inner voice was not going to let him off the hook.

You want to know the whole story. Why did she give you away? Who is your father?

Who are you?

Finally, *Who am I?*

Screw it!

It was too much. Cody suddenly stood up, nodded a thank-you to the clerk in the medical library as he walked to the elevators. He pushed the down button leading to the cafeteria. It was time to shove all this to the back corners of mind where it belonged. He would get some lunch and get back on the ER floor.

CHAPTER 17

August 22, 2005
Beaufort, South Carolina

As Shelby drove into her driveway she noticed that the mailman was down the street. *Perhaps that book is already here, Dr. Charlotte, Hum.* She pushed the garage door opener and entered the dark garage. Zoe and Tessie raced to greet her, wagging bundles of good cheer. *Ah, you sweethearts.* "Hey girls, let's see what the mailman brought?"

The dogs bounded out in front of her to the curb, sure enough a brown wrapped package was waiting for her. She tore it open, *No Longer Alone: The Power of Telling the Secret.* Walking back into the house she wondered just what was in store for her if she had the courage to actually read the book. She recalled that she had felt safe in the author's presence. Perhaps she would be safe to read the woman's ideas. She recalled their time on the airplane, she'd sensed then that there was far more to the woman than she had learned.

A cup of mint tea in hand, she perched on a tall stool at her granite kitchen island. She studied the familiar back cover and then examined the contents. She slowly leafed through the pages. The Forward quoted psychologist Eric Fromm, "Life is a constant process of giving birth to oneself." *Tell me about it.* Shelby scanned a few more pages and read "some of the most devastating secrets involve sexual crimes such as incest, others include giving up one's baby." She flipped through a few more pages. "The secret keeper is an imposter, living a lie, which produces feelings of isolation and despair."

She sat at the counter and looked out the window to the colorful blooms in her beautiful back yard. She thought about that for a moment. She turned to the index and looked up Post Traumatic Stress Disorder. "PTSD may result after a terrifying ordeal. Initially the body prepares its flight or fight response. People who suffer PTSD may feel stressed or frightened even many years after the ordeal." Shelby knew enough psychology to know that her panic attacks, nightmares, hair-trigger startle reaction, and acute anxiety, were classic symptoms.

She read on to treatments: "Talk therapy," "Exposure therapy," and "Cognitive restructuring," seemed the top choices. Shelby laughed. How ironic, *what I'm freaking out over is TALKING!!!*

She slammed the book shut. She knew she had to tell her story soon. A weird thought came to her. *I wonder if in some perverse Freudian way I have always been searching for Cody on some deep level. I wonder about my fascination with Native Americans, searching through their history, struggling to discover just when they migrated to America; from where they had come? How had they lived? Who were they?*

She stopped herself. She noticed her heart rate had suddenly escalated. She felt breathless.

My God, I have been searching for him all these years!

I don't know what to think. Perhaps I've always been looking for him and now that I've found him I'm at a loss for the next step. I understand the "looking for," I just never imagined what would come next...

Shelby, her wise internal voice began, *when it was the saddest time of your life you knew to find comfort by taking the nanny job with Cara. How about you call your daughters? You need to do something...*

Maybe Grant and I can keep the girls for the long Labor Day weekend, give Laney and Michelle a break.

***

Picking up the telephone in the kitchen, she dialed Grant's cell phone.

"Hey, Love, what's up," answered Grant in his typical warm style.

"Hi Grant. I just had an off-the-wall idea for Labor Day weekend. I've been missing our little ones. What would you think of instead of entertaining both families here all weekend, we just kept the girls, and let Laney and Michelle have a weekend off?" Her voice was hopeful.

"They were all here in July, maybe something different for them, and we'd get those cutie-pies to ourselves. What do think?" she asked.

"Honey, whatever you want. You know that most of the work lands on your shoulders. I'm game. I'm guessing this getting pregnant thing has been harder on Dale and Michelle than they're letting on. What would you think if we gifted both couples a weekend in the Big Apple, maybe treat them to a play?" suggested Grant.

"Really? Could we? That would be so nice for them, and we could have some Geepop and Grandma time! Grant thanks for not thinking my idea is whacky. How about I call the girls right now? I'm so happy… You're a genius!" added Shelby.

It had not taken much persuading to get her girls on board with the idea. They would bring the grandchildren to her on Friday afternoon. The two couples would fly into Kennedy. Shelby was pleased with the child weekend plan.

This is just what the doctor ordered! I know I'll feel calmer this weekend with the girls. I've been isolating. If I don't start seeing my friends and going out more, Grant is going to notice that I have not been myself. It's bad enough that Michelle noticed...

If I'm going to pretend that I'm okay,... I must do a better job of acting the part.

CHAPTER 18

September 3, 2005
Beaufort, South Carolina

"Oh Grandma, I can't believe we get to spend *three* nights with you!" enthused Ellie. Looking over at Gracie, Ellie said, "Gracie you get to sleep with me in the big bed! Isn't this so cool?"

"Me wants to wear Ariel jammies!" insisted Gracie.

Shelby laughed. "No problem, girls what would you like for dinner?" she asked pulling each girl into her arms for a big group hug.

"Quesadilla!" answered Ellie.

Looking up at her grandmother, Gracie said, "deeyaa."

"Okey dokey," answered Shelby steering the girls downstairs to the kitchen.

A few hours later Grant went upstairs with Shelby helping to get the girls ready for bed. "Geepop tell us a 'tory!" asked Ellie.

Smiling, Grant sat down on the side of the double bed in the guest room decorated for the girls. He smiled as he took in the complete girliness of the room; a colorful border of mermaids who seemed to be swimming atop the blue walls, gave the room a distinctive underwater effect.

"Oh so you want Geepop to tell a story? Hmm. Let's see,"

smiling, he settled himself more comfortably against the headboard and began, "Once upon a time in a far away kingdom by the sea, there lived a beautiful princess with fiery red hair. She would become queen some day and to rule kindly, she had to know all the business of the kingdom."

"One day she came to work in a part of the big castle where the knights were taking care of the legal business of the realm. One of the knights was a kind and lonely knight for an evil witch had cast a spell on him. When he saw the flaming haired princess he could not believe her beauty, for she was the fairest in all the land! But he was so shy from the spell that he could not speak! The timid knight held back, sometimes hiding behind a tree, admiring the princess from afar."

"The months passed. He wanted to say hello to her, but he was far too afraid. One day she passed by his desk, and he became so nervous that he dropped his quill pen, then knocked over his ink well which made a terrible mess on the floor!"

The girls began to giggle. "Geepop, he's so clumsy. He's so silly," commented Ellie. Both girls were laughing as their eyes glittered with pleasure. Sitting in the rocker in the corner of the room, Shelby remained quiet, enjoying the story.

Grant continued, "The poor fellow was so embarrassed that his face turned bright pink. The kindly princess smiled, but did *not* make fun of him. That was the beginning of the joy that came into his life; for her smile broke the evil curse. They got married and were blessed with two princesses and then two more, named Gracie and Ellie. They all lived happily ever after in that beautiful kingdom by the sea where the mermaids played and the dolphins jumped. It was a very wonderful place," finished Grant as he stood up and leaned down to kiss each child's perfect round cheek.

Both girls looked up at him and he recognized his own deep brown eyes in Ellie's. He turned his head toward Shelby and grinned, "And that, my dear, is a *true* story."

Shelby shook her head and grinned back. *Oh, you are something else fella! My love, how am I ever going to tell you?*

"Grandma, how about Pony Girl? Can we have another 'tory?" asked Ellie.

"Absolutely, I have a new one for you. I bet you didn't know that Pony Girl found a tiny little baby horse in the brush and she brought it back to her camp. Tomorrow I will tell you all about it," promised Shelby as she bent down and placed a kiss on each girl's forehead. "Right now it's sleepy time. I love you guys so much," she whispered as she tucked them in and turned on their night light.

"Night girls."

Grant waited for her in the hall. As she closed the door, he took her hand and they walked downstairs together. She realized that she did feel better, for now.

Much later, after she and Grant made tender love, Grant fell asleep beside her. As she listened to his familiar breathing, she reached across the pillow and stroked his dark hair, turning grey now at the temples. She thought what a truly good man he was and how hurtful his childhood must have been. He'd never been one to reveal his feelings, but across the years she came to understand, that the grandparents on his mother's side had been the stable ones. They had earned well and were fixtures in the community, but the fact of their wealth had allowed their daughter, Virginia, Grant's mother, to lead a life of temptation. After his father had passed away from complications resulting from hypertension, she had brought chaos into Grant's life. Grant had been only been fifteen when his dad died, and they'd been close.

His father had been twenty years older than Virginia. Shelby guessed that Virginia had married him in an attempt to curb her wild ways. Perhaps it worked while they were married, but once his father, Bernard, was gone, there'd been an endless parade of male friends, two more husbands, parties, and trips aboard. Shelby guessed that excessive drinking lay beneath Virginia's flamboyant behavior.

Shelby had always gotten along well enough with her. She understood what she was, most obviously a narcissist. Everything was about Virginia. Grant seemed to shrink around her. Early in their marriage, when Shelby had suggested that they celebrate the holidays with Virginia in Paris, Grant had dug in and refused. Shelby sensed a seismic wound beneath Grant's easy personality. Perhaps, he had felt second to the many men in Virginia's life? She wasn't sure, but he showed little of himself around his mother, and it was *not* a topic for discussion.

Shelby recalled a typical family Christmas when the girls were around ten and twelve years-old. This particular year, Virginia had joined them. She had swept in Christmas Day dressed in a lavish mink coat, blonde curls piled high on her head. When she had taken off the big fur coat, her bosom was displayed as if she were in a singles' club. Even that might not have been too awful, but she had paid little attention to the girls, and then had given them inappropriate gifts; real perfume from Paris and can-can burlesque costumes. Grant had paled when the girls opened the packages. Shelby kept her cool; saying to her daughters, who were stunned by the odd gifts, "Oh, how about at Halloween? That could be lots of fun." She had tried to soften the awkward moment.

As she lay there in bed, she wondered if Virginia had thought the girls might actually wear the can-can get-ups in town? She had no idea. The woman was pleasant enough, but not engaged in their lives. Shelby doubted she knew anything about Grant's cases, and she certainly had never shown any interest in Shelby's docent work at the museum, Pony Girl, or the girls' activities.

As an eighty-something, Virginia had mellowed some, but she lived in Paris. Now that she was getting older, she didn't make the trip home very often. Shelby doubted the girls had many feelings for her. And to think of it, her own mother, "Grandmother Avery," was not exactly in their lives either.

Poor girls. They lost out in the grandparent department. Shelby's dad never did participate much in her life after he divorced Avery, and the girls had never known Grant's dad. *Well, my grandchildren are not having that experience. I am there 100%.* Shelby smiled.

Then the dark thoughts came. *What about Willow and Kaitlyn?... Oh, dear.*

She stared into the dark bedroom. After a long moment, *I will figure my way out of all of this.* Exhausted now, Shelby, curled against Grant's warm back and fell to sleep.

THE UNRAVELING OF SHELBY FORREST

CHAPTER 19

September 6, 2005
Beaufort, South Carolina

"Oh Mrs. Forrest," said the receptionist at Dr. Becker's dental office. "I'm so sorry, we had a little emergency here this morning, there was a flood. All systems are a go now, but we're running a bit behind. Would you mind waiting, maybe just ten minutes for your cleaning? We're so sorry. Dr. Becker discovered that the toilet tank had cracked. Had a team in. Shop vacs. Lots of excitement. Can you wait?"

"It's fine. I had my grand girls all weekend. Won't hurt me to sit quietly for a while," replied Shelby as she took a seat in the waiting room and reached for a magazine on the sofa table. She looked past *Time Magazine* featuring an article on the War in Iraq. *When will this war ever end?* Knowing that Cody was in the military, maybe flying fighter jets, she now worried more about our troops involved in the Iraq War than she ever had before.

Noticing the familiar bright yellow cover at the bottom of the stack of magazines, she sifted through them and picked it up. *National Geographic. Ah, my favorite,* she thought opening it and settling into the soft couch. *The Hidden Southwest: Forgotten Treasures of Utah's Range Creek,* was the title above a striking image on its cover. A wave of adrenaline bolted through her body as she realized what lay between her hands. *Range Creek, I haven't thought about that trip in years.* Her stomach lurched. Shelby turned to the article. There he was, Waldo Wilcox who had been their guide so many years ago. The caption, "The Cowboy's Indians," was below his photo. He was shown holding the pelt of the huge mountain lion he had killed decades before. Shelby remembered seeing that pelt during that long ago school trip.

Instantly her memory transported her to that class field trip in the Fall of 1969. That was the trip which she labeled, "The Watching," for that was when she came to understand the character of Dr. Tom Steele, a person who used others and threw them away. She studied the picture of Waldo Wilcox. It was he, who had allowed their class into his 4000 acre ranch. His hair was white now, but he looked about the same, weathered and wrinkled, but remarkably hardy. She scanned down the article and studied Waldo's quote, his substandard English caused her to smile, "There *was* two different cultures here, you got the crude stuff and you got the good stuff on the same rock." He was describing the petroglyphs carved into the walls of a cave.

Dozens of mental pictures flashed in front of Shelby, most starring Tom Steele. Pulling her focus back to Wilcox she thought, *so he finally sold the property to the State of Utah. Interesting, it was just in 2001. The property is now a national history museum.* She thought more about it, considered obtaining a visitor's permit. *Would I dare to go back?* She read through the article. She soon learned that the Native Americans were enraged that their sacred remains had attracted the world's media. Waldo was quoted as saying that he had seen enough skeletons pulled out of the ground on his property to know that the earliest inhabitants were "little people," only four feet tall. The later people, the Fremont People, were larger. It was a big controversy.

Go back? No. That trip was a turning point for me. I learned a hard truth about character and trust. Until I met Grant there never was another man. I learned my lesson: once trust is broken, it is difficult to rebuild.

She sat there for long minutes recalling watching Steele as she and her classmates hiked the canyons, climbed the buttes, studied the ancient drawings. Others would not notice, but she watched and saw that Steele and that pretty girl were heavily into something. Her mind went back to the second night at the inn. She had made an excuse to Barbara, her roommate, about going out into the lobby to study because she couldn't sleep. Shelby had sat in the dark, in the same corner where she had sat when they first checked-in, as Dr. Steele handed out the room keys. She had waited. A few hours passed. Everyone was nestled in their rooms. The lodge grew quiet; sure enough around one o'clock she observed that girl's door slowly opening. She watched as the shadowy figure took the few steps across the hall and silently entered Dr. Steele's dark room. She had been so naïve. Had no clue about the after midnight wanderings that went on. *Oh Shelby,* her higher self was laughing at her, *you were so innocent. Silly girl.* Her inner voice mocked her young naïve self.

"Mrs. Forrest, Rebecca is ready for you now," called the receptionist.

"Oh, thank you Judy," replied Shelby as she thought, *Saved by the bell. There is no need to pick at that old sore.*

CHAPTER 20

September 8, 2005
Beaufort, South Carolina,

Shelby kissed Grant goodbye as he left for the office. She was happy to have the quiet house to herself for a change. It occurred to her that since the Water Festival, except for seeing the family, and working at the museum, she had been isolating.

*Shelby you may not feel normal, but you need to at least **act** normal. Did you notice that Michelle called you out on being "stressed?* Her annoying internal voice pestered her.

At that moment the phone rang. Shelby walked into the kitchen to answer it.

"Hello," she answered.

"Hey, Shelb, it's me, Karen. You'll not believe it, but Jeff was transferred to Colorado for some unspecified time. Guess who gets custody of his new puppy?" Her voice was filled with laughter. "Well, my son is darn right sorry, but what's a mom for?" enthused her friend.

"This all happened so fast," she continued, "apparently, I've got me a pup. He's all set to compete in two puppy matches; conformation and obedience, whatever they are? I've been practicin'. You would think I'd been to the Westminster Dog Show the way I have my prance on!" Karen chortled at her own joke.

"So Shelb, whaddaya say, want to come out with me and my

pooch today?"

"Hey, how can I resist seeing you strut your stuff?" Amused at the vision of her friend in the show ring, Shelby responded, "Sure, we'll come. Want to meet at the harbor walk this morning?"

The women set up the meeting.

This is good. I know I have not been right lately. I probably should not have taken the summer off from my docent job.

An hour later as Shelby and her dogs came across the park, they immediately spotted Karen's beautiful light yellow puppy. "Karen, you didn't tell me the dog was a *Goldie*! What's his name?" she asked, sinking to her knees to accept the wriggling puppy's enthusiastic kisses. With her free hand she pulled him in closer for a hug. Zoe and Tessie's tails vibrated in excitement. Thump, thump, as they admired the little dog.

"Oh, Karen, he's precious," Shelby exclaimed, rubbing her face into his downy fur, "and so soft."

"My girl, I would like ya'll to meet Lord Tanner," drawled Karen.

As they walked the crushed shell path, Shelby felt her body begin to relax. She realized that her muscles had been tense for weeks. She rolled her shoulders, calmed herself with a long inhale. *This is good being with Karen, being normal.*

Her dogs, invigorated by the puppy, went into a wild chasing mode the instant they were released from their leashes in the big field. "Oh, I have a surprise for you, Lord Tanner and I have it going on. Look out Westminster!"

"As soon as the wrestlers finish up, I'll give you a full demonstration!" exclaimed Karen, eyes sparkled in merriment. She was an attractive woman in her sixties, a real go-getter. Shelby had met her a few years back when Karen had trained under her to become a docent. They had been friends ever since.

About fifteen minutes later, they called in the exuberant dogs, latched their leashes. "Okay, wait up," called Karen as she took off prancing, impersonating a professional dog handler as if she were in the show ring, Tanner faithfully followed her lead. Shelby could not help but fall into laughter. With that encouragement Karen embellished her prance, topping off the parody by lifting her right arm in the exaggerated flounce of a true competitor!

"Stop! You're cracking me up!" shouted Shelby between giggles, which just egged Karen on all the more! Yelling between waves of laughter, "Hey lady, I see you've got your *groove on!*" The more Shelby enjoyed it, the more Karen strutted! Both women finally fell into welcome hilarity as they finished up their dog walk.

That evening as she prepared dinner, Shelby realized that for the first time in a long while, she felt a bit like her old self. With the confidence that feeling better brought, she promised herself that she would call the United Kingdom, soon.

CHAPTER 21

Chapter Twenty-one
September 8, 2005
Lakenheath, Suffolk, England

Cody drew in a deep breath of fresh morning country air. *I will miss this* place, he thought as he increased his pace on his daily six mile jog through the quaint village. As his muscles warmed up, he felt his body fold into an easy rhythm. Now that his tour in Europe was coming to an end, he could not help but think back to all that had happened while he had been stationed in the United Kingdom. He smiled, remembering his eager self as he brought his wife and baby here. It had been a good run for the family: Kaitlyn had thrived with the other military kids, and little Willow was born.

As the miles clicked by Cody focused on what these past three years had meant to him. He thought of Amber. She had discovered something of her own destiny here; an unlikely event, had they remained as civilians. He scanned the years, his thoughts turned dark. They had arrived in England in 2002 just before the Joint Forces invaded Iraq and captured Baghdad.

He thought about the 100,000 troops deployed to find the weapons of mass destruction, and the December 2003 capture of Hussein. Yet, here they were two years later, with thousands of lives lost, massive injuries, the end of Saddam, but no such weapons had been found. What remained was an ugly war which continued to rage on. Cody knew that by the time the Coalition Forces actually pulled out, there would be far more bloodshed.

As he strode along, his thoughts grew heavier. He flashed to the broken bodies he worked to save when he was transported to Germany, to Landstuhl Regional Medical Center, to deal with the results of the surprise attacks, the relentless uprisings against U.S. ground forces. Just last month a platoon of forty was ambushed by multiple IED attacks. The troops had been on night patrol. Drones spotted movement on the roof tops, somehow, the commander ordered them forward. The enemy trapped them in the dark alleys. Bombs were detonated using cell phones and wired up TV remotes. Broken bodies. Burned faces. Shattered legs.

Cody had nightmares, something he would never share with Amber. The dreams were filled with the smell of burned flesh as he unwound bloody gauze; visions of stretcher after stretcher, loaded with injured twenty-something young soldiers connected to machines, tubes running out of their noses, wires hooked up. Unconscious.

The dreams were vivid. Some nights as he struggled up through the fog of sleep, he seemed to smell the acrid stench of disinfectant, or the sickening sweetness of coagulating blood. In some visions there would be the line-up of uniformed doctors, nurses, and the chaplain, standing ready to receive the buses loaded with the wounded who had had been coughed out by the continuous grey stream of C-17 cargo planes. The planes from Kabul and Baghdad delivered their damaged goods from two and three thousand miles away. In his dreams he could hear the roar of the planes and the drone of the chaplain's greeting to each shrapnel-filled soldier, "You're safe now. You are in Germany." Sometimes a muffled sob escaped from him as he stirred to consciousness.

In his sleep he saw crutches and amputees. Five times he had been flown to Landstuhl, the combat hospital, to perform emergency trauma procedures. The most recent assignment to Germany was the result of one of the worst attacks on US forces. He'd put in forty-eight desperate hours, trying to save limbs and lives. Many injuries; concussions and brain damage.

Goddamn those fucking humvees. Those fucking canvas doors.

Goddamn it! Our own guys struggling to survive against an elusive enemy with only flimsy canvas between them and eternity. Godfuckingdamnit!

Anger surged up in him every time he thought of the inadequacies of our side's ability to protect its own troops. He tried to shake off the rage as he felt his blood pressure soaring.

As his legs stretched across the miles, he couldn't help but ponder the futility of it all, and now the Sunni and Shia factions were waking up. Cody was certain that the capture of Hussein had only been the beginning of violence in Iraq, not the end, as Washington had expected. Cody sensed that the underlying animosities between warring factions would heighten in the wake of the U.S. military action. As Coalition Forces pulled out, he worried that civil war would escalate. In the chaos of the civil war, his real concern was that the extremists of Al Qaeda would have the advantage, would find a foothold and take over Iraq. He didn't think the Iraqi people were ready for self rule. He sucked in a deep breath. It was too much.

All this is above my pay grade. If I can help our men and women taken down in military vehicles insufficiently armored against attack, if I can save a limb, an eye, cure an infection brought on by an injury from an IED, that has to be my best. But in his most secret thoughts Cody knew this war was a massive mistake in terms of dollars and lives, but this was not his call. *I'm not in charge.*

He'd been awarded a Joint Service Commendation Medal for extraordinary achievement for those horrific forty-eight hours, but he knew that those poor maimed sons-of-bitches deserved the credit. Those poor guys put their lives on the line. *But, Cody,* he heard his internal voice, *would you give up your life to protect your wife, daughters, ...your country?*

He knew the answer. *In a heartbeat.*

He thought more about the wounded he did his best to help.

They are the heroes. I know it. It just frustrates the hell out of me to see these life altering injuries, and they are the lucky ones who survived....

As he came to the end of his morning run, he thought of his wife, his girls and his country, *Maybe I will go the next thirteen years, become a lifer. The military seems to suit us; this seems like what I am meant to do...*

With that he was back at his place. It was time to clean up and get to the hospital.

CHAPTER 22

September 8, 2005
Suffolk, England

Luminous sapphire eyes held Amber's as she lifted her sturdy two-year-old, Willow, out of her highchair. "Momma, 'kool today?" she asked hopefully.

"You betcha, little lady," responded her very trim and petite blondish mother as she admired her daughter's translucent skin and glossy ginger curls.

"I think most of your friends will be there. I know Katie and Hannah will be for sure."

A big grin spread across Willow's face as Amber began to wipe the sticky peanut butter from her plump little pink fingers. *Oh baby girl,* she thought, *we're going to miss the everyday pleasure of our friends' company aren't we?*

Time was running short, before long they would be back in the U.S. Part of her was excited for the adventure, and the opportunity to see her mom, but the other part dreaded leaving her cadre of friends. They had become so *close.*

They had met at "Mommy and Me," the pre-school co-op. She joined when they first arrived in England, when Kaitlyn was little, and she had made acquaintances, but across the time and with her second child, a core group had formed. There were six mothers at its center, others had come and gone, but these six had become more of a sisterhood than mothers socializing their two-year-olds.

A familiar lump made itself known in her stomach. Her eyes welled with tears. She would miss these gals so much. Except for her husband and her sister, this was the first time she had ever experienced such closeness with others; originally connected through the children, now they were linked through a bond of trust. What fascinated Amber was that each of the women was so uniquely herself. They were in no way copies of one another; they were different ages and came from various backgrounds, but across the three years they had become each other's best friends. It was a safe zone. They had each other's backs. When a last minute baby sitter was needed or someone was ill, help was there, no questions.

Stop being maudlin Amber. No one has died. This is the military. Families move. It's not the end! she scolded herself. And suddenly her mind flashed to a recent film she and Cody had enjoyed, *Sisterhood of the Traveling Pants,* and she laughed out loud. In the film, the best girl friends were going their separate ways for the summer; the plan was to stay in contact by mailing their lucky pair of jeans around to each of them. It was a sweet romantic comedy but it spoke to the bond that is possible between women. *We could become the sisterhood of the traveling wipies, pacifiers, diapers, oh yuck, diapers!* She laughed again as she took Willow's little hand in her own strong one and walked her down the hall to the bedroom to get dressed for the day.

"Willow, what pleases you to wear today, my dear one?"

"Mommy, Ariel shirt," she answered smiling.

As Amber helped Willow into her clothes and checked on Kaitlyn's state of readiness for school, her memory tracked to how these friends, these "sisters" had been there for her back when her big idea had come to her. She thought of how they had encouraged her rather off- center-of- normal notion.

As an artist, Amber had been packing her easel and paints with her everywhere she went. She loved to paint out-of-doors, on location, whenever the opportunity presented itself. Her friends knew this about her: Amber has paints, will travel. It was her thing. They knew that each woman had a passion, some for jogging, another for cooking, handicrafts, blogging. Each had her special skill; it was part of what made the group so uniquely special. But after a certain weekend excursion, Amber had a vision that amped up her dream, her friends had supported her idea one hundred percent.

The turning point had its start on one of the typical short trips she and Cody and Kaitlyn often took; this time they crossed the channel to visit Claude Monet's garden. His home and gardens had become a museum and his prints were there for purchase in its store. As Amber toured Monet's spaces she took her time. She carefully studied the water lilies and their reflections in the still water of the pond. Later, in the exhibit area, she studied the details of the paintings. She compared Monet's inspiration, the actual lilies, to his paintings of them; doing so had expanded her mental picture of her own artistic life, maybe forever.

She recalled that they had walked the lovely gardens playing tourist, marveling at the beauty of the wisteria covered bridge, admiring the riotous colors of the tulips, and being captivated by Monet's talent. As an art student she had studied and appreciated the great masters' techniques, but on *that* day she came away feeling almost obsessed with the way Monet had caught the light. She could not get over his brush technique; how he captured the sense of the opening of the delicate pink and white petals. She could see that he had used the softest touch, but it was how he used light that fascinated her.

After that trip, back at home on painting days, she was inspired to further explore her own use of light. She strove to use a feather touch with her brush. Monet had worked in oil, her medium was watercolor. She painted everything she could find: the flowers in the church yard, the hollyhocks near the children's play area, a rose opening with glistening dew drops. Every where she went she noticed the light, how it played off Kaitlyn's hair, the shadows on the linoleum in the kitchen. She painted and studied.

One morning not long after that Monet trip, she was reading in her art magazine that a fundraising festival was planned at the museum at Stonehenge. They were offering a two week en plein air opportunity for local artists; granting a limited number of painting permits, with an art show as the culminating event at the patrons' elaborate fundraising gala. Museum donors from all over the world would be invited. The en plein air artists were to donate two original paintings created during the festival.

As Amber got her girls ready for school, she lingered in that life-changing memory. She recalled that the Stonehenge painting opportunity had shaken her to her core. She couldn't believe that for a small donation she might be allowed on the grounds to paint the mysterious monument? She was a little in love with the museum anyway, its title, "Museum of Unnatural Mystery," had thrilled her during a visit when they had first arrived in England. Without hesitating, Amber remembered going online and applying for a permit, which was immediately granted as she was one of the first ten to apply. She had contacted her women friends who volunteered to care for Kaitlyn so that Amber could participate.

The driving force behind her desire to paint the monuments was to apply the new skills she'd taught herself through studying Monet. Now three years later, she enjoyed thinking back to how desperately she'd wanted to capture the way the sun played against the famous stones.

Amber steered her thoughts back to the present. It was time for school. Satisfied that her adorable offspring were presentable, she collected Kaitlyn's lunch and backpack and ushered them both into the car, where, smiling to herself, she reflected on the fact that she was having a 'precious moment.' It was a simple thing really, buckling children into car seats; it was its very ordinariness that gave her pleasure.

Much later in the day, during the girls' quiet time, Willow in a nap, and Kaitlyn resting with a book, Amber picked up the earlier thoughts from that morning and the pivotal opportunity at Stonehenge.

Enjoying the little journey down memory lane, in her mind's eye she visualized the image of her very pregnant self standing in front of her art easel as she carefully worked to get the effect of the late summer afternoon sun as it fell against the ancient stone pillars. Monet's sensibilities had crept into her unconscious. She had become obsessed with trying to accomplish his gentle touch, instead of lilies she was after the effect of sundown on Stonehenge. And so on that certain late summer day, she was lost in her art.

It was then, when she knew what she was meant to do. She had felt called in an extraordinary way that day. A great desire had filled her soul. Her chest had tighten as she thrilled to thoughts of her future. *She would portray a sense of the past, celebrate the great monuments left by the ancients by showing them in various illuminations, the changing seasons, and times of the day.* Her heart had raced and she'd felt dizzy with excitement. She had realized in that moment that she could do this, if it took her a lifetime. She would raise her family, stand by her husband, and she would bring an aspect of the past to life through her paints and brushes.

Still focused on that day, when her racing pulse had finally settled down and her hand had stopped shaking from the rush of adrenaline, she had given the crazy idea more thought. She could not come up with any reasons why not. Her encouraging inner self had simply said, *Amber, who better than you? Daddy always promised you Stonehenge and here you are. He loved the Celtic tribes, the Druids, and respected their accomplishments. You have Daddy's passion. You have studied art your entire life, and heaven knows you have many paint brushes!*

She'd kept the idea to herself while she completed the days of painting outdoors in the field surrounding the stones. Finally, with the plein air days behind her, it was time to share her idea out loud. A few days later, after the co-op, she and the gals were enjoying coffee as they watched their little ones crawling around the outdoor sand box. She recalled the conversation. She could still feel the temerity which had overtaken her.

"Martina, Honor, Gina," and with that the other two, Debra and Farrah, turned their full attention to her. A wave of shyness had engulfed her, "Uh," she stumbled, stalling for time. "Last week, uh…um…" Her friends' faces were encouraging, "while I was using that painting permit, something came to me. Something *big*." She'd swallowed and stopped. Five pairs of eyes held hers.

"I… uh. I had a thought….what if.." With that she muttered out her idea about the ancients. She even shared with them how Andrew Wyeth had painted his favorite subject, Helga, 240 times! "Am I being crazy?" she had dared to ask, her blue eyes darkly serious. "My dear friends, is this Amber's OCD kicking in, or am I on to something?"

In unison, five lovely, accomplished, level-headed women nodded their support. Honor said, "If not you, who then, Amber? You know Van Gogh had to start someplace. What the great masters had going for them was that they painted, they were passionate about it, and they *really* painted. Amber you paint, and what I love about you, is your passion for it."

Martina, jumped in. "Amber the work you've been doing, those hollyhocks, for example, they could hold their own in any art show. This is not a dumb idea."

Farrah rose from where she was sitting and wrapped her arms around Amber, "You go girl."

Amber had embarrassed herself by bursting into tears.

Finally she asked, "Really?"

"Yes, really," replied a chorus of her friends.

She had one answer, but what would Cody think? A few days later it was time to share all this with him. By then her idea had grown, she would paint Stonehenge in all its angles and illuminations, then someday, maybe the Irish Stonehenge, Dromberg Circle, maybe the Coliseum in Rome. If they ended up in Texas, she could paint the Alamo, maybe the Indian village in Taos, New Mexico. Her imagination had soared. What about the great pyramids? She had her entire life ahead to paint.

She had planned it for a Friday night. She waited until Kaitlyn was settled into bed; stories read, kisses granted. Amber and Cody closed her bedroom door and tip-toed into the living room.

"Honey, I have something to discuss with you," she had begun. Her voice held a tentative quiver.

Cody heard her out, and when she dared to look up, she could not help but notice that her stalwart, handsome, tough-guy husband's eyes were moist.

"So Cody, am I being a crazy lady, or could this be something for my life?" Her words were rushed. "It wouldn't matter where we were stationed, my paints are mobile. The planet's mysterious structures are awaiting me."

Cody took a minute to process his thoughts. "Amber, I've always believed in your artistic talent. This could be a brilliant direction for your life to take. I think you've had a brainstorm here, maybe it's pure genius." He paused and riveted his bright blue eyes on her face.

"Amber, you've nothing to lose. These weeks since that day at Monet's…it's like you've been on fire. You seem infused with a new sense of purpose. It's intoxicating as hell to be around you! In fact, it's energizing me for our next challenge."

Cody reached for her. They remained together for long minutes, their hearts beating in unison, each lost in their own thoughts, contemplating the future.

CHAPTER 23

September 9, 2005
Lakenheath, England

Cody had fallen asleep in front of the television. His day in the ER had been brutal. Amber roused him up and into bed. By the time her head hit the pillow she wasn't sleepy anymore. Her thoughts turned back to that pivotal day at Stonehenge when she realized she could paint the antiquities, that she could somehow celebrate the ancients, bring them to the modern world. The epiphany had altered some of the plans she'd had for her life. She understood that it might seem silly, but she felt strongly about it. A faint smile traced itself across her face as she let herself drift into the memory of that life altering day three years ago.

True to what the museum promised, the patrons' gala for the "Museum of Unnatural Mystery" was filled with donors from all over the world. The event was held in London's Marriott Regents Park. The ballroom was festive, overflowing with the beautiful en plein air paintings. Each painting was identified with a short biography of the artist and a photo. They were to be auctioned near the end of the event. The artists were given complimentary tickets to the gala.

Amber had been nervous all week just thinking of her work being exhibited to a world class audience. She hoped that her blood pressure did not spike and get the contractions started. This was not a good time to have a baby!

Somehow she'd found an appropriate maternity evening gown. Cody, of course, looked more striking than ever in his rented tuxedo. They had booked a room in the hotel so Amber could rest between the reception, the art showing, dinner, and then finally the auction. She and the other artists and their spouses were assigned tables near the front of the massive ballroom. Her breathing had been a bit irregular all evening. During the opening reception, Cody kept her steady by holding her hand as she smiled nicely to the many strangers who approached her wanting to discuss her technique.

The event organizers understood that maximum bids would come from well fed, well lubricated guests. The alcohol had flowed freely. At precisely 9:30 p.m. the robust auctioneer took the stage. With microphone in hand, he warmed up the audience with jokes and funny stories. He planted the idea that original art by newly discovered artists had great economic potential. The crowd of four hundred quieted down.

The auction began. Two stunning young women dressed in black gowns strode onto the stage and with a flourish, unveiled the first piece, a smallish painting, maybe 18 x 24 of a wonderful view of the Stonehenge pillars caught in the vermillion of dawn.

"For this original piece the bidding will begin at 100 pounds, do I hear 100?" called out the vigorous auctioneer.

"Yes, in the back, do I hear 200 pounds?" And the bids soared higher. Amber could hear the rush of her heart beating in her ears. The idea of painting and exhibiting her work had been intriguing, but she'd not gotten her head around what it would *feel* like to observe the actual auction. She knew her pieces would soon be up. Her head had buzzed as she thought, *This could be humiliating. What if no one bids on my paintings?* She recalled how she had tried to shrink down in her chair, not an easy feat with a very swollen belly.

Two more pieces came and went. The auctioneer was a master at humor and speed. When a bid would stall he filled in with interesting trivia. "Did you know that the first, the center pillars, the blue stones, are now thought to be 11,000 years old?"

More bidding.

"Stonehenge was a religious burial site, bones have been dated back to 3000 B.C."

More bidding.

"Your donations will secure this site for future generations."

Extraordinary pieces came and went. "Historians once thought that Stonehenge was built by the Druids two thousand years before Christ. Carbon dating proves they merely *borrowed* the spot."

A rush of higher bids.

"Researchers now believe the stones were brought from such a vast distance, two hundred miles away, because of their acoustic properties. There are deep marks in them, probably from being struck to create sound. They think the pillars provided the original *rock* music!"

The crowd broke into laughter.

The bidding went higher.

Amber took a swallow of air, and dared to look up as the two assistants marched across the stage carrying a very large painting. *Oh my God, this one has to be mine!* Her heart thudded against her chest as the glamorous assistants threw back the black velvet revealing her very impressive four-foot wide vision of Stonehenge at sunset. The piece was framed in deep walnut to compliment the simplicity of the subject. The bidding began at three hundred pounds. She took another swallow of air and clutched Cody's hand. Cody squeezed back, as the bids flew faster than they could comprehend. The auctioneer was banging his gavel, "Going once, going twice, sold to the gentleman in back, for seven thousand pounds."

The audience burst into applause.

Heavens!! thought Amber, *I hope I don't wet my panties!* Cody turned and looked at her. His eyes were wide with astonishment. "Honey, did I get it right. Did your first piece just sell for seven thousand pounds?"

"Ah. I think so." The auction continued like that and Amber's second piece, a bit smaller, sold for sixty-five hundred pounds. Both Amber and Cody sat in stunned silence.

Once the auction wound down, during the last service of coffees and after dinner drinks, the art collectors descended upon the artists. Both tables where the artists were seated suddenly became surrounded by admirers.

Amber remained seated, all the better to rest her feet, considering the size of her enormous mid-section. "Mrs. James?" asked a petite middle-aged woman dressed in silver lame. "I'm Lydia Lane, and I'm very impressed with your work. I represent HomeCo America. We have retail outlets in hundreds of locations in the States and we are expanding to Europe. We are opening our first store here in London. We carry almost anything you can imagine for the home. I represent the interior design center. We bought both of your pieces."

Amber looked up at her and managed a smile and tried not to look as shocked and stupid as she felt.

"Here's my card," the woman continued, "do you think we could meet to discuss a future relationship? Our competitors carry a Martha Stewart line of home décor and furnishings. We want something fresh and original. I think you could help bring that to us."

The woman offered her hand. As they shook hands, Amber managed to grunt out a few words of agreement, and the woman walked away.

"Amber, was that what I think it was? Is she a buyer for a home improvement chain?" asked Cody.

"She is."

***

Amber recalled that she had been so excited at the hotel that night, she could barely sleep. Her thoughts churned on the baby coming. She considered her options; the reality of taking on work and caring for her children. She worried whether she could handle it all.

She knew that an office meeting in London with the buyer was out of the question. She could easily drive the ninety-four miles into London, but it became a much bigger trip when she considered making it in just one day. Amber had pondered the possibilities that Lydia Lane might provide until she'd fallen into a light sleep.

The next morning she and Cody had breakfast brought to their room. Settling into the chair next to the window, Amber finished her coffee and asked Cody, "Do you think I should call her right now?" she paused. "Cody, am I savvy enough for this?"

"Amber, find out what she's talking about."

"I don't want to be a sell out?"

"That's not possible. This could be the beginning of something huge. Call her," he urged.

Amber felt like her heart was in her mouth. Her tongue seemed thick, but she reminded herself that she had nothing to lose: her baby was coming, Kaitlyn was at home, safe, Cody's career was thriving. She did not need this. *That's right. You do not need this. Act like a big girl and call! Also what are you talking about "selling out?" Selling **what** out?* It was that impatient inner voice which sometimes scolded her.

She opened her cell phone and pressed the digits printed on the woman's business card.

"Hello?"

"Ms. Lane, it's Amber James. You gave me your card last night."

"Of course, Mrs. James. How are you this fine morning?" she asked in a cheery voice. "May I call you Amber? Would you call me Lydia?"

"Certainly."

"I'm so glad you called. My colleague and I love your work. We are international buyers, as I mentioned, for Homeco America, but this month we have been tasked with a special assignment. Our home office has been awarded the contract for a chain of boutique hotels. The design team has the vision of bringing in an historic touch, maybe a bit of the medieval. They plan to combine period antiques with contemporary pieces. Our part of the project is to secure the art. We are tasked with finding original work that is representative of the past. They are thinking of photos or paintings of crumbling castles, maybe monasteries falling to ruins, perhaps an ancient Irish circle, and of course some paintings of Stonehenge." Lydia paused. "Are you getting the idea?" she asked.

"I am."

"I know the designers are after something fresh, the heaviness of the antiquities contrasted with the buoyancy of the modern. My partner and I are particularly taken with the fact that your paintings are so open and airy. So subtle. Of course we're talking about reproductions of your originals, but it's that fresh, simple quality we're after."

"Well thank you," Amber hesitated, after a moment, "You understand that I am about to have a baby, right?"

Laughing, Lydia Lane replied, "Ah, that one I did notice. Kinda hard to miss it!" Her voice was teasing and friendly. "There's time. They are just breaking ground on the first hotel. We wouldn't need all the art for a year."

"Will my paintings be going into the suites?" inquired Amber.

"Yes, into the individual rooms and in the hallways; probably at the elevator lobby on each floor. Perhaps a large piece for there."

It was clear to Amber that this woman, Lydia Lane, had a sense of where the paintings would go, as well as a vision of their sizes.

"What color palette are you thinking about?" asked Amber, forgetting her nerves and considering the business aspects of creating product.

"The palette you used in the two paintings we bought, the gold and yellow tones contrasted with the green of the grass, and the sky. I think the palette you use naturally will work for us," concluded Lydia Lane.

"I'm interested. I need to talk to my husband about it and find out exactly how many paintings you are going to require, at least for the initial project."

"Of course, but before we go any further, we first need to know if this is feasible for you?"

"It is, but I don't know the next step," added Amber.

"Well, your people would have a sit down with our people and work out the financial details, develop a contract, a scope of work."

The women said their goodbyes. Amber closed down her phone and shared the proposition with Cody. "Honey, I don't have any people? She means attorney or business consultant, someone like that? Doesn't she?" Amber's expression was wide-eyed.

"I think so," answered Cody as he kneeled down in front of her chair and took her hands in his. "Amber, let's get us some people!"

***

Amber lay quietly next to Cody as the memory continued to spool across her mind. She recalled placing the call a few days later to her mother.

"Momma so much has happened since the Stonehenge Museum painting days. I'm overwhelmed. I talked with that buyer lady, as you know. She told me to have my people work out the details with her people. Mom, that's the problem. I don't have any *people*," she paused and took a breath. "I think I remember you saying that Dad's great uncle had a grandson who was an attorney, a prosecutor, something like that. Was he Fremont? Freeland? Mom, I need help!" pleaded Amber in a frantic tone.

"Amber, my daughter. This is so thrilling! Yes, your dad's grandfather had siblings. Some of them died young and we lost touch, but I do recall an attorney. I think he's over in the Carolinas, maybe its Savannah. I just *knew* that if I saved those awful family Christmas newsletters that someday they would come in handy," she said laughing. "I bet I can dig around and find out his name. Would that help?" Her voice dropped, "Sweetheart, this is all going to be fine. Don't get upset about the details, what's important is this big break with your work. Artists wait decades to be discovered, some never are. This will all sort itself out. Don't go scaring yourself. You know I could bust my buttons with pride over all you're doing?"

"Oh Momma, thanks."

"Now let's talk about what's really important! How is that baby doing?" Her mother's voice, as always, was filled with love.

The conversation was still fresh in Amber's memory even though it had been two years. She had felt herself relax. "Oh

Momma, thank you. You always reassure me that I'm not in over my head," she paused. "Oh goodness, our baby is kicking like crazy. I think she wants out!"

The next evening her mother called her back.

"Amber, I found what you wanted. I think I met him once. Yes, his grandfather was your dad's great uncle. He was a prosecutor in South Carolina last time I heard. I know he's out of the area but I'm sure he will know what steps to take in order to protect your intellectual property." Her mother's voice dropped an octave. "Amber, this will be fine. I am sure he can at least point you to the correct resources."

"Oh thank you. You always calm me down. I'm so glad you're coming out to help with the baby and Kaitlyn. Kaitlyn keeps asking how many more days til Grandma gets here. I tell her 'not much longer now.'"

The next day Amber had called this cousin, Grant Forrest. She easily recalled the conversation, "Ah, hi, Mr. Forrest, I'm Elma and Sharon Blake's daughter, Amber. I'm a few times removed cousin, and I need some advice, my Mom thought you might be able to steer me in the right direction."

"Oh, yes Elma Blake over there in Georgia. I met him once. He loved antique cars. We had a conversation at a family thing down in Atlanta. In fact," his voice trailed into laughter, "...it was at one of those reenactment affairs." There was more laughter. "We were at Stone Mountain Park. We had a big turnout of family, anyone related to a Mathews was there. One of the Confederate soldier-actors shot himself in the foot with his pellet gun. Funniest thing you've ever seen. All that drama and old-time regalia mixed up with modern day ambulances. He wasn't really hurt, his pride maybe, but it was awfully funny. Your dad and I chuckled over it." His friendly banter came through the phone.

"I remember your daddy, great guy. It seems to me I heard that he passed. I'm sorry about that. I liked him. So y'all are his girl?" In his gentle drawl, he brought the conversation back to the point.

Amber immediately warmed to his familiar Southern accent and told him her story.

"This is great news. I've just the man for you. Went to law school with him. He specializes in intellectual rights. Straight arrow. He's your guy."

They chatted a bit longer and Amber assured him that she would let him know how things worked out with her contract. By the time they hung up, she felt much more confident.

The next day, during Kaitlyn's nap, she placed the international call to the referral attorney, Jeff Newton.

"Hey, how y'all doin? Grant gave me a heads up. This is an amazing opportunity for you. By the way, any family of Grant's is family to me." He paused. His casual manner immediately put her at ease.

"So exactly what can I do for you?"

Amber explained the details.

With Mr. Newton on board she really did feel like she could relax and have her baby. Somehow, maybe because of the distant family connection, she felt safe. She trusted him to take care of things, and she had been right. He handled all of the business seamlessly.

She plumped her pillow and listened to Cody's rhythmic breathing next to her. She closed her eyes, but sleep failed to come. She continued to think about her career, how Newton handled the boutique hotel contract. The legal business had all gone so fast while Cody was on double shifts at the hospital. It was a few days later when she had a chance to fill him in one morning over coffee.

She remembered it vividly.

"Cody, the attorney, Jeff Newton, worked out our contract with HomeCo America. The initial phase is twenty paintings within the next twelve months, they have stipulated the sizes, and I have agreed to giving them reproduction rights to the work that I do for them under contract. I will retain the rights to any work I do for myself. They will pay for travel; hotel, food, all of it, when I go on location. They are thinking Ireland and maybe some sites in England. Wouldn't it be cool if I got to paint the Harry Potter castle at Edinburgh? Cody, I am so excited!" Amber's eyes had sparkled with energy.

"You amaze me. Harry Potter castle, now that could be fun!" grinned Cody.

"I've been talking with Lydia. I guess the designers' original concept for the hotel was to use big framed photos of ancient crumbling buildings, but after that Stonehenge event, Lydia created a demonstration for them, a kind of visual storyboard. She placed framed photos next to the framed plein air paintings. She said there was no contest when they saw them side by side. It didn't take much persuading after that. They abandoned the photograph idea," Amber's words vibrated with energy. "This is so thrilling!" she'd exclaimed. She recalled that big belly and all, she'd flung herself into Cody's arms.

"Whoa girl, you're not as svelte as you once were," he chuckled, stumbling as he caught her.

After a long interval. "So how's our baby bump today?" he'd asked embracing her. She remembered how he'd bent down on one knee and whispered to her swollen middle, "Hey there little girl, when are you coming out to meet us? We promise you a wild ride!"

Amber had massaged her pregnant middle as she smiled down at her gentle husband. "It won't be long now. I see the doctor on

Monday."

"Amber I'm so happy for you about all this. I know it won't be easy to have such a commitment along with a new baby, but you've always just dug in." He studied her face. "I've never kept it a secret how I feel regarding your art work. It transports me. It always has. There's a bit of magic in your brush. I knew that if others could see your art, they would appreciate it, but I never *dreamed* of anything like this."

Enjoying the rerun of the beginning of her fervent art life, Amber let herself relax against the pillow as she relived the rest of that conversation with Cody.

"Cody," she'd said, "I know. Me neither. It takes my breath away. There was more to what Lydia had to say. She has become chattier since I signed the first contract. Anyway, she was more forthcoming than before. Apparently this boutique deal is a side business; there is something bigger, a whole corporate vision. Lydia was full of info." Amber remembered catching her breath before she continued.

"Maybe you need more coffee."

"Coffee? No, I'm fine. Really, there's more than all this?" Cody had asked in surprise.

"For starters, they need artwork that can help sell their new fall signature line. They work a year ahead. It's to be "old world," with images on china, pillows, decorative throws, as well as a collection of framed reproductions in various sizes. In the past they have been industry forerunners in creating the next genre of interior design. This old world theme, if it catches on the way they think it will, would translate into masonry in the kitchens, rough stone floors, farm- house style counters, old fashion faucets, reproductions of antiques in the living spaces; all the decorating needs. Lydia said the last time old world was popular was in the early 70's and it was Mediterranean, she says, this would be earlier, more about antiquities, than Italianesque. I don't pretend to understand the marketplace, but Lydia thinks my work may be exactly what they need to compliment this new direction. Anyway Jeff Newton is working with them to draw up a contract with me for the next five years, maybe you can look it over before I sign it."

"You've got to be kidding! I thought the hotel gig was a big deal!" In her memory she could still hear Cody's words. "Amber not many artists get paid to pursue their passion. This is an incredible opportunity, especially when you consider how few artists are recognized in their own time." Cody's eyes had held hers. "This is big, really big!"

"Oh yeah, like my belly!" She'd said giggling and thus lightening the intensity of their future plans.

***

It had all come to pass. As she lay in bed next to Cody who was snoring softly, a warm feeling streamed through her. It came whenever she stopped to consider what this had all meant to her. It was not that she was now a known commodity. It was more about the work itself. In some ways she had come to revere the ancients. She imagined them rolling tons of massive stones across vast distances to immortalize their faith; their markers, for the future. She devoured the most recent research on them; learned that the village for the Stonehenge workers held a population of about 4000, was two miles away from the monument building site, and was carbon dated to 2600 B.C.

We are their sons and daughters, she thought. *I cherish what they accomplished. They have left us a rich legacy to decipher and if not that, at least to appreciate. When I think of Easter Island, the Great Pyramids, the Inca civilizations, the pyramids in Mexico… when I think of all they left for us, I want to cry out with joy.*

Amber noticed as she lay there, that her eyes had filled. *I don't think I've sold out. I feel blessed to bring attention to their brilliant achievements; to show the world, yes they were here, our forefathers were here. They struggled, they loved, they died, as they paved a pathway to the future, to us.*

Amber's thoughts continued, *I'm grateful. This is a privilege for me to celebrate who they were and what they did. Maybe this will be my legacy.*

A young, little girl part of herself whispered a thought, *This is a beautiful way to feel close to Daddy...*

He would be so proud...

Her more sensible self replied, Y*es, all this may be true, but you also need to get some sleep!*

With that she turned her pillow to its cooler side and turned onto her left hip. *Yes, sleep. We'll be moving soon. There's a lot to do.*

CHAPTER 24

September 10, 2005
Lakenheath, England

"Amber are these the last items for the biggest boxes?" asked Cody.

"Yes," she replied walking into the living room. "I can't believe how much stuff we've accumulated in three short years. This feels so weird to pack up, to start a new life."

"It's crazy," responded Cody. "I've felt sort of cocooned here. Safe. I'm glad we've had our "British" adventure, but it feels like it's time for the girls to experience life as Americans." He caught Shelby's eye as he playfully grabbed her bottom on his way to the boxes. "Hey, how about a quick run while Natasha is still here with the girls?"

Outside enjoying the quiet of a fragrant September evening, Amber whispered, "Cody, do you feel like we've been hiding out over here?" With your parents gone and all, their house up as a rental, sometimes I feel like we have been avoiding reality. I know Mom is okay with her nursing career, but sometimes I think of her at night, sitting there all alone watching "Let's Make a Deal" while we are raising our girls and basking in the comfort of life in England. I feel guilty."

Amber kept a nice even pace and after a few moments, "All those side trips and weekends away, my painting trips. It has been so great, but it feels like the party is over." Her voice trailed off as they jogged past the handsome row of red brick military homes. They turned left and ran through the quiet lanes of Lakenheath. They moved in step past the medieval church.

"I'm going to miss this," she nodded toward the ancient building. "It will take some getting used to, the freeways and congestion."

"If we don't like it, we can always put in for another transfer. Think of it as the next leg of our adventure," he said smiling, as he turned his head and gave her a dose of his bright blue eyes.

"You're right. I just don't deal too well with big changes. You know what I went through in the beginning of the art thing." They jogged silently for some time. "Also, lately, I'm worrying that I've pushed you too hard to find Shelby." Her voice was low. "Hon, I'm concerned she might hurt you. I know you have your hopes up that she's normal, but I fear that the outcome of all this might not be so good. I know she sounds okay, and I *want* to give her the benefit of the doubt, I do." She paused, "But something feels off to me. It's been almost five months since you made that initial call, and really, where are we with her?"

As the miles folded into one another, they grew quiet. Cody thought about how devastated he had been three years before when he had learned that his parents had been involved in a horrific fatal car accident. The driver of the car which had struck them had been a nineteen year-old girl who was trying to make a call on her Blackberry. She had been speeding, maybe going 50 mph on a curvy two lane road in rural Georgia, a few miles from where they lived in LaGrange. Cody's brain spiraled to the months after the accident; numb at first, and then, later, when the agony of the reality had sunk in, ruined.

The worst was when Willow or Kaitlyn did something new, took a step, smiled, got a new tooth, his instinct was to call his mom, then he'd remember. The hurt he felt was physical at first; an ache near his heart, a knot in his stomach. It had been a rough road. If not for Amber and the girls and his work, he sometimes wondered if the grief would have swallowed him whole.

A sweet feeling coursed though his body as he thought of his parents. He smiled to himself; they'd always called him "our chosen one." It had never been a secret about his adoption. In fact they made him feel special. All those years he knew how much they wanted him; his arrival had been the best thing to happen to them. He'd spent his childhood feeling cherished and adored, thus guaranteeing that certain *other* feelings would be forever kept to himself. He sensed on some instinctual level that he was a square peg in a round hole in his family, but they loved him so. The few times he did let himself think about how odd he felt compared to his parents, guilt muzzled any further thoughts. When it became apparent that he had an eidetic memory, his parents sought enrichment programs and saved up for special science camps in the summers. They encouraged him every step of the way in his studies. His acceptance into the Air Force Medical Corp residency program had secured his future. Without the Air Force and his parents' support, he doubted he would have been on this trajectory. He was playing a winning hand and he knew it.

He smiled as his reflections took him to one of his dad, Fred's, favorite games, his parlor game. When they had company over, his dad would bring out a magazine and show it to the guests, then Cody would look it over and give it back to Dad, then the fun would begin.

"Son, what color is the shirt on the boy in the granola ad?" his dad's eyes would glitter in anticipation as Cody easily answered, "Blue and grey stripes." Fred would beam and open the magazine to show the friends who would invariably be shaking their heads in wonder. It didn't stop there. "Son in the ad for Hertz rental cars is there something on the wall in the photo?" More smiles as Cody allowed his dad the pleasure. "Yes Dad, there's a photograph of a sailing ship on the wall near the window with the white curtains." His dad's smile would spread into a grin. By the time Cody was about twelve, however, he realized that it was more like a sideshow and he stopped performing. His father seemed okay with it.

For now, he missed that silly game and his dad's smile. Sometimes when he thought about how much his mom would have loved little Willow, the sadness would feel like a knife in his heart. He was thankful that his parents at least got to meet Kaitlyn, and know her for the short time they'd had with her.

As Cody and Amber jogged through their favorite last mile of the six mile course, Cody studied the quaint lanes of Lakenheath with new eyes. He would miss the unruly gardens filled to overflowing with hollyhocks, the sassy daisies springing up along the side of the trail, and the colorful roses in every yard. He would miss England. The military life seemed to suit them. For himself he thrived in the structure, and they had also enjoyed living in Germany. He had committed to nine years: he had two left to fulfill his obligation. Lately he was leaning toward becoming career military. There was time to decide. For now they were moving stateside.

CHAPTER 25

Sunday, Sept 11, 2005
Beaufort, South Carolina

It was the day she'd promised herself to place another call. Shelby knew that if she didn't get her act together, Cody and Amber could move back to the States and she could lose track of them. Surely they would give up their European phones.

You have their email. Quit catastrophizing! commanded her more rational inner voice.

Since resuming her normal schedule of walking with Karen, she felt a shift in her anxiety levels. Lately, the nightmares were less frequent, but the nervous knot was still there. She felt a certain urgency to know where Cody was moving. It was hard for her to believe that she had learned so little about him. She'd failed to discover if he had in fact gone to college. She had no clue what he did. She assumed that Amber was a stay-at-home military wife, but truthfully, she didn't know much. She'd not asked. *I don't feel entitled. I have not wanted to pry. I don't feel worthy...*

So make the call; it seems to me that you need some professional help. How much longer can you go on with the panic attacks, the anxious stomach and the nightmares? asked her internal adult.

She waited until Grant left for the club for his regular Sunday golf date. She went into the bedroom to her lingerie drawer and dug around for her illicit cell phone. That's how she thought of it; her dirty little secret. This was so not like her to skulk around. She hated it. *I really do need help. I need to get an objective opinion about how to go forward.*

Make the damn call!

She made her way downstairs to the office where she closed the door. Slowly she opened the cell phone, checked the clock, 1:00 p.m. in England. Heart thudding, she carefully pressed Cody's numbers. With each ring, her nervousness increased. On the third ring, a breathless, "Hello," came across the line.

"Hey, Cody, it's Shelby. Am I catching you at a bad time?"

"No, I'm just coming back from a quick run. I'm fine. I can talk. I'm happy to hear from you. How are things going for you, Shelby? You sound better."

"You mean I'm not crying?"

"Well, yes... that."

"I just want to make sure that I'll have your new phone number. I know you're moving soon. After all this, I don't want to lose track of you now. There's still so much I don't know about you, like where you grew up," she paused, "I was relieved to learn that your family took such good care of you. I stipulated that the adoptive family had to promise that you would get an education," she took a big gulp of air. Cody could hear a desperate, sad quality behind her words.

"Cody, *did* you get a college education?"

"I did. I grew up in LaGrange and went to Emory, majored in science. Shelby, I was fine. You seem worried that I had a bad childhood. I did okay, and I'm okay now." His voice was reassuring.

"I'm glad to hear that." In a sudden rush of bravery, Shelby revealed, in a ragged voice, "I used to look for you in crowds; you know, when kids got out of school, places like that." She hesitated and then blurted out, "I didn't want to let you go, Cody, but I couldn't see any way to give you the life you deserved. I worry that you won't forgive me."

"Hey, I'm grateful for my life. You could have aborted me, but you didn't. Shelby, you have to understand *that!* I have a wonderful life. We're doing well." His passionate words came across the distance. He thought, *Clearly she is projecting her own guilt onto how she thinks I feel about her. There's no way I'm ever going to share with her how it felt to be so different from my parents. Never*

"Thank you, Cody, I appreciate that." She took a breath. "So when do you leave the U.K.? Are your orders still to Lackland?"

"Actually the orders have not come through yet. We are just guessing. Nothing is concrete. We'll probably be out of here by the end of the month. It's hard on Amber. She's made some really great friends and she'll miss them. The girls are happy here too. Lots of little buddies."

"Oh, I'm sure that must be hard for her. Does Amber stay home with the girls, I've been wondering?"

"She does, but she also paints, a lot of en plein air watercolors, and often she can take the girls with her. It's been good here."

"That sounds wonderful. I loved that photo you sent of all of you posed in front of Stonehenge. It's one of my favorite places. I've always been interested in the Druids." Her words were warm with interest. "The girls are beautiful, well, you're *all* so beautiful!" Her voice cracked. "I want to meet you, see the girls, but I still have not settled things here at my end. Can you give me a little more time?"

"Shelby, we didn't connect with you to bring havoc down on your life. It sounds like you have some complications. There's no pressure from this end. Amber and I just wondered about the genetics. I never really asked about that, but your daughters obviously have been healthy, no horrible genetic surprises waiting..."

"Oh, don't worry about that. The gene pool from my end seems fine." Shelby realized the conversation was steering toward the rest of the gene pool, Tom Steele. It occurred to her that perhaps it had not been the smartest decision to keep him in the dark about there being a child. *Well, you are a bit late to be thinking about that now!*

In an attempt to maneuver the conversation in a different direction, she asked, "So you've been out for a run? Is that your exercise of choice?"

"Oh yeah, been doing some marathons. I love it. Keeps me in shape. Amber runs too. We do 10K races together."

"That sounds great. I'm a power walker. You saw in the photo that I have two big dogs? They help keep me fit."

"Power walking is terrific. Good cardio. We like dogs but with moving and all we don't have one. What else do you do to fill your time?"

"Oh, I am a volunteer docent at the museum here in town. I enjoy it. I supervise some of the exhibits, help put together the various shows, especially the Native American exhibits. I'm a bit of a history buff." Shelby could feel her strength for continuing the conversation starting to ebb.

"Cody, I know you must have a hundred things to do. I just wanted to touch base. Let you to know that I care." A sob choked out.

"Thank you Shelby. We'll talk again. I'll email you our new contact information when we have it. I'm glad you called."

"Bye Cody."

"Bye."

Once she hung up she realized she was in trouble. A wrenching dizziness overtook her, as hot sweat broke out on her upper lip. Her heart was pounding so furiously that she doubted she could make it out of the room.

I've got to sit, or lie down!

Am I having a heart attack?

This is not good!

My God, I am unraveling!

She collapsed onto the sofa and placed a throw pillow under her head. The room was spinning as she suddenly saw white lights. Her heart was still pulsing out of control, banging outrageously against her rib cage. She closed her eyes. Spinning.

Shelby, it's getting worse. You have got to get a grip. In fact.... slowly the truth dawned on her.

You've got to get professional help.

CHAPTER 26

Sunday, September 13, 2005
Beaufort, South Carolina

Shelby lay on the sofa like that for a long time. Eventually she had enough strength to sit up, to shut her phone. She inhaled a huge breath trying to steady herself. Now that her head had stopped whirling, she realized she was pleased to have mustered up enough courage to call Cody, but she still had not really moved forward. She'd steered far away from any commitment about meeting them, plus she hadn't learned a whole lot more about their lives, and for sure she had not explained to him why she had given him up. Exasperated with her weak behavior she understood that she was spiraling downward.

You need help.

Yes I probably do.

Did you notice that this week is the anniversary of 9/11?

Oh God.

She remained there, sitting on the sofa. With whom could she confide? Michelle was a good, solid sounding board, but she didn't want to pit her girls against their dad. If they held her secret, when Grant learned of it, he would feel more betrayed than ever. Tell Karen? She would understand. It would be a place to vent, but Karen could not possibly comprehend the effect of all of this on Grant. Shelby had always understood that his mother's behavior lay at the bottom of Grant's distrust of women; the way she'd flaunted a parade of meaningless men, drunk to excess. All this had deeply impacted young Grant. Early in their courtship, Grant had whispered a confession to her; he'd worried that he would remain a bachelor.

I feel like a really bad country song, torn between two loves, my poor child that I gave away and my beloved husband who finally trusted someone with his heart. If only I had a crystal ball and could see into the future.

A thought darted across her mind, maybe she had a good idea. She remembered the woman she had met on the airplane in May; the one whose book she ordered, Dr. Lewis.

She stood up and went into the library where she dug around the stacks until she found the book. Dr. Lewis' website was on the inside cover page.

Without hesitating, she walked into her office and sat down at the computer. She opened her browser and put in the website. She scoured the site, counseling via telephone, Skype, or in person. Dr. Lewis was in California.

She dashed off an email: *Dr. Charlotte Lewis,*

Hi. I had the pleasure of sitting next to you on the flight to Atlanta last May. I shared a bit about my issue, "I sort of have four grandchildren." I hope you remember me. Anyway, I got the impression that you understood about secrets. I bought your book and it has helped some, but I am still in a mess. I need someone who can offer me some objective guidance. If you have some time this next week or so, may I schedule a Skype counseling appointment with you?
   Sincerely, Shelby Forrest

With that accomplished, she thought, *Perhaps I am making progress. It's time for a walk.*

"Hey doggies, how about a nice walk?"

Two sets of tails began to thump against the hardwood floors. As she gathered up the leashes it occurred to her, once again, that she didn't know what she would do without her faithful dogs. Sometimes in the middle of the night when that nightmare woke her up, she would go down to the garage and cuddled up with them. Their trusting, eager natures calmed her.

CHAPTER 27

September 14, 2005
Beaufort, South Carolina

Shelby picked up the ringing telephone on her desk, "Hello."

"Mom, hi it's me. That trip to New York City rocked!" said Michelle, her excited words spilling across the line.

"Michelle, I'm so glad. Dad and I hoped you girls would have a wonderful time. We loved having the kids with us. It was marvelous."

"Mom, I know Laney told you all about the play we saw, *Mamma Mia*. It was just so much fun. I loved the music, all of it. We cracked the guys up singing *Dancing Queen* as we boogied down the sidewalk. Dale says I am his 'dancing queen' and now he's all hot to go to Greece." Michelle paused, "Good luck, with baby number two coming. But it was amazing; after the play we stumbled onto the wildest diner ever, the Stardust, craziest singing waiters and more Mamma Mia songs. We had banana splits while dancers tapped on a raised floor right next to our booth! It was great. Thanks so much! The guys got along well, and the next day, Laney and I shopped 'til we dropped," laughed Michelle.

"So anyway, Laney and I had such a great time having a girls' afternoon, that we want to make a date with you, just the three of us, for a spa day. We'd each have childcare, actually Dale's mom can take Ellie, and we can book a day at The Sanctuary Spa in Hilton Head. One of my friends at school spent a day there, and raved over it. I'd come to you, we'd drive to Hilton Head and meet up with Laney, then I'd spend the night with you. What do you say?"

"Sounds perfect, great idea! We'll coordinate our day planners. You don't mind that much driving? We could come to you," offered Shelby.

"Thanks Mom, but this is something Laney really *needs*. She doesn't say much, but I know she's struggling trying to get her catering business going and with Gracie… This will be good for all of us. We can make a whole day of it, besides if I spend the night I get to see Daddy."

***

The following Saturday, Shelby and her two daughters were enjoying lunch on the spa's terrace overlooking Hilton Head Harbor. As Shelby gazed across the placid water at the iconic red and white lighthouse, she could not help but think how much she has enjoyed her life in the Lowcountry.

"Girls, what a lovely gesture this is. I don't have you to myself so much anymore. When you were little, your dad and I would bring you here. Once he rented a ski boat and tried water skiing. Do you remember that?" asked Shelby enjoying the memory.

"Mom, oh yeah, that was when you were driving that Boston Whaler and we were dragging Dad for what seemed like forever, while he thrashed about in the water trying to get up! I thought we'd snagged Big Foot or something," Laney was laughing.

"He got up though," added Michelle. "That *was* pretty funny."

Both Michelle and Laney grinned at the mental picture of their dad's dogged determination to get up on those skis.

"Hey do you remember the rest of it?" Michelle asked, "Once he finally got up, he insisted on pantomiming that he was falling. The more he acted it out, the more we all broke up laughing!"

"Girls, we had good times, didn't we?" A thoughtful expression crossed Shelby's face. Turning more serious, she asked, "What did your childhoods *feel* like to you?"

A little taken aback by the turn in the conversation, Michelle responded, "Mom, growing up my friends all wanted to have my life. I've got no complaints. I just hope Dale and I can do half as well as you and Dad with our family."

"Mom, I'm with Michelle, the safest place I could ever be was home with you guys. I still feel that way. During the Water Festival, with all of us under one roof, that same comforting feeling was with me. It's the sense of truly being home. That's how it is for me when I'm with you and Dad," replied Laney with a wistful smile as she held eye contact with her mother. "Mom it was key having you at home all those years."

"That's part of why I'm stopping teaching for now. I want to be home with Ellie and baby bump," offered Michelle.

"Your growing up wasn't like that was it, with Grandmother Avery?" asked Laney.

"Well Bellingham was beautiful, a lot like Beaufort in terms of the small town, the water and all," Shelby waited a minute to collect her thoughts. "Grandmother Avery is a tough customer as you probably know."

"We figured, I noticed that as we got older the trips out West grew less frequent," observed Michelle.

"My mother kept a tight hold on me, on all of us. She was probably the hardest on me because I was the first born. It was suffocating. I know that part of it was how she was raised. Her parents were passive. It was Avery's grandmother who ruled with the iron fist." Shelby held eye contact with her lovely daughters, two sets of soft brown eyes encouraged her to continue.

"There was an interesting story my mother once told me. It gives you a sense of her mother and grandmother. I'll tell you, *her* grandmother was a negative influence. It seems the grandmother was in charge when it was time to register young Avery in school. I guess her parents were out of town. Anyway, that grandmother enrolled her under an entirely *different* name than her own!"

"What? Who in their right mind would do that?" asked Laney, disbelief clouding her face.

"She enrolled her as 'Constance Marie' when her name was 'Avery Ann.'" When six year-old Avery told her parents, they just smiled and did nothing," Shelby paused. "Seriously, can you even imagine?"

"Mom, no. I cannot! So what happened?" persisted Michelle.

"The kids called her 'Connie' until she finally got to junior high when she marched into the school office and set the record straight."

"That is just plain wicked," remarked Laney. "So why did her grandmother do that?"

"My mother guessed that her grandmother never liked the name Avery so she just changed it. How confusing would that be for a kid to be called the wrong name for seven years!" questioned Shelby.

"Yikes, that explains a lot about Grandmother Avery," said Michelle.

"Girls, the weirdest part is that Grandmother Avery laughed about it," continued Shelby, "It's bizarre. On some level she must have understood what an invasion of her boundaries it was, but perhaps, due to the viciousness of it, she had to minimize its effect on her."

"Mom, that's hateful!" exclaimed Michelle.

"What interests me about that story is that the grandmother's power play was aimed at both Avery and her daughter who was Avery's mother. I find the whole thing chilling; to imagine that Avery's mother did not fix it or come to her aid," concluded Shelby.

"When I'm at my wits end with my mother, I try to imagine her as a little kid who wasn't even called by her own name. I try to see her as a victim and show her grace. At least by the time she was thirteen she had enough confidence to change things up, even cut her pigtails off with the pinking shears," concluded Shelby.

"It's a bit ironic," added Michelle, "Grandmother Avery had her boundaries invaded and yet she does the same thing."

"Oh don't get me started on that!" interjected Shelby with an edge to her words. "Once when I left you two with her while I had lunch with Aunt Mandy, Michelle, you were just four years-old with beautiful silky curls. Anyway, your hair was finally getting long enough for a little pony tail. When I got back from lunch she had cut off all your curls! *Gone!* Oh I could have killed her that day!"

"What was her excuse for doing that?" asked Michelle.

"She said your hair was in your eyes."

"Hey, how about when I was seven," chimed in Laney, "and she threw my favorite glittery little sandals out, said they 'weren't appropriate,' that they were 'hooker shoes!'"

Shelby looked at her girls. "Perhaps becoming the control freak that she is has allowed her to move from the powerless position to one of power. Whatever. You can see how annoying it was for me to live with her. I couldn't get far enough way!" confessed Shelby.

"Mom I always wondered how you got so far away from home;

why you lived with "Aunt" Lily," observed Michelle.

"That was part of it," commented Shelby in a soft voice.

"Well, Mom, good job breaking the generational cycle," commented Laney, as she placed her hand on top of her mother's which was resting on the table.

Michelle, reached over and squeezed her mother's other hand.

Shelby felt a rush of tears, but held them back. "Thanks my dears, enough of that ancient history; so glad that it's behind me. It was very nice to become independent, and then meeting your father," she inhaled, "in a lot of ways I've always felt like finding him was the beginning of my *real* life!" She smiled wistfully at her graceful daughters, "Enough of this seriousness! What do you say we head for those massages now?"

As they settled the bill, Shelby considered her childhood in a fresh way; she understood that the temerity and indecisiveness she sometimes suffered were rooted in that long ago family dysfunction. She imagined that if she peeled back another layer beyond her "mom stuff," a scalding shame would be lying in wait for her as well.

I've done better in the parenting department than my mother. She inhaled deeply and forced a smile as she silently assured herself, *I WILL figure all this out!*

As they ambled back into the spa's elaborately decorated reception area, Shelby came up between her daughters and placed an arm around each of their capable shoulders. *These two have anchored me all these years, and Grant has been my rock.*

CHAPTER 28

Monday, September 19, 2005
Beaufort, South Carolina

Shelby felt nervous as she prepared for the 10:00 a.m. Skype meeting she had set up with Dr. Charlotte Lewis. She could feel her heart racing and a new thickness to her tongue. This would be the first time that she would share the impact of giving up Cody. She walked into her office and shut the door. The house was quiet, she could hear the antique wind-up clock as it struck its ten chimes. One. Two. Three…

Suddenly her computer rang. She pressed the answer button and came face-to-face with Dr. Lewis.

"Oh, hello, Dr. Lewis. Thank you for taking this meeting. I told you some of my story on the plane back in May, but I didn't share with you anything about my feelings."

"Hi Shelby, I do remember. How could I forget? You told me that you, 'sort of had four grandchildren,' that was pretty memorable. I'm glad you contacted me and shared a bit of your current situation in the email. You want to feel better don't you?" asked Charlotte Lewis in a warm, comforting voice.

"I do. I hate to admit that I am more of a wreck than I was when we met. The symptoms have escalated. I have frequent nightmares, panic attacks, and most of the time I have a knot in my stomach. It is hard to sleep for more than a few hours at a time," Shelby stated in a rush of nervous words.

"From your email I know you've already figured out the

problem. You're suffering Acute Post Traumatic Stress symptoms, and it's no fun. What happens is that when there is a trauma, and for you it was giving up your baby, one's sense of reasonable mastery of life is disrupted. Victims of this have trouble making sense of what is happening to them. In the case when a mother must give up a child, she experiences the grief one would feel with a death, however in this situation, there's no memorial, there are no social and emotional supports. The young mother must simply suck it up and go forward as if she did not have a gaping hole in her heart. In your case, when your son made contact with you, the fragile coping mechanisms you had in place to deal with the loss, were ripped apart. This disruption manifests itself in the symptoms you have been experiencing," explained Charlotte Lewis.

"If left untreated the symptoms will continue to disturb your sense of well being," she paused. "I'm so happy that you felt safe enough to call me. Shelby this can be treated."

Shelby told Dr. Lewis more about the situation; the struggle she had growing up under the shadow of a controlling mother, the devastation she felt when her father left, her guilty feelings about not telling Grant earlier, and the shame of sneaking around with the burner phone to make contact. She admitted that she mostly cried during two of the four calls, that she intended to call Cody more frequently but didn't, and finally, that Cody and his family were soon moving to the States.

"Shelby no doubt the moving is part of the trigger. There is a certain urgency going on here. You have been confronted with an unexpected, very threatening circumstance, in terms of interference with your marriage and your family life. It must feel like a time bomb about to go off. Your natural reaction is fear and anxiety. Your body and mind react by going into emergency mode. It is this hyper-vigilant state that feels so uncomfortable. I'm sure you feel out of control."

"It's true. I do. I find myself isolating from others," confessed Shelby. "I have to work so hard to fake seeming normal that I'm exhausted!"

"We call this being in a state of crisis." Dr. Lewis paused, "The longer the symptoms remain untreated, the more likely you are to fall into depression and isolation."

"How are you doing with your husband and children?" asked Charlotte Lewis.

"When I first told my husband that there had been a child, he was terribly hurt and angry. I know he felt betrayed. He didn't touch me for weeks. We have not discussed the topic since the first time I told him. His reaction was so strong and so negative that I was afraid to tell him that Cody had called. I'm terrified to revisit the subject." Shelby dabbed at the tears that were streaming down her cheeks. "Mostly I feel afraid."

There was a long pause in the conversation. Dr. Lewis waited, knowing that Shelby needed to share her story.

"Last week my daughters treated me to a spa day with them. Just the three of us. I have been trying to act normally around them. One of my daughters has noticed that I'm off. She attributed it to a recent community event that I was working on. I'm trying to stay connected with my daughters and granddaughters, but it is taking all my energy. In the past I was social, having frequent lunches with friends, and enjoyed being interactive with the staff at the museum. Now, I go in early before the museum opens to avoid talking to people. Mostly I sit in my chair and stare out the window, trying to figure out what to do."

"It's a good sign that you know instinctively to maintain the most important relationships; if you can keep up regular exercise that will help too. I think that during our sessions we can work to develop a game plan. When will your son and his family be moving back to the States?"

"Anytime now," whispered Shelby.

"You know, just because they are moving closer doesn't mean

that you have to suddenly rush to see them, or tell your family. You can take your time. I don't think you're yet ready to face more upheaval," added Charlotte Lewis.

"There's something else, Dr. Lewis," said Shelby.

"Please Shelby, call me Charlotte."

"The guilt I feel for abandoning Cody, and then not racing to him the minute he called is overwhelming. That's a big part of what wakes me up in the night. The guilt, it feels like an avalanche is falling on me," confided Shelby.

"Oh, Shelby this is natural," affirmed Charlotte Lewis. "From the little I know about the circumstances of giving up your child, and the difficulties with your mother, my best guess is that your personal boundaries were invaded as you grew up. Controlling parents often cross the mental as well as physical boundaries of their children. A young child loses a sense of self and often turns to people-pleasing for survival."

"I feel responsible for Cody's feelings, even though he keeps assuring me he's okay, I can't seem to believe him. I feel guilty that I betrayed Grant, and I am deeply troubled about keeping the knowledge of a brother and two nieces from my daughters." She paused for a long minute as she surveyed all that was bothering her.

"My youngest daughter has a two-year old and I sense that she is overwhelmed trying to start her catering business. She is determined to bring in some income, but right now she cannot really afford to pay for a baby sitter while she gets her business going. I know I *should* volunteer to help her a day a week or so, but honestly..."her voice trailed off. "...I just can't right now..."

"So shall we work on a game plan?" asked Charlotte Lewis, her voice was confident.

"Can we? Can you help me?" murmured Shelby.

"Yes, if you'll commit to moving forward. Let's start with strengthening your boundaries. You have gotten yourself away from your mother, but you still feel in charge of Grant's feelings, as well as Cody's and your daughters'. You're probably 'shoulding' on yourself as well." Dr. Lewis, waited a moment for the little play on words to sink in. "I suspect that you're projecting your own sense of loss over your father's leaving onto how Cody feels."

"You need to learn a new way of being. You must come to a place where you understand that you simply cannot be *responsible* for their feelings. We are each responsible for our own feelings. I'm going to teach you how to reframe events so that you can choose your response instead of simply reacting. This is what we are going to work on."

For the rest of the hour they discussed specific strategies and a payment schedule. Charlotte gave Shelby some homework to help with the symptoms, and she reassured her that she could take all the time she needed to move forward.

"Our time is up," explained Dr. Lewis. "It is important that you continue to exercise, that will help with the anxiety. Also, Shelby, talk to yourself. Oftentimes victims of PTSD tend to catastrophize, blowing events out of proportion. Slow yourself down. Keep up the positive self talk. Give yourself permission to breathe. Many victims suffering like this find comfort through prayer or meditation."

"Is Cody pressuring you?" she asked.

"No, nothing like that…"

"You have time."

Charlotte Lewis' voice softened, "It's a big thing to have one's child turn up unexpectedly after thirty-five years! Don't discount the enormity of all this. It creates emotional mayhem, like riding a rollercoaster, between joy and terror. I think you are very brave. Many birth mothers will not see, nor acknowledge the adult-child when he or she comes knocking. You have talked to him, and reached out. Give yourself credit."

Both women were silent.

Charlotte began, "We will schedule another session next week. Now do you want me to arrange for anti-anxiety meds? Prosac might help against the angst?"

"No, thank you. You've helped me. This idea about boundaries and people-pleasing resonates with me. I still go home every year to Bellingham, partly to "fix" my family's feelings and to assuage my guilt about moving so far away. This was a big help. Understanding my feelings brings me a bit of peace. I see that I have made a practice of taking on the feelings of those closest to me." Shelby paused. "Thank you for the help, for the insights."

After they ended the therapy session, Shelby sat for a long time at her computer. Without thinking about it, she clicked on her pictures and scrolled to the one of her red-headed granddaughters. She studied their perfect images; Willow in her two-year-old glory, and Kaitlyn looking wise and vulnerable. She sat for a long time as she imagined them running into her outstretched arms yelling, "Grandma. Grandma is here!"

Tears rolled down her cheeks.

CHAPTER 29

September 20, 2005
LaGrange, Georgia

As the massive jet touched the ground in Atlanta and rolled to the gate, Amber turned on her cell phone and left a voice mail for Cody. "Hey honey, just checking in. The girls and I arrived safely. Mom is picking us up at the airport. We miss you. I love you."

Amber guided her girls out of the plane, collected the stroller and headed for Customs. After checking out of the busy international airport, she spotted her mother's blue Honda mini-van. Navigating the stroller, with a close eye on Kaitlyn, she waved to her mother. Once suitcases and stroller were secured in the back and the girls strapped into their seats, Amber remarked, "Good job finding us Mom, it's a bit of a mob scene here. Thanks for picking us up. It's so much easier than trying to find a taxi with all our gear."

"My pleasure," replied Sharon Blake, a sweet-faced sixty-year old with short curly grey hair. "I can't wait to get some sugar from you girls," she said turning her head toward the back seat as she drove through the busy airport. "Grandma has some new Barbies for you and I made your favorite vanilla cake cookies, I thought we would decorate them. They are in the shape of mermaids. Anyone have an idea about that?"

"Ariel. Our favorite!" exclaimed Kaitlyn.

"Me a mermaid, Grandma," added Willow.

"Mom, we're so happy to have some time with you. It's been

pretty crazy getting ready for the move. Once the Air Force packed us up it was a good excuse to grab a week or so with you. It's weird. Our orders have not come through yet. We were pretty sure it would be Lackland, but now there's a hold up. Anyway, Cody was in the middle of an important case, but after that attack the other day, they've flown him to Germany again to care for the wounded. It's been a hell hole for him. More of those eighteen hour shifts, like he had last time."

"He's glad we came early. He's exhausted. He encouraged me to come before this most recent insurgence. I think in general he feels guilty for taking me and the girls so far away from you. Anyway he's glad we can have this time with you."

"Honey, he's pure gold. Having Cody join our family is worth any sacrifice, besides the planes clearly have flown back and forth across the pond," said her mother turning and smiling at her daughter.

During the hour long journey to La Grange, Amber brought her mother up to date with her HomeCo America commissions.

"Mom, that boutique hotel turned out beautifully. It's like a little jewel. The designers understood so many details; you almost feel like you stepped back into time about five hundred years, but in a very elegant and comfortable way!" laughed Amber.

"My paintings adorn the lobby, elevator landings, and the suites. I got lucky in that Lydia Lane and her team got excited about the florals, the ones I had already done. You saw them; the hollyhocks, some wild daisies, and the Icelandic poppies that were growing so uproariously in the church yard. Do you remember that in some of them I painted in hints of the old iron work? I also included suggestions of the masonry in the old cemetery." Amber was quiet for a while as she studied the passing countryside. "One day I entertained myself by painting wild heather growing around a five hundred year-old grave marker. I was goofing off, but believe it or not, they liked that too."

"Amber, I'm not surprised. Of course I remember your paintings, especially that Celtic cross, weaving the wild vines and blossoms through its arms. That blew me away; it literally took my breath away! And girl, you've spent your entire life amazing me!" Sharon looked meaningfully across the front seat to her daughter. She continued, "That cross painting was truly brilliant; it was beautiful and sad all at once."

There was silence in the car for the next minutes.

"Cody can feel guilty about moving you away, but I think something out of the ordinary has resonated with you as an artist. And I think it has to do with your being in the old world." Pausing, Sharon added with a twinkle in her eye, "Maybe a past life somehow seeped into your unconscious?" Sharon chuckled, but then her tone became solemn, "Seriously, there is a new essence to your work, a hint of nostalgia. It almost feels other-worldly to me. I know it's your way of bringing the antiquities to life, of reminding the world of the eons of humanity who walked the Earth before we got here." She hesitated. "Daughter, what you're revealing in your work is something rare, something precious."

"Thank you, Mom. I don't say much about it. I don't like thinking about stuff I don't understand, but you might be right. Something is definitely up with me. During those en plein air days at Stonehenge, I could almost feel the presence of others, of a spirit world. I don't believe anything like that, but I notice a sense of what I was feeling as I painted, has eked its way into my work," Amber's words were thoughtful.

"As I'm painting, there is another dimension to the subject. It's like my mind's eye can *feel* back in time. I know it's just my vivid imagination." She stopped.

She turned to check on the children in the back seat; both auburn-haired little girls were fast asleep. Willow was sucking her two fingers, her index and middle finger. Kaitlyn's teddy bear was tucked under her chin.

Whispering, "It almost feels like the watercolors are painting themselves, like I'm just the vessel which holds the brush," she hesitated, "Mom, it kinda creeps me out. Also when I'm deep in the flow of some of these paintings, in some odd way, I feel closer to Daddy. He always loved the ancient Celts. Remember how he dreamed of a family trip to Stonehenge before he got so sick?" Both mother and daughter were silent for a while. Finally, Amber asked, "And why with all those accomplished artists at the festival would they choose *me*?"

"There is just so much we don't understand Amber. I know it is a cliché, but God moves in mysterious ways," Sharon waited a long moment, "Whatever it is, it's your gift. I'm so proud of all that you are doing. I admit I was worried about the HomeCo account on top of that hotel, on top of the baby. I worried you'd work yourself to death, but it seems like you have things under control."

"I do. But it will be good to rest for a week or so. Do you have any days off from the hospital?"

"I traded some of my shifts with another nurse. I have a whole week," Sharon grinned at her daughter. "We will have a great time! Guess what? Your sister can come for part of it!" Feeling content, the women remained quiet for the remainder of the drive, both lost in their own thoughts.

The next day Sharon and Amber packed the girls up and took them for a day at Playland, an entertainment park geared for young children. All four of them climbed aboard the miniature train that circled the park, fed the llamas, held the guinea pigs and bunnies, and the children enjoyed pony rides on real ponies.

Much later in the afternoon, both excited and exhausted, the little girls went down for a nap while the equally exhausted mother and grandmother fell onto the living room sofa. "Mom, I'm too pooped to even talk! There's nothing like that in Suffolk. The girls loved it. We're going to be hearing about those pony rides for a long time!"

"Why don't we turn on the tube and vegetate for awhile," suggested Sharon.

"Great idea."

Sharon picked up the remote and began scanning through the channels. She passed the Oprah show, and two channels later paused at Oprah's new competitor, the highly advertised "Counter Point with Caroline," a 3:00 p.m. show.

"Amber is this okay? They've been promoting it for weeks. I'm curious."

"Sure. Anything. I'm so tired that my hair hurts!" groaned Amber.

The television screen showed a kitchen table around which were seated three guests and the glamorous host, the remarkable and assertive, Caroline Gardner, known for her outspoken position on women's issues. The voice-over announced, "Society's Coercion of Unwed Mothers!"

The cameras zoomed in on the face of an angry middle-aged man whose acid words choked the airways. "A horrific injustice was leveled against the unwed mothers of the 1950's through the early 70's. Using the social weapons of guilt and shame, combined with economic and religious pressures, a conspiracy of coercion was foisted upon those unwed mothers in both America and England." He paused and glared into the cameras, "Thousands upon thousands of babies were ripped from the arms of their young mothers through the guise of the betterment of society, bringing children to the childless, while relegating the young mothers to the shadows. They were forced to live with the damning secret, that they *dared* to conceive out of wedlock!" The man's face was fierce with rage.

Amber was suddenly riveted by the angry guest's hostile words.

The camera moved to Caroline Gardner who tried to interrupt the tirade. The furious guest ranted over her words. "Social workers, attorneys, adoption agencies, the foster care system, all have been complicit in this crime against young women." He stopped and again stared angrily into the camera. "It is beyond time for the conspiracy of secrecy to end. The U.S. Congress must enact legislation to open the birth records of adoptees. The concealment of birth records continues to promote the injustice. Darkness and secrecy promote shame. Open the birth records!"

Caroline Gardner tried once again to interrupt his forceful argument. "Mr. Raymond," she inserted with an equally ferocious edge to her voice, "we understand that the stigma surrounding unwed motherhood has fallen away, but since Roe vs. Wade you must know that something like fifty million pregnancies have been terminated in the U.S. alone. This is a very real counterpoint to the secret of adoption! If birth records were to suddenly open there is no accounting for the consequences." Caroline Gardner glared at him.

Another guest, whose face was covered with a gauzy fabric to protect her identity, interrupted, "I gave my daughter up the day she was born. If I had not been guaranteed that my privacy would be maintained, I would *never* have considered adoption. My mother wanted to take me out of the country for an abortion," she inhaled her own angry breath, "Mr. Raymond you are dead wrong on this. It is hard to imagine now in the 21st century, the shame that used to center around illegitimate births. Had my secret come out, I would have been considered a degenerate. My character would have been stained. It was an untenable situation. I built a life and I will take my secret to the grave. There is no way those birth records should be opened!"

Caroline Gardner and the other two guests stared at her. "The escalating abortion rates are proof of the importance of privacy!" Her tone was emphatic.

Attempting to tone down the rhetoric, Gardner interjected, "For the viewing audience, I think it is important to understand the social climate of fifty years ago. This was before the birth control pill and the most recent wave of feminism. It was virtually unheard of for a woman to give birth to a child outside of marriage. If she did, the stigma was horrendous. The child was labeled 'illegitimate,' or worse yet, 'a bastard.' Those terms are no longer even in use. Today something over 40% of births in the U.S. and the European Union are outside of marriage. The social landscape is completely different. It is important to understand the power of that stigma just a generation ago."

The red-faced Mr. Raymond cut in. "What is *stigma* in the face of the frustration of not knowing who you are!" He was shouting, his face a mask of molten emotion. "I have been desperate to know who I am my entire life!" He suddenly stood up, banging the table with his fists. "A person should have the right to know who they are! This is so much bigger than a mere privacy issue!"

Both Amber and her mother were spellbound by the emotional scene playing out in their living room.

The third guest, a poised brunette woman in her late 50's jumped into the discussion. "I became pregnant when I was twenty years-old. The boy I was dating turned out to be dating another girl, who also became pregnant. He married her and left me. My family and my church forced me to give that baby away. I wanted to keep her, but it was not feasible without support, money, or a place to live. I had to give her up. The taint of that secret and the shame I have lived with for the last thirty-seven years, have crippled me. I have battled depression and alcohol. I have never recovered from giving my baby up. There is hardly a day that goes by that I don't wonder where she is; if she is alive out there somewhere." The woman sobbed, "Giving her up was the single most devastating action in my life!" The camera rolled in on the woman's contorted face as tears cascaded down her cheeks.

Caroline Gardner brought the interviews back into focus. "We cannot solve all the problems of the past. Surely we cannot undo the pain, but we can understand the negative emotions which those birth mothers have suffered. As a society we must be more compassionate. We can lend our hearts and understand that so many did not want to give their babies away. It is up to our representatives in Washington to figure out the issues involved with unsealing birth records. For now our time is up. Thank you to our guests."

A commercial for Tide detergent filled the television screen.

Amber leaned back against the sofa. "Mom that was sure a downer."

"They made some good points. When I was a young nurse I heard real horror stories from the emergency room team; girls hemorrhaging from having tried to abort their fetuses with coat hangers, or ingesting toxic substances like dried henna. I remember a case in which a sixteen year-old girl threw herself down the stairs. It worked, she terminated the pregnancy, but as I recall she damaged herself so badly that she had to have an emergency hysterectomy. It is a risky business trying to get rid of a baby." Sharon paused. "For the girls, the fear of being disowned, and bringing shame on themselves, was worse than any harm they might have done to their bodies trying to abort the fetuses. It was a terrible time." Sharon's voice was husky with sadness.

After a while she continued, "Even now, with so many immigrants coming from conservative cultures, we encounter high-school girls delivering their babies in the lavatory and then putting them in the dumpster; the price of being ostracized by their families is too high." She waited a long beat. "Amber, it is a tragic situation, for the young girl, for the innocent babies. Every time I think about it I am filled with anguish."

Amber and her mother remained silent. Sharon picked up the remote and turned the television off. After a long while, Amber began, "Mom, I shared with you that Cody was in a bad way after his parents died," she looked at her mother. "You know I pressured him to look for his birth family and that he found his mother."

The two women held eye contact. "With the contracts for the paintings, I haven't kept you up with all that," said Amber.

"I haven't pressed, Amber. This is really Cody's personal business. It has to be his deal."

"Well, he and the birth mother, Shelby Wells, have had some conversations," Amber hesitated. After a moment, "I guess in my magical thinking, I dreamed she'd hear his voice and come running. We'd have our happy ending. Hasn't happened!"

"Sweetheart, it's a big deal, especially for her. No doubt she has built a life. Cody's sudden emergence may not be welcome."

"He says she mostly cries. From the little he shares with me, it sounds like she wants to know us, but yet nothing… It has been nearly five months since he called her, and still *nothing*. I don't get her problem," remarked Amber in low tones, "Cody is so amazing I can't imagine a soul who would not want to know him, especially his *mother!*" Her voice throbbed with emotion.

"Oh honey, Amber. Give her a chance." Sharon's tone was filled with compassion. "Don't give up on her."

CHAPTER 30

September 29, 2005
LaGrange, Georgia

Amber and her very put-together, fashionable sister, Heather, found themselves alone in the living room of their mother's cozy Craftsman home. They could hear Sharon in the kitchen talking to the girls.

Willow's little trills rippled through the rooms. "Grandma me want cocoa and some mar'mellows!"

"Oh do you *now*, young lady?" responded their serene, plumpish mother in loving tones.

"Grandma, how about you let *me* make the cocoa for Willow?" asked Kaitlyn who had recently learned about the microwave oven.

"Alrighty then! Let me pull up the stool."

Amber and Heather could hear the scuffing of the metal stool across the kitchen floor. Amber looked at her lovely, curvaceous younger sister and confided, "It calms me down to be around Mom."

"I know. Me too," admitted Heather. "She might be the most positive person I know. It feels right being here under her roof. Of course, it makes me miss Daddy all the more," Heather inhaled, "I can hardly believe it's already been *ten* years since we lost him."

After a moment, looking at her big sister, Heather remarked, "Dad would have loved those little girls!"

Laughing now as she thought of her father, Amber replied, "Oh he'd have spoiled the daylights out of them. I'm guessing the red curls would have sent him into orbit!"

"Well, I do declare you're right on that score. Who'd of ever dreamed up red curls? He would've flipped for sure. In fact, Sis, after our brownish locks, it's pretty wild. I bet people stop you in the market to talk about the gingers?" asked Heather.

"Oh yes. They sure do. If only Daddy could have known the girls..." whispered Amber.

Both young women sat quietly on the sofa.

"It was hard with him being sick for so many years and Mom having to work double shifts." Amber paused. "I miss him so much."

"Me too."

The sisters held eye contact for a long moment.

"Changing the subject..." Amber swallowed hard. "I'm so happy you traded flights to spend some time with us." Looking meaningfully at her sister, "I miss you little Sis. At least with you being in the airlines we've gotten to see more of you than, say, if you were an accountant. The girls are wild for you. Sometimes when I walk by their room at home, I can hear them in tea party play and there is always a place for Auntie Heather."

"Hmm," Heather's blue eyes sparkled with mischief, "so maybe it helped that I sent them the world's most magnificent tea set from China?"

"Oh hey there, I forgot about that! You're a clever one!"

After a long while Amber observed, "Isn't it odd that you and I have both moved so far away from home?"

Heather was pensive, "You know Amber, I never really intended to, I was always happy here as a small town gal, but once I got a taste of flying, was offered the New York to Sydney trip, well. And then those two other flight attendants invited me to share a brownstone with them....in the Big Apple! What can I say? You know the rest. One thing led to another, and now I'm something of a New Yorker." Heather once again looked at her sister and raised her eyebrows as if to say "who knew?"

"Do you think you'll settle down one day?"

"I do. I want it all Sis; what you have: the hottie husband and some rug-rats!" she said smiling.

"You'll be a cool mother, I know you will."

"I haven't said anything to Mom, but well...I'm seeing someone."

"Really? You're always seeing someone. Is this different?"

"It is. He's Jonathon Jake Lannings. He goes by Jake."

"I'm listening," urged Amber, turning her torso more fully to face her sister. Both women wore ear-to-ear grins.

"He's pretty dreamy."

"More!"

"He's older. He has eight years on me; he is turning thirty-nine this spring. He's delicious to look at; six feet, thick brown hair, green eyes. Good build. He's lots of fun, but that isn't it. He wants what I want." She seemed lost in thought for a moment. "He's no player, I'll tell you that much. In fact the other flight attendants can't believe that he's even dating. He's private. I don't know what they assumed, maybe that he's not available, or gay? I'm not sure."

"Heather, I haven't heard this much detail about a man from you in a long while…"

"I'm trying not to get ahead of myself. But I'm kinda crazy about him."

"Should I guess? Is he a pilot?"

"He is, but he talks about retiring after his twenty-five years and opening a cargo flight service, settling in one place…Maybe running a ranch…" Heather's expression had again taken on a faraway look.

A while later, Heather began, "So big Sis, are you still heading to the Southwest?"

"Cody's supposed to call, soon I hope. They flew him over to the field hospital in Germany. He's up to his eyeballs in urgent cases. Fallujah is boiling over. Cody says our troops are putting up a ferocious battle against the insurgents. The military is estimating that there may be up to 2000 hard core Al Qaeda and they won't stop at anything. The Iraqis themselves are getting the worst of it. Something like 600 of them have been killed in bombings this year alone."

Amber looked at her sister. "Heather, it's so horrible. Those poor soldiers. The one good thing that is coming out of this, at least according to Cody, is that battlefield medicine is getting better. The advances in neuroscience and prosthetics are helping, but what an agonizing road."

There was a long pause, finally in low tones Amber confided, "We don't talk about it, but sometimes he cries out in his sleep. I know he's reliving the mayhem in his dreams. He gives me the tough-guy act, but I know this war is shaking him to his core. It's more awful than they report on the news. The guys are so young, and so brave. Even after they suffer horrible injuries, they're determined to heal so they can go back in. It blows my mind that our country can produce such men and women, who volunteer…"

"Anyway, Sis, sorry. Cody's going to try to break away and call, maybe tonight. We are living in limbo until our transfer papers come through. All along we've thought Texas, then New Mexico, but the fact that the orders have been slow has Cody thinking that the military has other plans for him."

"What're the big picture plans?" asked Heather changing the subject away from the violence of war.

"Truly, I think the boy is leaning toward career military. It's not that many more years and then we have a guaranteed income while we go to Plan B. I'm okay with that idea. Some families seemed suited to military life. We seem to have taken to it, but if I'm truly honest with myself, I have two issues; I worry that the girls might not understand that they are Americans!" Amber sighed, "And the hardest thing for me," she paused to collect her thoughts, "is leaving my group of women friends. Heather, except for you, this is the first time I've known other gals in such a close way. They feel like family; we all help each other. I'm really going to miss them."

Heather could hear the sadness behind her sister's words.

"Sister, two things," began Heather, "the girls will know they are *Americans.* The second thing, in my experience, distance cannot dissolve true friendships."

Heather patted her sister's hand. "Plus with the air passes, Skype, and email. I think you'll be okay, but I hear you. Those everyday friendships are so dear."

After a few minutes, Heather encouraged more detail, "Now catch me up on this incredible painting career of yours. You know our apartment in New York is almost a shrine to Amber James' work! Our throw pillows and china patterns are all yours. My roommates are crazy to meet you. A big framed print of your Celtic cross hangs above our couch. We even did our colors to match your work!"

"Really?" Amber's eyes suddenly pierced with tears. "Really?" She stopped and blew her nose. "Heather, never in my wildest dreams did I think my playing in paints could turn into something like this." She sucked in a big breath. "HomeCo America is talking about extending my contract…"

The sisters continued their catch-up conversation. Amber brightened as she described the weekend painting excursions she and Cody and the girls had taken. She shared about the Blarney Castle, the Celtic Rings of Ireland, the ancient churches of Belfast, and more. Amber had delighted in painting Notre Dame. There had even been a recent short trip to Rome where she turned out watercolors of the Coliseum and the Palatine Hills, while Cody played with the girls in the ruins of antiquity.

Finally winding down, "Heather, I've photos and sketches of European monuments to help me while we are stateside. I'm not sure that HomeCo will welcome American points of interest. We'll see. I feel pumped by the way the painting's gone. I'm just sad about leaving my friends."

"Ah Sis," said Heather as she grabbed for Amber's hand and squeezed it. "I know. It's never easy to make these changes, but I think things will work out. I bet next time you see your friends you'll take up right where you left off. You'll see. It'll work out."

"I hope so."

CHAPTER 31

September 30, 2005
La Grange, Georgia

As Amber cleared up the girls' breakfast dishes and wiped Willow's high chair tray, her cell phone rang.

"Hello?"

"Hey sexy, guess what?" teased Cody in a delighted tone.

Laughing, Amber responded, "Hey sexy yourself. What's up, you? I haven't heard joy in your voice for quite some time Dr. James. With what you've been though in Germany, I wasn't sure when I'd ever hear happiness from you again. I know it's been vicious."

"Amber, you've no idea. But hearing your voice helps. How are my girls?"

"Mom's spoiling us. I've gotten some rest and Heather has been here. We're all great. Willow's sentences are getting longer and Kaitlyn is crazy about trying to cook. How are you really?"

"The team here is amazing. It's devastating to see the results of these attacks, but we've worked hard, had some positive outcomes." Cody paused and lowered his voice. "For sure, if the politicians in Washington were ever in the OR with us, I think they'd seriously cut back on the war machine… Amber, when we're alone, when I get back to you, we'll talk about it. For now I have some news."

"Cody, I know we'll make time for the details later. At least I know you're holding up okay. I sensed that your good mood must have some news behind it. So did our transfer orders finally come through?"

"They did."

"Ah, so are we about to become Longhorns?"

"Not really!"

"Cody James you are killing me here! Tell me," she said chuckling.

"Amber we're being transferred to Charleston Air Force Base and I'm to be number two in charge of trauma cases in the medical center. I will be part of the Medevac team, of course working the ER, and managing cases." He took a breath, "Amber, I'm blown away to be offered this challenge. I'm really excited as hell about it. It's good work, but I'm also pleased that you can be closer to your mother."

Squealing now, Amber responded, "Honey, Cody, are you kidding? You mean I'll be within driving distance of Mom in LaGrange?" Exuberant words tumbled out of her, "Only three hundred and something miles; not thousands! We can see each other on a regular basis. The girls will have their grandma in their everyday lives! Oh, I'm so happy!" Amber couldn't help herself, she was out of her chair, and her feet were doing a happy dance.

"Amber, I have to tell you I never expected this. It's a good hospital too. This might just seal the deal on us serving a full career, that's if you're with me on it?"

"Absolutely, I'm always with you. Do you realize that with Heather's airline passes, I'll be close enough to be able hop over to the UK and see the gals! This is great news! So give me the details so I can make some plans."

Forty minutes later, Amber closed her phone and went in search of her mother.

"Momma, you won't believe this!" Amber's infectious grin covered her beautiful face.

"Oh yeah?"

"Momma we are going to be within driving distance of you! We're moving to Charleston! Cody will be number two administering the Trauma Center at the military base. He wants me to find a house and start getting us settled right away! Oh Momma!" exclaimed Amber as she grabbed her mother and whirled her around.

Laughing, Sharon grinned at her daughter. The two women poured fresh cups of coffee and went out on the patio to expound on all the benefits of life in Charleston; the wonderful harbor, the Painted Ladies homes, the aquarium, Fort Sumter, the Magnolia Plantation Gardens, beautiful kid-friendly parks." She beamed, "Oh Momma, this is a dream come true. There'll be endless activities for us. What a place to raise a family!" Amber leaned back in the patio chair with a huge smile plastered to her face.

They were quiet for a while.

"This is really happening! Mom, I need to get myself a car! The Air Force will store our things until I find us a place. I'm so excited!"

***

Later that day as the excitement turned to creating a game plan, Sharon reminded her daughter, "Don't forget we've got that cousin of your dad's over there somewhere near Charleston. I know he practiced there at one time. He may have some connections. That might be a good place to begin."

"Mom, you're a genius, great idea! I still have his contact info somewhere. I will call him first thing tomorrow." She looked at her mother. "When the girls go down for their naps this afternoon, I'm going to jump online and see what I can find about a car and perhaps check out housing prices. Mom, you realize this will be the first time we'll have bought a home? Wow. I can practically feel the roots growing out of my feet!" she laughed.

The next day Amber placed a call to Grant Forrest's office. "Hey, Grant Forrest. Do you remember me, Sharon and Elma Blake's daughter, Amber? You helped me with that rights attorney, Jeff Newton, a few years back."

Grant's soothing Southern drawl filled the line, "Well, hello there, of course I remember y'all! How did all that work out for you? It was about your art work, your intellectual property, am I correct?" asked Grant.

"Yes! It has all turned out very well. You put me with Jeff Newton and he took good care of my rights. Thank you," said Amber.

"So any chance of some more advice?" she asked.

"Oh Amber, I always have a lot of advice. It might not be good, but I've always got a lot of it," he chortled.

"You recall my husband is in the military?" asked Amber.

"I do. Y'all stuck in my mind," his tone turned serious. "I didn't mention this the last time we chatted, there was no need, but I served two tours in Nam. Army. It was a rough time, terrible really." He paused and took a breath, "But all this Middle East business is brutal. Weapons of mass destruction; IED's. Horrible. Has your husband deployed to Iraq?"

"He's at the big military hospital in the UK, but he's been flown into Germany a number of times for special circumstances. Works in the ER at that combat hospital. It's rough. He doesn't talk about it much, but I know it's bad," Amber's tone was heavy with emotion. "The injuries sustained are sometimes so massive…" her voice trailed off. "Anyway, he does his best."

Neither said anything for a long moment, finally, "So cousin Amber, what kind of advice are you looking for?"

"Well on a brighter note, our orders came through. We're so happy, we're moving to Charleston! Cody happens to be detained now, actually he's over in Germany. I need to find somewhere for us to live. I wondered if you know which areas are best for our young family. Also maybe you have a contact that I can trust?"

"Oh this one is easy. First of all you'll love Charleston and its true Southern hospitality. It's a beautiful, majestic city, rich with history. A great place for families. Do I recall you have children? Am I correct?"

"We have two little ones. Yes."

"There are lots of good neighborhoods with a wide variety of price points. South of Broad, we call it SOB, is going to be pricier with a lot of penthouse living. There's James Island, West Ashley, and Harleston Village, which boast affordable family homes and good schools. Actually there are a number of good neighborhoods," offered Grant.

"What are your time parameters?" he asked.

"Oh this is good news." She paused. "Hmmm, time parameters? Well, I'm here at my mother's over in LaGrange. I plan to book a room at Embassy Suites or Holiday Inn Express, while we go on the hunt. Maybe I will be lucky enough to have a short escrow. Anyway, I'm just getting started. We can always rent an apartment short-term if we need to." Amber paused and lowered her excited voice. "This helps so much Cousin Grant. Thank you, I appreciate the 411."

"I can do better," he paused. "My son-in-law, Dale Whittaker, is the broker over at Golden Door Realty. He's a great guy and I know he'll help you. Let me get his cell phone number for you and I will tell him y'all will be calling."

"That's great! Thanks again. Once we move in and get settled, I owe you a few nice dinners, one for the rights' attorney and another for this! Will you and your wife come if I promise you something delicious?" asked Amber in a teasing tone.

"Wouldn't miss it. You cook. We'll eat!" he said laughing. "Hey, it would be nice to see your mother again, maybe invite us sometime when she's there?"

The next few days were a whirlwind of activity as Amber took action. She left the girls with her mother; after considerable research, she bought a new burgundy colored Jeep Grand Cherokee. She contacted the realtor whom Grant had recommended. He was lining up houses to view while she secured temporary accommodations in Charleston.

CHAPTER 32

September 30, 2005
Beaufort, South Carolina

Heeding Dr. Lewis' advice, Shelby focused on slowing her racing thoughts, and trying to convince herself that she did not *have* to take immediate action to meet Cody and his family. Her fantasy life had been simmering for weeks. She might be working in the garden, dead-heading roses, while imagining herself sneaking off to Texas to meet Willow and Kaitlyn, or she could visualize herself standing in the terminal of the San Antonio Airport, studying the map to locate their street, and then climbing into a rental car, a little white Ford Escape. She would be wearing linen slacks and a colorful blue tee-shirt.

In one of her favorites, she saw herself handing over her passport to the British Airways agent; later, exiting the terminal at Heathrow, concentrating on driving her rental car on the left side of the road as she headed to Suffolk…Then suddenly the picture would stop.

What then?

These frequent fantasies involved elaborate schemes for not stirring up Grant's suspicions. She thought about saying that she was visiting Cara, the child she once cared for who was now a mother in her own right. She could make up that story, but Cara was practicing law, and lived in California. That would not work. She could pretend to be visiting Lily, her mother's friend, but that seemed complicated, and Grant might just call Lily's house, though she supposed he would use her cell.

Daydream after daydream played across her imagination. She loved the one where the two little girls, perhaps hungry to have a new grandmother, climbed up into her arms and planted exuberant kisses against her cheeks. She imagined the fresh vanilla scent of their little-girl skin, the weight of their sturdy young bodies pressed into hers. She envisioned their squirming and the sound of their giggles as she played "I'm-going-to-get-you" with them. When she got to that part of her fantasy, she could feel an ear-to-ear grin across her face. But soon enough, it would float away, as her thoughts crashed back to reality.

There was no way she could sneak off behind Grant's back. He already felt betrayed, if he caught her skulking around, he would think she was having some sordid affair. *That*, for sure, would be the end of her marriage.

The weeks passed. Shelby arranged three more Skype sessions with Dr. Lewis. She practiced what she was told and absorbed the lessons. She was forcing her wandering brain to practice something Dr. Lewis called *mindfulness*. It was hard. Her brain wanted to kneed and ponder; it wanted to sniff at the Cody conundrum.

Post-It reminders were stuck where only she could see them. She placed a rubber band around her wrist, and snapped it each time she'd began to feel guilty about Cody and Grant. She made an effort to walk every day, some days with Karen and her dog, Lord Tanner.

Dr. Lewis taught her that new neuroscience studies revealed more of how the brain operates, that people have deep neural maps for thoughts they've held across time. She'd said, "People tell themselves stories." She was certain that Shelby's story was something like: *you should have kept Cody and figured out a way to raise him; he would have been better off with you, instead of a family.*

She could hear Charlotte's wise words. "Shelby, that story is making you *crazy* with guilt. Practice telling yourself a different story. Let yourself off the hook! Write a new story: *I did the **right** thing in giving Cody to a good family who could raise him properly. I'm proud that I didn't terminate the pregnancy.*

"Give yourself a break!" Charlotte's vehemence made an impression. Shelby was *trying* to live a normal life. September had been the start of the docent year at the museum. She met with the five new trainees and instructed them in the techniques for making the history of the Lowcountry come alive. The museum's exhibits spanned from ancient times with the indigenous people, to the arrival of the Europeans, through the Colonial Period. The basic requirement for the trainees was a passion for sharing the past, as well as an ability to interact with others. The museum hosted 200,000 school children annually. As the culmination of the four day training sessions, she invited them to her home for a kick-off luncheon which featured their period costumes.

On this day, as she went about her morning routine at home, straightening up and placing the breakfast dishes in the dishwasher, she thought about that kick-off luncheon. She had hosted it in her home, the week before.

The five new docents had arrived about 11:30, where they met the six returning docents. Shelby had welcomed them with Mint Juleps. The dogs, Tessie and Zoe, calmly mingled with the guests. As Shelby passed around a tray of her stuffed mushroom caps, she was aware that the guests were relaxing under the influence of the gentle animals, and possibly the Mint Juleps.

One of Shelby's skills, and probably why she had been installed as the volunteer leader, was her ability to coordinate and manage people. She knew how to put people at ease. She smiled to herself, as she continued to think back on the luncheon. One of her tricks for having a successful event was interaction. She laughed a little as she recalled how startled they seemed when she offered up a game.

"Hi everyone! What do you say we play a little game?" she'd announced. "I have a basket of delights from the Cup Cake

Boutique for the winner!"

It had only taken a minute for the docents to get into the spirit. "So who will play my Secret Scavenger Hunt game?"

The game had been a big hit, with laughter ringing out from the veranda. As she brought out the first course, the Chilled Cucumber soup, she'd noticed that she was humming to herself. And as the luncheon continued, and she'd served the second course, a Roasted Salmon Nicoise Salad, thanks to Laney's menu ideas, she had found that she'd actually felt *happy*! It was one of the first times she'd felt relaxed in a long while.

She recalled her thoughts that afternoon, *I don't think I've hummed one note since last spring. Perhaps talking with Charlotte is helping. I'm using her tools; envisioning a bullet proof vest secured around my heart, something removable, but a boundary to keep me from being so reactive to everything. Charlotte wants me to stop feeling responsible for everyone's feelings.*

As her memory continued to examine the luncheon day, she remembered hearing little wisps of what, Bert, a returning docent, was saying at the other end of the table. He was asking, "So have any of you followed the discovery of that 12,000 year-old skull in the Yucatan Peninsula?"

"It's something, isn't it?" replied Emory. "They're saying its morphology is like that of the "Kennewick Man," discovered near the Columbia River a while back."

The rest of his sentences had floated away for Shelby, but now, a week later, vacuuming up dog hair, she examined that part of the conversation. It had been lively, hypothesizing what that skull meant in terms of human migration, but for her, the mention of Kennewick Man triggered a replay of a similar argument she had defended one evening on the African safari.

As her vacuum powered through the dining room, she became aware of an ironic twist as she considered that old debate with Tom

Steele. *Oh how vociferously I'd argued for multiple migrations of early man!*

Becoming more self-aware, she was now clear on what that conflict had *really* been about. *Of course it wasn't about migrations. I was furious that Tom Steele was on my safari! It galled me that he had not the faintest memory of my existence... I was not about to let him discount me once again.*

She paused and looked out the window as she thought, *Poor Grant, he couldn't imagine why his usually lovely, calm wife had become so contentious!*

As she wrapped the vacuum's cord around its guides, she thought, *That argument seems so petty now in comparison with the real issues facing me.*

***

A few days later, Michelle called. "Mom, hi. How are you?"

"Honey, I'm well, thank you. The question is, how are *you?*"

"Oh? I'm okay... Well, sort of stressed." She stopped.

Shelby could hear something in Michelle's tone.

"Listen, Mom, the week after next, there're mandatory in-service training sessions for us. It's that new computer generated reading system the district has adopted. We have to learn it, and I have to stay late at school. I need help. I'm hoping that you can drive up and read to Ellie's class that day, and bring her home. Can you stay until Dale and I get in that evening?"

"Michelle, of course. What date exactly?"

" Friday, October 21st. Thanks so much, you're a lifesaver."

"No problem at all. I look forward to it. You know I enjoy being a part of Ellie's activities." Shelby paused. "Do you have a minute? Some exciting opportunities have opened up on the Pony Girl front."

"Oh, sure. I have time, Ellie's working with her magic markers, and dinner's in the oven. Shoot."

Shelby explained that the children's television producer they'd been working with had completed a pilot cartoon of Pony Girl. He'd pitched it to a few networks, and PBS was the most interested.

"Michelle, if it goes forward, they propose ten Pony Girl episodes. They'd most likely air next Fall," concluded Shelby.

"Momma, that's wonderful! I adore your stories. They're captivating and rich with history. We like how Pony Girl always weaves in a life lesson." Michelle continued, "Mom, I'm so proud of you! You just never stop; you are always moving forward!"

"Oh thank you, dear, I'm not so sure about that." Shelby sighed. Her words were ripe with meaning only she could comprehend.

CHAPTER 33

October 8, 2005
Charleston, South Carolina

On Saturday morning Amber and the girls climbed into their shiny new SUV. Sharon came around to the back windows and gave Willow and Kaitlyn each a little packet with crayons and a coloring book.

"Girls, for the ride. Grandma will come see you just as soon as y'all are settled," she explained, as she reached in and patted each girl on the head.

The girls smiled contentedly as they accepted the coloring books. "Thanks Grandma. Love you!" said Kaitlyn.

"Love you," whispered Gracie as she busily opened the package.

"Thanks Mom. I'll call when I get to the hotel. You were a huge help. I'm so wired. You realize this is another beginning of the rest of our lives, right?" she said laughing. "Cody and I seem to have a lot of new beginnings!" She was smiling as she put the car into drive.

"Amber, there are worse things! This is going to be wonderful. I love you! Be safe," called Sharon as the SUV pulled slowly away from the curb.

"Girls, is everything okay back there?" Amber asked, as she sneaked a look into the back seat where twin car seats secured her auburn-haired darlings.

"Momma, are we gonna see Daddy?" asked Kaitlyn.

"We will, but not for a while yet. Daddy's helping people who got hurt. He will come as soon as he can. You, Willow, and I, are going to find us a new house! It's going to be an adventure! We're staying in a hotel tonight, actually for the next few days, until we decide exactly what we're doing about housing. We're going to meet a man who will show us different places. How does that sound?"

"Good." With that Kaitlyn went back to coloring in the new coloring book.

"Willow, you okay darlin'?" asked Amber.

"Okey dokey," she smiled as she placed her favorite two fingers into her mouth and looked out the window.

Amber checked her side mirrors as she changed lanes heading for Charleston and the beginning of a new life.

Twenty-four hours later, she and the girls arrived at the Golden Door Real Estate Company where they met with Dale Whittaker.

"Hi. I'm Dale," announced an energetic, sandy haired man, in his mid-thirties as he walked toward Amber, extending his hand. "I'm so happy to meet you. It's interesting to learn that we're cousins-in-law!"

"I can use more folks, we might only be shirt-tail relatives, but what's wrong with that?" Amber turned her 1000 watt smile on him. "I'm delighted to find more family, especially now when I feel kind of out here on a limb looking for a house without my husband."

Turning toward her daughters, "Here are my girls, Willow and

Kaitlyn."

"Girls, this is Mr. Whittaker, he's going to show us some houses." Two sets of blue eyes studied Dale, as they nodded their acknowledgement of him.

"As the girls and I were leaving England two weeks ago, that attack on our troops in Iraq occurred. Cody, my husband, has been detained. They transported him over to the hospital in Germany. It's bad. A lot of trauma. He's working almost non-stop to save limbs. He manages trauma cases. It's awful." Her thoughts went to Cody and his struggle to save lives.

"Anyhow, Dale," she began, forcing her thoughts back to the moment, "our work is cut out for us. We need a place to live."

"No problem. My father-in-law gave me a heads up about what you require, and since our telephone conversation, I've narrowed down the possibilities. I think I understand what you're looking for. I've lined up six houses to show you today, that seems about right, and some for tomorrow. If that's too much with the girls, we can pull back."

"Let's just see how it goes. When the girls begin to wilt we can take a lunch break. Is there a McDonald's with a play zone where they can relax a bit? They would love that. Then we can view more houses."

"I have a daughter myself. I'm up to speed on parks and fast food. We'll do whatever it takes. I usually drive my clients around to show the houses. I know you don't know the area yet. Should we move the girls' seats into my SUV?"

"It's a big hassle. What if you just got into our car and showed us around?"

"Perfect."

"Before we get started, I noticed a wall map over there. Would you mind showing me the areas where we will be looking?"

"Great idea. Absolutely."

For the next few minutes, Dale gave a rundown on the pros and cons of the various family neighborhoods in Charleston. After the quick primer on "SOB," South of Broad, James Island, Wild Dunes, Island of Palms, and more, she was overwhelmed.

"Hmm, I think the best bet is for us to just go and look."

"That's fine. I have a nice range of houses lined up. There is one house, however, that might really be right for you. It just came on the market. It's almost brand new, a custom home, over on Daniel Island. The family moved in last year, and then suddenly, earlier this summer, the husband was offered an exec position in Atlanta. He couldn't turn it down. They just moved out. It's immaculate, priced right, and ready to occupy."

"Really? It's empty, ready to occupy?" repeated Amber, as excitement spread through her.

Though Amber was intrigued with the idea of a house that was ready-to-go, she performed her due diligence. Two days and ten houses, including drive-bys, gave her a good idea of the values in the area. She emailed photos and links to virtual tours to Cody in Germany. Luckily, late one night, he had time to review them, and could discuss options with her.

Their conversation kept coming back to the big Antebellum that was ready for occupancy.

"Cody, it's gorgeous. You see the wrap-around veranda and the hardwood floors in the photos? I love the granite in the kitchen," enthused Amber.

"I like the big tree-filled double lot," added Cody.

"The girls are thrilled about the swing in the backyard. It's hanging from a big magnolia tree. There's a wood-sided shed in the back corner of the yard that could be transformed into a playhouse. I remember when I was little, Daddy made Heather and me the cutest little playhouse you could imagine. He lined the path leading up to it with pansies. I have the best memories of us playing in that little house. Mom even sewed real curtains for it. Heather and I would color and eat snacks in there. We'd stow away candy bars, and then when Momma wasn't looking, we'd sneak them into the playhouse and have a feast!" Amber's words danced with joy.

"Oh Cody, I'm so excited, but I'm getting off the subject. I'm sorry." She stopped.

"Where were we? And babe, you need to grab some sleep while you can."

"Amber, you know I can get by on a few hours. This is important. You weren't off the subject. This is our first house. We need to get it right. I want our girls to have memories like you and Heather have. What else do you like about it?"

"Well, it's in a gated community, and only three miles from the elementary and middle schools. Dale tells me that there's a great pre-school five miles away. In fact his daughter goes there. Downtown Charleston is only a ten minute drive and your medical center, the 268th, is under twenty minutes away." She forced herself to slow the rush of words.

"Also, I met another mom, with two boys, when I took the girls to the park today. She said she loves Daniel Island because of its quaint little downtown; lots of coffee shops, and farmers' markets. She might be a potential friend. I got her name and number. Anyway, Cody, the house is beautiful, very much the epitome of the Southern style and the neighborhood has other young families. Honey, I do think it's the perfect choice."

"So why are you looking at all these other homes?"

"Because, my dear husband, this Antebellum is much more house than we'd thought about. It has a huge great room and five bedrooms!" Her words were light.

"Maybe we'll just have to fill them up with kids!" joshed Cody.

By the end of their second over-seas call, Amber pressed, "Cody are you sure you want me to go in there and make the offer without you? All this could wait 'til you get here." The worry was heavy in her tone.

"Amber, I've seen the photos, been on its "tour," and you love it. We haven't touched my inheritance, nor your earnings from HomeCo. If this house makes you as happy as you sound, then I think we should go for it. What really is the downside?" Cody paused. "If we don't feel comfortable in it after a while, we could always move. Right?" His tone was playful.

"Hey, seriously, I hadn't thought of that. That helps me realize that living there doesn't have to be so permanent. Besides, the military might move us again, or crazy idea, like you said, we have a bunch more kids to fill it up?" teased Amber.

By Wednesday, she and Cody firmed up their decision to purchase the big Antebellum even though it was more of everything than they had considered. It was even more than a dream house, it was perfect.

Cody instructed Amber to cash out three of their CDs so they could pay 30% down, thus keeping their house payments at a workable sum. They made an offer, it was accepted, and they opened escrow. Dale arranged for them to rent the home for the weeks before escrow closed, while Cody gave the Air Force the heads up to deliver their furniture and personal effects.

THE UNRAVELING OF SHELBY FORREST

By Friday evening, Amber got the children bathed and into bed. She poured herself a glass of Merlot, and pulled a chair around to the window in their Embassy Suites sitting area. She put her feet up, and leaned back in the wing-backed chair, smiling to herself, as she looked out the window.

Dale had also organized a cleaning crew to come in the house to get it ready, his treat. That was nice she thought, continuing her mental check list: the furniture will be delivered next week. If I'm lucky, Cody will be here by then. I need to enroll Kaitlyn in the pre-school that Dale recommended. Oh. I need to call Mom and see if she can spend the weekend and be a part of the move-in. Amber smiled, knowing that 'being a part of the move-in' was code for helping with the girls. Everything was falling into place. She inhaled the fragrant bouquet of her wine and then slowly sipped its rich body, as a sly smile came across her face.

I'm not dreaming. I am pretty sure this is my true life; we are moving into a dream home, it looks like my husband will soon join me; we have two wonderful children and careers that are rich with meaning for each of us.

Amber leaned her head against the back of her chair. It does not get much better than this.

THE UNRAVELING OF SHELBY FORREST

CHAPTER 34

October 20, 2005
Beaufort, South Carolina

As Shelby finished slicing the roast beef, she looked up at Grant who was seated across the table from her.

"I can't believe that after all these years I can look at you and my heart does a little flip," she said. "Today, when I was in the grocery store buying this roast, and putting the potatoes into my shopping cart, I had the sweetest feeling, it was like when we were newlyweds and we would both go grocery shopping. Do you remember that? I had that sense of new beginnings. Strange, isn't it?" asked Shelby.

"Not so strange." Holding eye contact with Shelby, Grant's tone was husky as he whispered, "Red, sometimes when I watch you playing with Ellie or Gracie, it feels like when Laney and Michelle were little, I imagine it like it was; that we have all those years stretching in front of us."

Shelby put down her carving knife and reached for Grant's hand. She squeezed, and he squeezed back.

"Grant, you remember that I'm driving into Charleston tomorrow. I'm reading to Ellie's class and then I'm watching her until Michelle and Dale get home. Michelle has that in-service after school."

"Are you spending the night?"

"I was thinking I'd play it by ear. I sleep better in my own bed, but if I feel too tired, I'll stay. I'll call you either way."

The conversation moved along companionably. After dinner, they took the dogs out for a walk. They were strolling along the path that edged the harbor, when they stopped to watch a lone sea gull make its dive. They smiled. The noisy screeching of the birds was familiar. They both cherished their life near the water. Shelby filled Grant in on the new docents and how well they were doing.

"You met Bert at the Water Festival. He's such a character. He's taken on the persona of an old English bard, as he spins the docent tales. He's so entertaining that several of the new ladies are trying to copy his style. It's pretty funny to watch." Laughing, Shelby tried out her own silly accent. "Ah Matey doth thou knowith from whence comen these many olde English accents?"

Grant enjoyed her antics. They ambled along, as they had done for so many years, the dogs racing ahead, when the path was clear of others. After a while, Grant said, "There's been so much going on at work lately, I forgot to mention to you about a call I had a few weeks ago, from those distant cousins I have over in Georgia. You remember? We met them once at Stone Mountain, at that reenactment? Elma Blake. He seemed like a nice sort; passed away about ten years ago, was sick for a long time. Anyway, his daughter called me, looking for a realtor. I put her with Dale. Small world isn't it?" Grant smiled down at Shelby. Their footsteps crunched on the crushed shell path as they strolled along.

"It is," answered Shelby, "and nice that you could help Dale with a referral. Changing the subject, you know I'm not caught up on those people in your money laundering case. Did they finally plead out?"

"They did, and turned state's evidence, gave the police some valuable intel. They're getting off easy; just house-arrest and then probation. It always fascinates me what can pass as justice." remarked Grant.

Darkness was falling as they headed back up the hill toward

home. Shelby felt at peace... for the moment.

THE UNRAVELING OF SHELBY FORREST

CHAPTER 35

October 21, 2005
Daniel Island, Charleston, S.C.

Cody came up behind Amber as she was standing at the kitchen sink, gazing out the window onto their large, lush backyard. She'd been watching the girls as they played with their Barbies under the magnolia tree. She could see that Kaitlyn had changed Barbie's clothes once again, while Willow seemed to be struggling to get her Ariel doll into the tiny upstairs bedroom of the dollhouse. Cody put his arms around Amber as they silently observed their daughters contentedly playing in their new yard.

"We're lucky they get along so well. Do you think they're missing their playgroup friends very much?" asked Cody.

"With all this excitement of moving and then my mom's visit, they're fine. Wait 'til they get to exploring all the new nooks and crannies around here! That could keep them busy for years!" joked Amber.

"How's their mom doing?"

"You know me. I won't relax until I get us on some kind of schedule. I'm just thankful I managed to get Kaitlyn settled in preschool. There's so much to do, it's fine, but I admit I'm a bit of a stress case. Next week there's a Welcome Wagon tea for the new residents at the community center. Willow is invited too. We're going to go. Maybe there will be some gals I click with. I'm going to scout around for some kind of Mommy and Me program."

She paused and looked at Cody. "I miss Honor and the others.

We've been Skyping, but it's not quite the same. I'm needin' my posse!"

"I know you are, but Mrs. James, I think you've done an amazing job of getting us settled in a very great home," Cody murmured as he turned her around and pulled her close.

"Thank you my darlin'. I think so too." She reached up and kissed his cheek. "Do you think this new position at the medical center will work out? Do you like the people?"

"The staff seems great. Of course I've only been there a few days, I think sharing some of the administrative work along with the ER trauma rotation will be a good fit. I feel useful and I doubt the work will be quite as stressful as it's been. Those transports over to Germany are rough. God, the injuries our guys sustain are unspeakable."

"I can only imagine. I admire what you do Cody." She studied his handsome face. "You make a difference."

They embraced at the kitchen sink. "I missed you," whispered Amber.

"I know. Me too."

"Cody, on a lighter note," began Amber, "what a relief it's been that you got here in time to help with the move. I'm sure I could have managed the details, but it was so much easier having you with us…Ah…about the move. Have you noticed that our furniture hasn't put a dent in what this place needs?"

Laughing, Cody exclaimed, "Oh I *have!*"

"Maybe on your next day off we could go furniture shopping?"

"There you go, and that will give us a chance to think about what pieces we want. Amber I hope the great room is high on your priority list!"

"What are you saying? Dude, are you wanting to *sit down* to watch TV? What a crazy thought!" joshed Amber. "Also I need to interview some mother's helpers and find a weekly house cleaner. Maybe the people I meet at the welcome meeting will have some contacts for me."

Turning around, once again to look out the window at their daughters, Amber remarked, "Cody aren't our girls great?"

"All three of *my girls* are great, more than great." He nuzzled her neck. "You're my life."

"Oh, Cody," Amber leaned into him. She was grinning, "and my friends wonder how it is that I'm still in love with my man!"

They stayed like that for a long time. Finally, Amber began, "Back to this furnishings business. As soon as we have a dining room table and some outdoor chairs, I need to invite my dad's cousin and his wife for dinner. He's who put us with Dale. I should invite Dale and his wife and daughter as well."

"No problem, but let's get more settled first, plus there's going to be an officers' spouses reception in a week or so. I'll get the exact dates for you. Seems like our new life is off and running." Cody smiled at Amber.

THE UNRAVELING OF SHELBY FORREST

CHAPTER 36

October 21, 2005
Beaufort, S.C.

"Charlotte, thank you for taking my unscheduled call. I don't want to be a drama queen; I know it's early in California, but last night was the worst one; the most graphic nightmare yet. Worse than the black marbles falling out," confessed Shelby as her voice cracked. "I'm sorry to need help so early…"

"It's fine about the call. Tell me." Charlotte's voice was warm and comforting.

"You know I've been doing better. Practicing telling myself a new story, but last night the dream was so vivid. I was running somewhere. It was dark. There was a lot of blood. I was afraid for my life. I was running through a long dark alley. I woke up sweating and my heart was racing. I sneaked out of bed so as not to awaken Grant. Then I emailed you," sobbed Shelby.

"Oh, Shelby, I'm so sorry. That was another panic attack along with the nightmare. You know that Acute PTSD doesn't suddenly dissolve. It can take months, years even. Many of the vets and many of the folks involved with 9/11, and the Oklahoma bombings, are still symptomatic. Shelby, sit down if you're standing. Take a deep breath," directed Charlotte.

"My best guess is that the chase in the dream represents your past. It is struggling to catch up with you, to make itself known. Why last night? What's going on?" asked Charlotte.

"Oh God. I don't know. I was doing better. This morning I'm driving into Charleston. I'm the storyteller in Ellie's class this afternoon. It should be fine. I've done it before. I enjoy it."

Whispering, Shelby asked, "Do you think I'm okay to drive?"

"I do, but you've got to settle yourself down. Do you have time to take the dogs out before you get on the road? At least for a half hour?"

"I, I ,...I think so."

"Walk briskly. Get the endorphins going. Talk to the dogs and take those big deep restorative nasal breaths. Blow out of your mouth. Take a shower. Also you've got to eat something. Your blood sugar is probably low. You can do this." Charlotte's tone was commanding.

"Once on the road, play some lively music. Do you have something like the old Beatles', *Yellow Submarine?* Find some songs that make you smile, upbeat tunes, Whitney, maybe some hip-hop! Practice positive self talk. You're going to spend the day with your *granddaughter.* This is a happy day for you Shelby. You can do this!" Charlotte reassured her.

***

Four hours later, Shelby felt much more in control, as she arrived at Good Times Pre-school. She signed in at the office and walked to Ellie's classroom. The colorful characters adorning the walls made her smile. This was a safe place. *I'm fine.*

She glanced around the room looking for Ellie, who was busy at her desk with two other little girls. The teacher, Miss Jennifer, greeted Shelby. They chatted for a few moments before Miss Jennifer said, "We'll finish this project in about ten minutes. We are working on our letters, and then we'll create our circle on the floor for your story. The children have been talking about you and Pony Girl all week!"

The women smiled at one another.

As Shelby took her seat in the rocking chair at the front of the circle, Ellie looked up and caught her grandma's eye. Instantly she was out of her seat rushing into Shelby's arms. They embraced. Just as quickly Ellie floated back to her desk and whispered something to the little girl she'd been working with. The little girl got up and came back with Ellie to meet Shelby.

"Grandma, this is my new friend. She just moved here last week. Her name is Kaitlyn," explained an enthusiastic Ellie.

As recognition flowed through Shelby's awareness, she became dizzy. Bright white lights seemed to go off in front of her eyes. She took a breath, and did her best to look at Kaitlyn, trying to appear normal, while her heart was flipping and banging horribly. Her hands began to shake.

"Well, hello Kaitlyn. I'm so happy to meet you." Her words felt prickly against her tongue. She inhaled. Her breathing was irregular. "I'm going to share a story with you girls and boys today."

Kaitlyn smiled, "Hi," and both girls scooted back to their desks to complete their project.

Shelby sat frozen in the rocker. She wished she had worn the rubber band around her wrist, though she realized snapping it was not going to fix this.

Kaitlyn, Oh my God! You're so sweet and beautiful. You're just exquisite! Oh Kaitlyn, you're even more perfect than in your picture and here you are, right in front of me; Ellie's new friend. Her breath caught again. The room spun.

After a short while, the children took their places on the rug. It was all Shelby could do, not to stare at Kaitlyn. It was essential that she appear *normal*. She needed to somehow deliver an Oscar worthy performance. She was the star in her own drama, perhaps it was *The Great Unraveling of Shelby Forrest*. She enjoyed a moment of gallows humor, as she prepared for one of her most important roles, appearing put-together in the midst of the most hellish internal conflagration of her life!

She inhaled long deep breaths and began the tale of Pony Girl and Tangle Boy discovering an orphaned kitten. The words came easily as she described the two children bringing the little kitty home to their village. As the story unfolded, another part of her brain studied Kaitlyn; pretty bright blue eyes, *iridescent blue, hmmm*. She studied the spray of freckles across her perfect nose, the curve of her chin. As Kaitlyn sat spellbound listening to the story, Shelby noticed the yellow polka-dot ribbon which held back her voluminous auburn curls. She was conscious of how well groomed and tidy was the child's appearance. *Amber is a good mommy.*

The twelve children were rapt listeners. As the story continued, "Tangle Boy and Pony Girl had fallen into a deep affection for the kitten. They loved to show it off to the other children. When their father, the chief, studied the kitten, he declared, 'Pony Girl, Tangle Boy, that's not the kind of cat that you think it is, it's a *wild* animal. It's a bobcat and will grow to be as big as Little Dowgy, your dog. There is *no way* you can keep it!'"

"'Oh Daddy. We love him. What shall we do?'" cried Pony Girl.

"'Daddy, his name is Shorty Tail and I want to keep him!'" wailed Tangle Boy as he threw himself on the ground, kicking and yelling, in a temper tantrum."

The story continued. "There was much upset in the camp because soon *all* of the children were begging their parents to let Shorty Tail stay. The issue came before the tribal council. Finally, the elders agreed, but only under certain "wild animal" conditions could the animal stay. The children had to promise to follow strict rules in order to live safely with Shorty Tail. The children took solemn oaths. And so it was. For many long moons after, Pony Girl, Tangle Boy, Shorty Tail, and the other children, ran and played in the tall green grass near the village. Their favorite game was hide-and-seek. Shorty Tail would climb a tree, hide, and then suddenly pounce down and surprise them! This made all the youngsters laugh. When Shorty Tail became tired, he would curl up on one of the children and purr, but his purring was so loud that it sounded like a rainstorm brewing in the distance, which also made the children giggle. It was a happy time, and they all lived happily ever after."

As Shelby ended the story, she thought, *And they all lived happily ever after... We'll just have to see about that.*

Miss Jennifer came to the front of the circle and led the applause, thanking Mrs. Forrest for her wonderful story. School was finished for the day, and the parents were beginning to line up outside for pick-up.

As Shelby glanced through the classroom window she could see Kaitlyn's mother, Amber, walking toward the door with a little russet-haired child in her arms. Willow. *Oh Willow. Oh baby! Look at you.* The hot tsunami once again surged through her body, leaving her shaken. *Oh sweet little Willow...*

She stood up quickly, turning toward the white board, pretending to be straightening the pages of her story. Her hands quivered with emotion. *Oh please do not come over here.*

She surreptitiously studied the reflection in the window. She could see Amber collecting Kaitlyn's backpack and talking to the teacher. She was aware that Willow had two fingers in her mouth. She watched Willow as Miss Jennifer said something to her. The fingers were withdrawn and a big smile crossed Willow's face, revealing a dimple on her left cheek.

A dimple? She is more precious than I even imagined...

After what felt like an eternity, but could only have been a few minutes, Amber, Willow, and Kaitlyn left the room.

Breathe. Breathe! She implored herself.

She had no clue as to how she managed to get through the rest of the afternoon, preparing dinner for Ellie, and waiting for Michelle and Dale. When Michelle invited her to spend the night she made an excuse about needing to get home, something at the museum the next day, the new docents.

During the long drive home her internal dialogue raged on. She knew what she had to do.

You have to tell Grant. Soon.

At this rate I will stroke out.

Shelby you must! No matter the outcome… this simply cannot wait any longer.

CHAPTER 37

October 21, 2005
Daniel Island, South Carolina

Amber latched the plastic lock on Willow's highchair as she scooted it up to the table. "Kaitlyn did you wash your hands?"

"I did."

The evenings when Cody was home for dinner were special. Amber treasured the times when they all sat down together.

"Momma, what's in the pan?" asked Kaitlyn.

"Well, it would be your favorite. Twice baked mac and cheese!" announced Amber, smiling to her family.

"Hey, that's my favorite too," said Cody, as he sat down at the head of the table.

The conversation was sparse as they dug into their delicious, crusty entrée and enjoyed the goat cheese and arugula salads. Willow gave up using the spoon, and was delicately putting noodles into her mouth.

"So how was everyone's day?" asked Cody.

"May I share?" asked Kaitlyn.

"Sure, are you enjoying your new school Katie-cat?" asked Cody.

"Daddy, I am. But that's not what I want to tell you."

"No?"

"No. Today a lady came to our 'kool and told us a Pony Girl 'tory. It was so much fun. About a lost kitten that Pony Girl and her brother saved and made into a pet, but it was not a real kitty, it was a wild *bobcat*!" Kaitlyn's blue eyes sparkled in amazement as she described more of the story.

"That's pretty cool. I know how much you like those books that Aunt Heather sends you. That's great Katie-cat!" remarked Cody.

"The new school's going to work out. I've met a few of the other moms. They're all so welcoming," added Amber.

Turning toward the highchair and his youngest daughter, Cody asked Willow. "What do you think about all this, little lady?"

"Good."

"It's so great to have dinner with my girls. I'm on the ER rotation tomorrow night and Sunday, but I'll have Monday and Tuesday night at home."

"I'm happy about that," replied Amber, "I hope this rain lets up. I was thinking about taking the girls to the zoo tomorrow."

CHAPTER 38

October 21, 2005
Beaufort, South Carolina

Somehow Shelby managed to drive home without getting herself killed. It was late. Grant had already turned out his reading light. She silently completed her night-time ritual of make-up removal and tooth brushing, and slipped into bed next to her sleeping husband. He grunted a groggy greeting as she curled in next to his back. Soon he was again sleeping soundly. His rhythmic breathing, in and out, was comforting in its ordinariness. She scooted in closer, pressing her torso against his strong, warm body.

Inhale. Exhale. His long slow breaths continued as she thought about him and her marriage. *This may be the last night of the life I've known for the past thirty years. How I have gloried in being the wife of this good man. When I look back on this night and on our marriage, the words "honor" and "integrity" will stand out. That is the kind of man Grant has been. He has been loving and kind to me, has cherished our daughters, and has conducted his professional life in an exemplary fashion, always upholding the law. I admire him for never shaving corners off the truth; for never betraying his family.*

Dear God, please hear me now. My prayer to you is that you allow this genuinely good person to find forgiveness in his heart, for I have failed to live up to the example he has set by withholding the truth from him. My prayer is that somehow, after tomorrow, my marriage will be spared.

Shelby lay in the dark staring at the ceiling, finally as dawn broke, she dropped into a restless sleep.

CHAPTER 39

October 22, 2005
Beaufort, South Carolina

It was Saturday, Shelby and Grant followed through with their plans to go to the dedication of a new park in Beaufort, even though the sky threatened rain. It was a lively affair with a jazz band playing, a festive balloon arch, all kinds of walking-around Southern-style food, and of course speeches. As with most of the town's community events, the usual players were in attendance. Grant and Shelby enjoyed conversations with their friends and neighbors, greeting and smiling. They had missed the Labor Day festivities preferring time with their granddaughters. This was the first big event they had attended since the Water Festival.

Everywhere they went, "Shelb. Hey, that festival was the best one yet."

"Couldn't believe the turn-out! You did an amazing job."

"Shelby, that opening dinner-dance was fantastic, especially when Grant danced you around the floor!"

The compliments rolled in. She smiled appreciatively, all the while feeling the hard clump of nerves knotted in her gut. *Four more hours.*

Back at home, later in the afternoon, Grant relaxed in front of a golf tournament on television while Shelby worked in the kitchen. She was preparing one of Grant's favorite dishes, chicken enchiladas. She had introduced him to Mexican food when they first got together. She did not serve it very often, so when she did, it was a cause for celebration with Grant. She hoped so, for tonight she would reveal the rest of her secret.

You really think a good casserole is going to fix this? jeered the pessimistic side of her nature.

After quietly enjoying his meal, Grant exclaimed, "Darlin' those enchiladas were delicious! Moist and just spicy enough. I don't say enough about your cooking. You've managed to conquer our Southern recipes even though you weren't raised with them, and then to top it off, you brought us these incredible Mexican dishes. It has been divine, mi amorita."

"Thank you, Grant. She reached over and filled his cup with freshly brewed decaf. "I have something I need to talk to you about." Her voice was steady. She had determined that this would not be the tearful, sobbing, repeat of her last confession.

Grant lifted his coffee cup to his lips, as his warm brown eyes encouraged her to go on.

"Grant, it's about that conversation we had in May. The one we have not gone back to, the one about that infant I gave up for adoption."

Grant gently set his coffee cup down on the table. He studied her with non-blinking eyes.

"There was more that night, but I saw how upset and betrayed you felt. I knew you were furious with me. I didn't share all of it with you. I know you sensed that there was more. You pressed me, 'why am I hearing this *now*?' Obviously it didn't make sense to you that suddenly, thirty years into our marriage, I up and decide to tell you that horrendous secret." She took a deep breath.

After a long pause, "Of course your instincts were correct. I told you because that child, grown now, had found me and called me that day. There's more. He has a wife and two children. I couldn't keep it all in, but when I saw how hurt you were, I froze. The truth is, I chickened out."

For the longest time Grant just sat there, then he picked up the coffee mug and moved it back and forth in his cupped hands.

Shelby could read his body language. He was not one to anger easily, but once the fuse was lit, there was trouble. She could see the volcanic pressures building inside of him.

She sat still. She did not cry, nor try to defend her actions.

"There's more."

Finally, "Oh I don't need any *more* of this shit. Yes, Shelby you are dead on correct about hurting me with that disclosure last May." He paused, spinning the empty cup back and forth between his hands. His deliberate words and ominous tone were far more ferocious than if he were yelling.

"The betrayal was not that you had an out-of-wedlock pregnancy, nor that you had given the child up; the betrayal was in the failed trust. It's not even broken trust. Something has to exist before it can be broken." He paused. "To imagine that we bore two children together and yet, I wasn't worthy of your confidence on something this *monumentally* important, is beyond my capacity to understand. In fact, it has proven to me that you've never trusted me at all. This secret had to be so foundational to your being, that it was life altering for you. You can't sit there and tell me that you've not thought of that little boy across the decades of your life."

Shelby remained silent. To divulge her pain, her vain searches for him in crowds, her imaginings of where he was and how he was, would only add fuel to the fire that was very obviously engulfing her husband.

Back and forth, Grant rotated the empty cup in his hands, studying it. Finally he looked up and held eye contact with her.

"I don't think I can be with someone who has so little regard for my character, who trusts me so little."

With that pronouncement, he very carefully set his coffee cup down, placed his napkin deliberately at the side of his plate, slowly pushed his chair away from the table, and standing to his full height, walked out of the room and up the stairs.

She could hear him pulling out drawers in their room, the muffled sound of the closet doors opening and then closing. After about ten minutes, he came down stairs, and without a word, went out the kitchen door to the garage. She heard the garage door open and the low purr of the Lexus, then the garage door. It was closing, perhaps forever, on life as she had known it.

Her movements were almost robotic as she cleared the dining room table and cleaned up the kitchen.

She called in Zoe and Tessie and the three of them went into the living room. Like a sleep walker, Shelby moved to her favorite chair, slowly sat down, and looked out the window into the darkness of the rainy evening and her bleak future.

CHAPTER 40

October 22, 2005
Beaufort, South Carolina

Grant's movements were those of a man on autopilot, as he backed his sleek black Lexus out of the driveway, lowered the garage door, and slowly cruised down the quiet street. Overpowered, perhaps for only the third or so time in his life, he felt such blinding emotion, that he feared for his health. He could imagine a massive coronary. His chest constricted in a wicked jab of molten heat. He felt dizzy; as his breathing became irregular, coming in awful staccato jabs; blow after blow.

The intense moments had been far between. He recalled the first, the horrific secret, as its lurid details filled his mind. That too, had been a rainy night like this one. He'd been only nineteen. He could see it now. It was late. His mother had stumbled through the front door of their pretentious Queen Anne home. She was coming in from one of her endless dates, and she was drunk. She staggered into the parlor, leaving a trail of confusion in her wake; then she had tripped over a chair, knocking the blue and white porcelain Ming Dynasty vase, one of his father's treasures, off the end table.

As if in slow motion, he recalled watching it fall to the floor, shattering into a dozen pieces. His memory still held his mother's shrill laughter as she declared, "I never liked that dynasty anyway."

The old rage still knotted his gut. He saw his young self, "Mother, you're drunk. Go upstairs." He'd put his hands on her shoulders trying to turn her around.

"Dad would be disgusted by your behavior. Go to bed, Mother."

He'd tried again, to physically steer her toward the stairs. She would not budge.

She became angry. "Don't tell me about your father, that old fart." Her brittle laughter had stabbed the air, "Besides what do you care? He wasn't *your* father anyway." Ironic amusement turned into a macabre giggle.

Grant recalled the ice that seemed to seize his heart. He'd stopped, and with careful deliberation, asked, "What are you saying to me, Mother? What do you *mean*?" the ferocity he felt slammed through his words.

"I mean that fucking old man was not your father!" Her gaze was defiant.

"What do you *mean*?" he had implored. By now the adrenaline was savage as it raged through his blood stream. His heart pounded.

"What I said! Have you never wondered where you got your height? Your dark good looks? Look around, Sonny Boy; Bernard was 5'9' and bald." Her acid words tore at his soul.

"What? Who?" Tears were streaming down his cheeks.

"It was one of my art trips to Paris. Claude. He was an impressionist. Sexy and virile." Her laughter taunted him.

"Did you have a relationship with him? Who is he?" He could barely form the questions as it dawned on him what his stunned brain was straining to grasp.

"Yes, a relationship." Virginia's smile was smug. "I thought I loved him those weeks in Paris." She stared past Grant, seemed lost in a memory. "His apartment had lots of tall windows. You could see the Seine. It wasn't far from the Louvre. We'd walk the art bridge…Pont des Arts…"

"What was his last name?"

"Claude. I told you." She'd paused. "Oh, *last* name? I don't know. I might have known once." With that Virginia turned and stumbled up the stairs to her room.

Grant's attitude toward his mother, his father, in fact his whole life, was forever changed that night. Grant was aware that Shelby's admission last May had brought all that back; the pain of a child not truly knowing who he is. However it was the secret keeping which was the real hot button for Grant.

On some level he understood that his disillusionment with his mother had colored his attitude toward women. He had never really trusted any of the many he had known across the more than fifteen years he lived as a bachelor. He'd almost resigned himself to life as a single, until the flaming-haired paralegal came to work in his office.

As memories continued to swirl into his consciousness, he looked up at the road marker. He came back to the present. He was on the 315. Savannah, twenty miles. *Oh Jesus,* he thought. *Where am I going?* He exited the freeway at the next off ramp, turned around, heading north again toward Beaufort. His driving was erratic. A few times he noticed that he was driving well below the speed limit. Other times, he observed that the odometer reading was above 90 mph. A light rain had begun to dampen the highway.

Once again heading north, he was drawn back into the memories. He thought of Shelby, the early days, and how he studied her for weeks before he made his move. He'd not wanted to scare her away, she was younger than he, and there was a sense of vulnerability, sadness even, that hung in the air above her.

His mind slipped to their wedding day, a simple garden affair in his mother's verdant backyard. The rawness of his yearning was still fresh. He recalled standing nervously under the rose covered arbor, looking down the gleaming white wedding aisle, petals strewn beautifully across its surface. His heart had been hammering. His palms were moist, when finally, the cords to "Here Comes the Bride," filled the air, and he glimpsed his future; the woman with whom he planned to spend eternity. She had been radiant in a long strapless cream-colored satin gown, as she walked gracefully toward him, her vibrant hair pulled into a slick chignon. A sparkling tiara had adorned her head, as an impish smile played on her lips.

In that moment he had understood that he was lost forever. He was hers for better or worse. He'd never dreamed that he would find a partner such as she; a person of exquisite beauty, keen intellect, and goodness. She inspired him to be a better man. That day was merely the first one in a long parade of days when he knew himself to be one lucky bastard.

As the Lexus continued to pierce the darkness, he sped by the Beaufort exit as his mind kept to that wedding day. Now cocooned in the privacy of the car, a knowing came to him. He realized that on that day, he had missed something important. Shelby's choice to walk down the aisle, *unescorted*, was a metaphor for her life to that point. Now in hindsight, it suddenly became obvious to him, she had gone it alone, and then years later, when she'd tried to share her truth, she was shut out. Alone.

Grant now saw that solitary walk down the aisle in a new way.

He scanned to another significant emotional milestone; the birth of Michelle. The picture was clear; he was sitting next to Shelby's hospital bed, timing her contractions. Ten minutes. Five minutes. Two minutes. He watched as the movie of his memory reeled forth; the doctor pulling down the lights above the bed, the nurses racing to get things ready, being gently escorted out of the delivery room. Then, thirty minutes later, great joy as his wife held his baby daughter up for him to hold.

He lingered in those long ago memories, taking measure of his life. As he drove north on the most deadly section of Route 17, he was aware that he was near Green Pond and the Donnelley Wildlife Management Area. He pushed the down button on his driver's door window. Moist Lowcountry musk filled the car. He loved that smell. It was the smell of home.

As he made his way toward Charleston, and perhaps the comfort of Michelle's home, perhaps seeing Ellie in the morning, he completed the measure of his life. He realized, as he thought of Shelby, what she and being a family had meant to him across the years. It came to him, that his huge reaction to her secret was tied to the anguish he felt at his mother's betrayal.

Perhaps another kind of man would not have reacted so strongly to her May admission. He forced his thoughts to examine his over-reaction. Perhaps another kind of man would have understood what it must have taken for her to give that child up; would have comprehended the decades of pain resulting from that heart-wrenching decision.

For better or worse…

Across his life he had pushed down his own soft internal voice when it had wondered who he was, who his father had been. There was a seam of hurt that lay under his charm and easy ways. He knew there was a part of himself that was left in limbo, wondering.

Grant was locked in that old puzzle, when he looked up just as a young doe suddenly leaped in front of him, darting across the road. His instantaneous response was to protect her. He swerved hard. The pavement was wet. He could feel his car sailing, as it careened off the road, gaining more speed before it crashed heavily against a tree. He had the sense of being airborne, heard the hard crack as the car landed, the shattering of glass, the noisy deployment of the airbag, and then only blackness as he lost consciousness.

THE UNRAVELING OF SHELBY FORREST

CHAPTER 41

October 22, 2005
Beaufort, South Carolina

Shelby was startled awake by the invasive ring of the telephone. She'd fallen into a troubled sleep, sitting there in the chair, after Grant had driven away. The dogs stirred to wake her. She opened her eyes and tried to clear her head. *The phone.*

Another shrill ring pieced the quiet. She made her way into the kitchen.

"Hello?"

"Is this Mrs. Forrest?" asked a deeply masculine voice.

"It is."

"I'm State Police Officer, Sergeant First Class Dwayne Wright. There's been an accident. You should come as soon as you can. It's your husband, Grant Forrest."

Fear's blinding force seized Shelby. *I knew there was a price to keeping that secret, and dear God, don't let the price for the truth be Grant's life!*

The officer related the details of the accident, over at Donnelley Wildlife, how fortunate that the park ranger had come along shortly after the crash.

"He's being medevaced and should arrive at the ER in the AFB hospital in Charleston within the next twenty minutes. The ranger found your husband's military ID in his wallet. They're doing all they can. Can you get someone to drive you into Charleston?"

Shelby pulled herself together as best she could. *Think.* The clock said 11:20 p.m. She hated to wake up Michelle and Laney, but she knew the girls would never forgive her if she didn't bring them in on this.

Oh dear God. I have to call the girls.

Shelby dialed Michelle's number. A sleepy Dale answered the phone. She reported the details; that the helicopter carrying Grant would arrive at the base ER very shortly.

"We'll get there," responded Dale suddenly all business. "Mrs. Wilson across the street will come in and stay with Ellie. We'll be there to meet the chopper within twenty minutes. We can order a car service to bring you up here."

"No, I can drive myself."

"Shelby are you sure you're okay to drive? It's raining here."

"It's faster if I drive myself. Dale, I'm okay to drive. I'm going to call Laney. Then I'll leave for the hospital... in a few minutes."

"Do you want us to call Laney?"

"No, it's better that she hear this from me. Thank you, Dale. Pray for him," choked Shelby.

She dialed Laney's number. Her daughter sounded awake as she answered. "Mom, it's late. What's wrong? I was still at the computer finishing a report."

Shelby shared the details.

"Mom, Conner and I'll load-up Gracie and get on the highway.

We can be to you in less than an hour. Shall we collect you and drive in together?"

"Laney, thanks, but I'm heading out in five minutes. I'm okay to drive. Dad needs me."

"Mother, Daddy is strong and in good health. Let's not panic until we have more information. Are you sure you don't want to wait for us?"

"No, Laney, I'm not going to panic, but I *am* leaving now. I can be there in an hour and a half. I'll be careful. I know the roads are wet."

Calm settled over Shelby. She rushed upstairs, stuffed a few clothing items in her over-sized bag, placed a black felt cloche on her head against the rain. Breathing calming breaths, she knew that she had to keep her wits about her, just as she knew that her husband had to live. She needed him, they all needed him. Her story could not end like this.

Shelby put the dogs in the garage, checked their water, left extra food, as she propped open the door to the backyard.

The miles clicked away as her big Navigator headed north, toward her husband. Her thoughts pulled her back across their years together, to the joy he'd brought her. She had always known that when she found Grant, that was the real beginning of her life.

Sweet memories drifted before her. She could see the smile on his face as he leaned against the door jamb as she finished telling Laney and Michelle one of Pony Girl's tall adventures. He would have that sweet look on his lips, his dark eyes swimming with pride. One time during a shared confession, he revealed that when a case became untenable in court, he would pull out one of his favorite mental snapshots, to calm himself down. It was the image of her seated against the girls' headboard, a daughter tucked under each arm, telling a tale. In her memory, she could see him waiting for her as the last kisses were distributed to foreheads, the light was turned off, and the door gently closed, as they walked down the stairs together, hand in hand.

They had shared a big life; a community-centered life with galas, travel, friends and activities; but the private family time across the decades had been the most precious of all. She knew Grant loved her with all his heart and she sensed that his huge reaction to her secret, was not just about her. Somehow his childhood and his mother lay in a dark heap at the bottom of it all.

She carefully negotiated the wet roads as she offered up a little prayer, *Dear Lord, help me to make this right. I do not believe that Grant really wants to throw away what we have. He is my life, please help me to mend this fracture in our marriage.*

CHAPTER 42

October 23, 2005
Hospital, Charleston, S.C.

Michelle and Dale stood silently by the double doors of the ER as the medics wheeled in the gurney carrying Grant. There were no details offered as his unconscious form was rolled past them. An IV bag was being held above him, while a paramedic was squeezing the pulmonary pump covering his grey face. Michelle could see rust colored stains on his clothing and the gauzy wrap covering his forehead was crimson with blood.

There was nothing more for Dale and Michelle to do but wait. They walked back into the seating area.

After about fifteen minutes, a strong looking male doctor, clad in blue scrubs from head to toe, came out to talk to the family.

"I'm his daughter, Michelle Whittaker, this is my husband. My mother's on her way. Doctor, how bad is it?"

Kind blue eyes studied Michelle. "I won't lie to you Mrs. Whittaker, Mr. Whittaker," he looked at Dale. "Mr. Forrest has sustained multiple critical injuries. The biggest threat is the ruptured spleen. I'm taking him into surgery to stop that internal bleed. We're going now. He has a collapsed lung, his femur is broken, and I'm concerned about possible traumatic brain injury." The doctor's gaze held Michelle's. "We're doing everything within our power to save him." Competence emanated from him. "Stay positive. I need to get back in there."

As he walked back into the emergency room, Michelle buried

her face in Dale's shoulder as he held her.

A short time later, a state trooper approached them. He confirmed the earlier report that the patient was injured when his car careened off the highway near Green Pond, that it was good fortune that a park ranger had come along the desolate stretch shortly after the single car accident.

Dale and Michelle sat numbly in the visitors' area waiting for Shelby. They said little as Dale held Michelle's hand and she shed silent tears. She knew her dad was where he needed to be in the OR.

An hour and a half later, Shelby found them in the metal visitors' seats. Michelle looked up when she sensed her mother's presence and Shelby folded her into her arms. Dale embraced them both. Dale brought Shelby up to speed; the ruptured spleen, collapsed lung, the broken femur and the concern regarding possible head trauma.

***

Several hours later, Laney and Conner with sleeping Gracie in his arms, came quietly into the waiting area of the ER. In whispered sentences Shelby and Michelle filled them in. So as not to awaken Gracie, Conner walked over to a darkened corner of the lobby area.

The women held each other. There were tears.

Finally, "Momma," asked Michelle. "Why in the *world* was Daddy out driving around in the middle of the night?"

Laney's dark eyes studied Shelby.

Shelby took a deep breath. *It was time to tell. Her secret had already caused enough damage. It has to end here. Now.*

Sensing that the ensuing conversation needed to be between Shelby and her daughters, Dale moved over to the quiet corner to sit with Conner and Gracie.

Shelby's tone was low as she began her confession, "A long time ago, when I was a college freshman, I made a huge error in judgment. There was a very brief liaison."

Michelle and Laney held eye contact with her. They remained silent.

"It was a professor. One life-changing afternoon. I meant nothing to him. There was a pregnancy. My mother argued for termination. I stood up to her. I refused." Shelby was weeping softly.

"I carried the child." Looking into Michelle's eyes, "*That* is why I moved in with Lily. My mother was crazy with shame. For her it was all about the disgrace I was bringing down on the family. She couldn't get me far enough away from Bellingham. I had no choice but to give the infant up." There was a long pause as Shelby choked back strong feelings. After a moment she whispered, "It tore out my heart."

Michelle reached over and put her hand on Shelby's. Laney pulled her chair around to close a circle.

"I didn't know what to do with the grief." Shelby's words were desperate. "It took me a long time to begin to feel somewhat normal, and then I met your father." Her daughters remained silent.

"Girls, Dad never knew," Shelby's voice was clogged with emotion. "I lived a lie."

Tears rolled down her cheeks. She did not wipe them away.

More silence.

"Last May, that child tracked me down and called me. That was when I told your father that there'd been a pregnancy, a baby, a boy; that I'd given him up. Dad took my secret as a betrayal. I could feel the fury rising up in him. I was too frightened to tell the rest of the truth, that is until tonight. Your father is horribly hurt. He walked out on me at the dinner table. He packed a suitcase and left."

Tears continued down Shelby's cheeks.

"This is all my fault. I'm not sure that I can put it right." Shelby choked on her words. "Girls I'm so terribly sorry, for all of it. For keeping this from you, too. I wanted to tell you, but I didn't want you to have to hold a secret from your father. That wouldn't have been right. I cannot go back and undo the damage. I pray that your dad will pull through this."

"Oh, Momma. I'm so sorry," offered Michelle.

Laney slid to her knees and put her head in her mother's lap. "Oh Momma you had to carry that awful pain across all these years." Laney was sobbing now. "I couldn't imagine having to give up Gracie."

The little group huddled like that for a very long time.

After awhile, "But Mom, why *tonight*? Well, last night, I guess. Why now? You had such a nice time with Ellie in her class on Friday, didn't you?" asked Michelle.

Once again Shelby's blue eyes spilled over. "I did." She took in a breath.

"There's more. I've had four conversations with him. He's Air Force; they've been stationed in England. He has a wife and two young daughters. They've been waiting for their transfer orders. I've seen photos."

The girls studied their mother.

"Yesterday in Miss Jennifer's class, Ellie brought her new friend over to meet me." Shelby choked on her words. "Michelle, the little red-headed girl that I bet Ellie has been talking about, her new friend, Kaitlyn." She coughed, paused for a very long moment.

"I knew the minute I laid eyes on her who she was. That child is his daughter. That child is my granddaughter, Ellie's cousin, your niece."

"Oh my God!" exclaimed Michelle.

Laney studied her mother as her mind absorbed the information.

"Oh Momma, you *had* to tell Dad," said Michelle.

"I did, and now look."

After what seemed like an eternity, Laney began in a thoughtful tone, "Mom, I've known my father for a very long time. In my heart of hearts, if we are lucky enough that he pulls through, I think he will come around." She held eye contact with Shelby. "Mom, I do."

THE UNRAVELING OF SHELBY FORREST

CHAPTER 43

October 23, 2005
Charleston, S.C.

Cody and the team fought hard to repair the rupture in the spleen. The bleeding had stopped. They were finishing up that part of the surgery and working on stabilizing the collapsed lung to keep it from progressing to cardiovascular impairment; while he concentrated on the brain injury, the TBI. He knew that when a patient was rendered unconscious there was a good chance that the head had slammed against something like the window. There could be a bleed, at the least, severe swelling.

As Cody stitched up his patient's abdomen, he focused on the brain injury. *If I get his body temp down to 33 C for 24 hours we can minimize any neurological damage. Induce a coma to prevent shivering and heat generation.*

Cody issued those orders to his team.

I'm worried about that broken femur. Below the waist injuries run a high risk of blood clots. We don't want a pulmonary embolism.

He made a decision.

"We're going to put in an inferior vena cava filter. We don't want to risk a clot.

Several hours later, an exhausted Dr. James, walked out of the operating room. As he pushed through the double doors, he shoved his surgical mask down from his mouth. It hung near his chin.

He spotted the patient's family and went over to them. They were a silent, pained group, seated miserably in a corner of the waiting room. They stood as he approached, eager for news. He greeted them; met the patient's wife and the second daughter and son-in-law who had arrived while he was in surgery. He was explaining that at the moment, the patient was stable; the spleen repair had gone well. He had concerns, but he was optimistic about a positive outcome.

"The internal bleeding has stopped. We inflated the lung and it's functioning properly." He paused. Riveting blue eyes emphasized his words, "I'm concerned that he may have sustained some brain injury. I don't like that he lost consciousness. I'm taking his body temp down. Twenty-four hours." As he relayed these vital facts, he was sliding the blue surgical cap off his head.

Shelby was listening. *Stable condition.* She knew that Grant's general health was excellent. He was strong, worked-out all the time. She felt her body relax a millimeter. She dared to take a breath as she aimed for cautious optimism, praying that her husband would survive. *He had to.*

She was wrapped up in those thoughts, her eyes fixed on the doctor, on his words. She was feeling more hopeful. She observed him, as in slow motion, while his right hand reached up, and in one slow gesture, removed the blue surgical cap; she noted brownish hair, military style haircut, a square jaw, familiar features, and *unmistakable* blue eyes. Suddenly, recognition flooded her.

"Doctor," she interrupted. "Er… uh… ." She felt embarrassed for interrupting. All eyes were on her. She took a gulp of air. "Hmm." She stumbled. "Are you…are you… Cody James?" There was a desperate intensity to her whispered question.

Her daughters looked at her. It was out of character for their mother to interrupt something as important as a medical briefing.

"I am."

"You think my husband will make it?" she asked, her voice cracking.

"I do. I think he will, but I want to be on the safe side. I'm taking down his temp, in case of head trauma."

Shelby inhaled.

Holding eye contact with him, she very slowly removed the cloche hat she wore, revealing a flaming cap of hair.

Bit by bit, something new came into the doctor's expression.

Shelby lifted her reading glasses from her face. In words pregnant with meaning that, for now, only she and Cody could fully comprehend, she replied. There was strength behind her words. "I'm Shelby Wells. These are my daughters and my sons-in-law." She took another sharp inhalation. Paused.

"These are your sisters. We are your birth family."

For a millisecond Shelby observed the capable doctor as he morphed into a much younger version of himself. She saw him swallow twice; hard. His face reddened.

Tears reflected in his brilliant eyes.

"What?" he gasped.

"My *people*?"

Shelby could see him fighting for control.

"You're *my people*?" His incredulous question filled the space.

Just as quickly, the adult in him reappeared as he fought to reign in his emotions.

He pulled off the surgical mask which was now dangling from one ear. He waited a long beat. He swallowed as he crossed the short distance to Shelby. Holding eye contact as he looked down at her, he opened his arms. She melted into his embrace.

Michelle and Laney, dumbfounded, looked on. Relieved that there their father was stable, at least for the moment, they looked at each other with wide eyes. They held eye contact, subtly raised their shoulders in a silent sisterly communication, as they, too, folded into the impromptu group hug.

Conner and Dale stood at the edge of the circle looking bewildered.

Struggling to control his emotions, Cody James, stood back, "I'm so happy to meet you all." His words trembled with intensity.

Shelby could tell that this was too much for him. He needed to escape, to cope with it. He had been in surgery for hours. He had to be exhausted.

"I... um. I need to go check on the patient. We need to get him moved over to Intensive Care. I want to get that body temperature down. Can we take all this up later?"

Shelby thought he looked about ten years old as he made his excuses and went back through the double doors into the OR.

The family sat down. Shocked expressions remained on their faces, as each person processed the remarkable turn of events.

Much later, Dale approached Michelle and Shelby who were sitting quietly. Dale had time to think about meeting Cody James.

"Shelby, Michelle." Both women looked up at him, nodding slightly. Dale chose his words carefully. Slowly he explained, "I sold the James family a house over on Daniel Island. It's in escrow. They are renting it until the paperwork is completed."

Shelby and Michelle stared at Dale. "Michelle, that's the family I've been talking about. Remember? I was happy they took my recommendation for Ellie's preschool." Dale looked at his mother-in-law and wife. He took his time. "I've been working with the doctor's wife, Amber."

By now the hushed conversation had Laney's attention. All three of them looked at Dale. "Amber is Grant's cousin. Grant gave me the contact."

THE UNRAVELING OF SHELBY FORREST

CHAPTER 44

October 25, 2005
AFB Hospital ICU

Grant had been recovering in intensive care for forty-eight hours, while Shelby sat silently next to his bed. Cody checked on Grant each morning and evening. He reassured her that the fact of Grant's unconsciousness was part of the protocol. She should not worry. The next step was a very slow rewarm to prevent reperfusion injury to other organs. There was an unspoken promise between them, that once Grant was more stable and conscious, there would be time to get acquainted. She promised herself she would provide full disclosure when Cody finally got around to asking for his story. She would tell; she had learned her lesson. No more secrets.

Michelle and Laney came every day to sit with their mother.

On the third morning, Shelby was alone in the room, looking out the window, when she heard a raspy, "Hey there, beautiful," coming from the bed. She turned abruptly from the window toward her husband. She could make out a warm expression on his pale face.

"Oh, Grant, honey. We've been so worried… You hit a tree. Ruptured your spleen, collapsed a lung. We were so afraid. The girls will be back soon."

Shelby held back, not sure whether he would welcome her, once his memory circled back to their last conversation.

"Hey, Red, come over here," he croaked.

"Grant. Really? You want *me*?" her voice was tentative. Vulnerability showed on her tired face.

"Oh, yes," He paused. "*really*." Though weak, and difficult to understand, his commanding prosecutor's determination lay below the request.

Through strangled syllables, "Please…Come here to me." His eyes held hers. "I've been a total horse's ass. Please Shelby."

He slowly found his right arm and tentatively reached out from the metal guard rail on the hospital bed. "I overreacted." His words were a rough whisper as he groped for her hand.

Shelby moved silently to his side.

"What you told me got all mixed up with my mother and something she did a long time ago." He paused to gather his strength. "I'll tell you about it some time. For now, Red, will you forgive me?" His words were halting. "I'm so sor..ry." After a long moment trying to pull in some strength.

"*You're* the best thing that's ever happened to me… I should never have walked out on you. I'm so ashamed." His eyes were wet.

Shelby reached for his hand and squeezed it. "You forgive *me?*" Her words cracked.

Holding Shelby's eyes, Grant stammered, "I messed up. Please?"

She pressed his hand in affirmation.

They were quiet for a very long time.

After a while, a groggy Grant offered, "I remember there was a doe. I swerved."

They were studying each other as the doctor slipped into the room.

They both looked up at Cody.

Shelby searched for her voice. "Grant, this is your doctor, Cody James." She inhaled. "He saved your life; stopped the internal bleeding. It was pretty bad." Her anxious tone exposed the recent tumult which had engulfed her. "He............ ," she choked over her words, "put you back together again."

Grant managed a weak smile as Shelby's eyes filled and she stepped away from the bed.

"Well, hello there, Doctor," he whispered. "Have I been out for a while?" He studied the doctor's face searching for clues about his condition.

"You have. We've kept you out. Induced a coma. Wanted to make certain that there was no brain trauma. MRI looks good."

"So Doctor," his voice was feeble. "How bad's the damage? I see my leg..." his words trailed off.

Cody held Grant's eyes. "You'll be as good as new when that femur heals. I put in a plate and some bolts. In a few months you will be up and around; even playing golf." Cody smiled his encouragement to Grant.

Shelby had learned a grueling lesson about not saying all of it when she had the chance. She was not going to repeat *that* mistake. She inhaled and stepped closer to the metal bed.

"Grant."

He looked at her, noticing that her tone had changed.

"Grant," she breathed in, "that child I had to give up; the son who tracked me down." She hesitated. "Well, it turns out that he's a trauma surgeon for the military." She paused, took in another gulp of air. "Grant, I would like for you to meet my *son*, Major Cody James, of the United States Air Force, your doctor."

Grant, a man almost always comfortable with words, was speechless. He waited, digesting this unforeseen information, then, he stuttered out, "What? ...No shit?" He searched both somber faces, grappling for comprehension. His arm banged into the metal hospital rail as he struggled to stretch it toward Cody, to make contact.

He continued to stare, as if mesmerized by Cody's strong profile. Finally, in a voice raw with feeling, "Come *here* young man!" Another wave of emotion seized him. He fought to control it. He hesitated, his eyes welled, "*Welcome* to the family."

Cody, a boy who had always wondered who he was, who his *real* people were, grasped Grant's outstretched hand. Shelby came in closer and placed both of her hands around theirs.

The three of them exchanged meaningful looks, but no one said a word. They couldn't. They knew their voices would fail them.

CHAPTER 45

December 25, 2005
Beaufort, South Carolina

Christmas Day: As Shelby finished putting her signature mushroom caps on the white porcelain serving platter, she was keenly aware that these next few hours would be time dividing for her; that as she looked back on this day, across all the rest of her life, it would be significant. Before Cody and his family: and after.

They were all here, something she had only dared to contemplate in her most private dreams. Grant was home from the hospital, and finally, had some mobility using crutches.

She had delighted in decorating the house. Happily, a teen-aged boy down the street was eager to earn extra money and had helped set-up and decorate the 12' fir they installed in the great room. Shelby took pleasure in dressing the table. She arranged a series of hurricane lamps sporting chunky white candles filled with shiny cranberries along its length. Fresh pine cuttings were woven between the lamps, accented with poinsettias and red roses. She knew that when the lights were dimmed, and the candles lit, the effect would be intimate and festive.

The turkey was roasting, stuffed with the traditional cornbread and sausage recipe that her husband and daughters adored. She had prepared the cranberry sauce the week before and was going to whip up mashed potatoes and gravy at the last minute. Amber's mom, Sharon Blake, had brought her She-Crab Soup, Michelle was making Divinity. Laney, the real chef in the family, was on sweet-potato pie, country style green beans, and pecan brownies. Amber had prepared crescent rolls and layered Zucchini Parmesan. This

Christmas dinner would truly be a feast.

When she thought about the new additions to her family, she almost needed to pinch herself; she could hardly believe this was her *actual* life. Having her amazing and talented son with her was a fantasy come true, and of course she had yearned to know Kaitlyn and Willow. In her imagination though, she had not contemplated knowing Amber.

During the long weeks in the hospital they had all gotten acquainted, and then Amber and Cody had hosted Thanksgiving in their new home on Daniel Island. Michelle and Laney needed to be with their husband's families, so the group consisted of Cody, Amber, the girls, Sharon, Amber's sister Heather and her boyfriend Jake, and Grant and Shelby. They had made a festive day of it, sharing the cooking and lots of stories and laughter. In fact, they had turned Thanksgiving into a ten hour long celebration involving two meals! Shelby was intrigued by Sharon's easy manner, and she admired her nursing career. Heather and her man were fun and upbeat, but learning of Amber's passion for the earliest inhabitants of Stonehenge had truly captured Shelby's interest. Very often they would find themselves sharing theories about the earliest inhabitants of the planet. They enjoyed discussing the mysteries of Stonehenge. Especially, whether the blue center stones were part of a healing ritual, or were a pilgrimage site. They described what they knew of the carbon dating evidence; about the charcoal, which shows human activity at Stonehenge as early as 7000 B.C. Shelby liked to talk about her theories of the earliest migration of humans to North America, long before the Ice Age and the land bridge.

Shelby could not believe she had found such a kindred spirit in Amber. She felt she'd known her for years, not just weeks. With each visit she grew closer to Kaitlyn and Willow. Their hilarious antics made her laugh, and when they learned about the *real* story behind Pony Girl and her adventures, they could hardly get enough of them. At every visit they urged her to tell more about Nano and her escapades as a little girl.

As she finished arranging the garnish around the edges of the platter, she smiled to herself, turning to take the tray out into the living room. She noticed that Michelle was standing near the fireplace in what appeared to be an earnest conversation with Cody. She caught snatches of it. "Cody, I sure could've used *you* around when I was in middle school. I was taller than the rest of the kids. They bullied me. It was awful. I fantasized that I had a big brother who would beat the tar out of them!"

Shelby couldn't hear what Cody was saying, but he reached for Michelle and gave her a quick hug. Laney and Heather, across the room, were in an animated discussion, when suddenly they both laughed out loud.

Heather's Jake was discussing sabot racing with Conner and Dale. All four of the little girls were being entertained by Geepop who was teaching them how to do wheelies with his wheelchair. It was getting pretty rowdy in their area of the room.

Earlier, Shelby had discovered the girls behind the sofa in the parlor, dressing Zoe and Tessie in Santa hats. As Shelby approached, she'd been shooed away, "Grandma we're practicin' our show," warned a serious Ellie, as Kaitlyn added, blue eyes sparkling with anticipation, "Grandma we're making a dance for after dinner!" Shelby had heeded her cue and skedaddled!

"Here, let me do that," offered Dale as he lifted the tray from Shelby's outstretched arms and began to pass the mushroom caps around.

As Shelby soaked up the happy vibes shimmering through the room, Sharon came quietly over and hugged her shoulder. Both women paused as they admired the animation in the room. "You know," Sharon whispered earnestly, "after I lost the girls' dad." Shelby looked at her. "I wondered if I'd ever have that feeling of being a *real* family again." She stopped. Shelby noticed a mist of tears in her serious hazel eyes. "I have that old feeling back, of *really* being at home." Both women held eye contact. "Thank you,

Shelby for being so welcoming to all of us."

Shelby turned to her, "Sharon, it's my pleasure." She paused, and then in hushed tones confessed, "I realize now, that across my entire adult life, I've been waiting for something. I never quite let my guard down. I've held a part of myself back. Now, with all of you here, I see that I've always been waiting for Cody." She stopped. Neither woman spoke; they did not trust their voices.

Finally, after a long moment, brightening, "Sharon, this is the beginning of my new life," big grin, "and I'm so pleased that *y'all* are sharing it! See I can do that whole Southern thing too!" Both women laughed, breaking the intensity of their disclosures.

An hour or so later, the two highchairs were pulled up to the big dining table, the booster seats were in place for Ellie and Kaitlyn, the turkey was carved, and the countless delicious dishes lined the table.

"If I may," began Grant in welcome, clinking his glass as he stretched up from his wheelchair. The conversations quieted as everyone turned to him. "Shelby and I welcome y'all to this Christmas feast. It's a milestone for us, and frankly, a mighty turning point in my own life." Grant made eye contact with his wife. "Speaking for Shelby, as well as myself, it's difficult to put into words what we feel." He paused, "Our hearts are full. We can't believe that life's journey has somehow brought us all together. We're blessed to be here with y'all." He inhaled. His dark eyes shone.

"Years ago, back when we were just dating, one of our favorite things to do was to go to the Folly Beach Pier and watch the children on the merry-go-round." Smiling wistfully at the old memory, he continued. "We'd sit for the longest time, enveloped in the magic of their laughter, dreaming about having a great noisy family of our own. Well," Grant gestured, "look around!" His eyes found Shelby's once again.

"Shelby, my love, I'm thinkin' those dreams have come true!"

Shelby simply nodded as a single tear slid down her cheek.

All around the table, earnest faces responded, "Merry Christmas! Cheers!" as they lifted their glasses.

A minute or so later, Cody stood, clearing his throat, as he raised his glass, "Grant, thank *you* for that." He looked meaningfully around the table, "Shelby, Grant, Michelle, Dale, Laney, Conner, Gracie, and Ellie," he began, "today is *epic* for me, getting to know all of you," he took a long beat, "*my people...*" He waited, "...and being accepted so completely..." he swallowed, "it's difficult to explain... It feels like a light has been turned on in a dark room." He hesitated, "For the first time in my life..." his voice cracked, "I know who I *am*."

Smiling as he regained his composure, once again offering up his glass, "And of course, to my amazing wife and girls who have sustained me; to Sharon and Heather, and our new friend, Jake. You all mean the world to me. Cheers!"

"Bravo! Merry Christmas!" They responded enthusiastically.

Dinner was served and a very exultant and noisy group devoured the feast.

THE UNRAVELING OF SHELBY FORREST

THE UNRAVELING OF SHELBY FORREST

EPILOGUE

December 25, 2014
Beaufort, South Carolina

"Ellie, Kaitlyn!" called Shelby to her competent, teenaged, assistant chefs, "How are those pecan brownies coming? Do you need both of the shelves in the top oven?"

"Grandma, I think so, but please come here for a taste," requested Ellie, as she turned the spoon in the thick batter, lifting it toward her grandmother, who dipped her finger in. As Shelby enjoyed the rich mixture, she exclaimed, "Whoa! Good job girls." Kaitlyn smiled impishly through startlingly blue eyes, as she licked the big spoonful.

"You girls are just too funny! I'm glad you doubled the recipe." Shelby smiled at her granddaughters who, at fourteen, were both taller than she. The cousins had been inseparable since the day they first met at preschool.

"We've been wondering," asked Kaitlyn between licks, "any chance you might let us help prepare the turkey?"

Laughing out loud, Shelby exclaimed, "I have been waiting forty years to hear that! You bet! I think you will be shocked to learn that it's way less hassle than adults seem to make of it. Oh, this is becoming more fun by the minute!" Shelby pulled the twenty-five pounder out of the refrigerator.

By 8 p.m., the big Christmas dinner was finally winding down. The toasts had been made, the food consumed. Everyone was relaxing around the long table simply enjoying being part of a large family. Some of the younger children had sneaked into the corners to play Legos or race new Hot Wheels cars. As the conversations mellowed, Grant, his thick hair now grey, moving gracefully despite his years, took his cue to bring in the large stack of elaborately wrapped boxes that had been attracting attention all day.

With the dramatic flair of a winning prosecutor, Grant handed a colorful red box to each of the families. Suspense registered on faces. *What?* Everyone waited until all the packages had been handed out. Questioning looks were exchanged. On his go, fervent unwrapping began. As the recipients realized what the gift was, a hush settled around the table. Grant studied each face as his family slowly began to examine the pages of the large coffee-table style photography book he had created. The air crackled with energy. Awed into silence, they slowly turned pages, scrutinizing the images within.

Michelle came to a photo of herself on the morning that she gave birth to her son Jamison. The camera captured the primal ache she felt gazing at her newborn. Dale's face was naked with emotion.

"Oh Daddy..." she gasped, "Oh Daddy, it's... beautiful," as she burst into tears.

Around the table the exclamations and accolades followed, as each family glimpsed what Grant had achieved. He had used his photographic genius to capture each loved one as he or she lived. The book was a candid look at one man's family. The gold letters on the cover read, *Our Family Circle: Love that Binds.*

Heather and Jake opened their book to view an intimate close-up, which showed their expressions as they exchanged vows. The camera caught the depth of feeling in their eyes. Sharon, Amber's mother, turned her book to an image which showed her first moment with baby grandson Max; Cody and Amber's son. Kaitlyn and Willow were positioned behind her; all three faces reflected awe, as they admired newborn Max.

Laney dabbed her eyes, through silent sobs, as she took in her father's image of her. It was a shot taken during the ribbon cutting of the opening of her bistro, A Little Bit of Heaven. Conner was standing to the right of her, with one twin five-year-old son, under each arm. The boys, Jared and Josh, held serious expressions as they eyed Laney's shiny scissors. Laney's countenance told her story; she was beaming with pride.

The group became more animated as more and more pages were revealed. There was a close-up of Dale in front of the Golden Door Realty. He was the new owner. Grant had managed a photo, unbeknownst, to Shelby, of her on all fours, playing hide-and-seek, "roaring" out from her hiding place as the twin boys doubled over in giggles. Grant's hard bound pages were filled with freckled, sun burnt faces, sticky hands, and cotton candy expressions.

There was a big color portrait of Shelby and Amber taken at the museum, signing books for their documentary study, *The Ages of Man*, researched by Shelby and illustrated by Amber. Both women were smiling as a line of enthusiasts formed to buy their books.

Sabot trophies, serious faces, radiant eyes, Cody's strong arm garbed in full dress military uniform around Shelby's shoulders. The camera found Shelby silhouetted against the sunset at the harbor, two Golden Retrievers chasing seagulls in the background. Grant had even managed to include a shot of himself giving wheelie rides to young Kaitlyn, Ellie, Gracie, and Willow, in the old wheelchair from his accident. There were pages with images of Cody as a child, as well as Amber's original family. Grant, showing off his golf swing. Shelby splendid in her Pony Girl outfit.

The last page was the one which tore at their heart strings. Grant had filtered and blurred the edges, so that the eye was drawn in, past the verdant landscape, to focus completely on Grant and Shelby as they joined hands, renewing their vows during their last wedding anniversary. It had been a day layered with meaning for all of them and Grant had included it. For Shelby the day symbolized the past ten years, all of her loved ones united. It was the perfect final photo for his book.

That night, after all the sleep-over people were tucked into their beds, and Grant had climbed into the shower, Shelby was sitting at her vanity. She was reliving the magic of the day, especially the gift of Grant's remarkable book. It was a monument to the life they had created, and a testimony to the power of love.

As Shelby removed her make-up, she could not help but think back to the very anxious woman she had been during the difficult months in the summer of 2005; the summer of "The Telling," as she had come to think of it. Before the telling and after: before Cody and after.

The young girl who found herself pregnant and who went it alone, was but a distant memory now.

Finally, when the waiting ended, when I found what I had waited for, I was able to venture out of the shadow of the reticence that had followed me across my life. I was able to find my voice, to become the woman I always suspected was hiding inside.

With that she placed her make-up remover cotton balls in the trash container next to the vanity. She smiled to herself in the mirror, and walked over to the bed to turn back the comforter. Grant would soon be joining her.

REFERENCES

Achenbach, Joel. "Girl's 12,000-Year-Old Skeleton May Solve Mysteries of the Origins of Earliest Americans." *Orange County Register* May 16, 2014, Science sec.: 10. Print.

Cahill, Larry. Psycho-biologist, The Cahill Laboratory at the University of California, Irvine. Lecture: *The Brain at Work.* Inside Edge: January 2013.

Cvijetic, Christine M. "*No Longer an Alien: Leadership Autobiography.*" Dissertation, University of La Verne, CA. 2011. Print.

Csikszentmihalyi, Mihaly. *Flow: The Psychology of Optimal Experience.* New York: Harper and Row, 1990.

Forward, Susan. *Toxic Parents.* New York: Bantam Books, 1989

Frankl, Viktor. *The Will to Meaning.* New York: Meridian Book. 1966, 1989.

Friess, Donna, L. *Circle of Love: Guide to Successful Relationships,* 3rd Edition. California: H.I.H. Publishing, 2008.

Glasser, William. *Stations of the Mind.* New York: Harper and Row, 1981.

Goleman, Daniel. *Social Intelligence.* New York: Bantam Book, 2006.

Jung, Carl. *Memories, Dreams and Reflections.* New York: Pantheon Books, 1963.

Kline, Christina Baker. *Orphan Train: A Novel.* 1st ed. New York: HarperCollins Publishers, 2013. Print.

Kurzweil, Ray. *How to Create a Mind: the Secret of Human Thought Revealed.* New York: Viking, 2012.

Lemonick, Michael D., and Andrea Dorfman. "Who Were the First Americans?" *TIME* March13, 2006: 45-52. Print.

Lifton, Betty Jean. *Journey of the Adopted Self: A Quest for Wholeness.* New York, NY: Basic, 1994. Print.

Lifton, Betty Jean. *Lost and Found: The Adapted Experience.* New York: Harper Perennial, 2009. Print.

Lowery, Malinda Maynor. *Lumbee Indians in the Jim Crow South: Race, Identity, and the Making of a Nation.* Chapel Hill: University of North Carolina, 2010. Print.

MacGowan, Kenneth, and Joseph A. Hester. *Early Man in the New World.* Garden City, NY: Anchor, 1962. Print.

May, Rollo. *Love and Will.* New York: Norton, 1966.

Mellody, Pia, Andrea Wells. Miller, and Keith Miller. *Facing Codependence: What It Is, Where It Comes From, How It Sabotages Our Lives.* San Francisco: Perennial Library, 1989. Print.

Miller, Alice. *Thou Shall Not Be Aware: Society's Betrayal of The Child.* New York: Harper and Row, 1981.

Miller, Alice. *The Drama of The Gifted Child.* New York: Harper and Row, 1997.

Roberts, David. "Guardian of the Ghost World." *National Geographic. Vol 20.* Aug. 2006: n. pag. Web.

Roberts, David. "Waldo Wilcox: Range Creek's Fremont Artifacts." *National Geographic Adventure* n.d.: n. pag. Web. 27, June 2014.

Ruby, Robert H., and John A. Brown. *A Guide to the Indian Tribes of the Pacific Northwest*. Revised 1992 ed. Norman: U of Oklahoma, 1986. Print.

Rock, David. *Your Brain at Work: Strategies for Overcoming Distraction, Regaining Focus, and Working Smarter All Day Long.* New York: Harper Business, 2009.

Shimoff, Marci. Lecture: *Happy for No Reason.* May11, 2013.Women's Journey Conference,

"The Fremont People." *Forlean Times* 24 June 2004: n. pag. Web. University of California, Irvine.

University of Washington Digital Library. http:content.lib.washing.edu/sipn/

www.airforce.com

Made in the USA
Charleston, SC
02 January 2015